Up All Night

Mount Hope, Book 1

Annabeth Albert

Up All Night

Copyright © 2024 by Annabeth Albert

All rights reserved.

No part of this book may be reproduced in any form or by any electronic or mechanical means, including information storage and retrieval systems, without written permission from the author, except for the use of brief quotations in a book review.

Photo Design: Reese Dante
Cover Image: Furious Fotog
Cover Model: Caylan Hughes
Edited by: Abbie Nicole

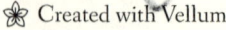 Created with Vellum

Up All Night

What happened to my predictable life?

I had a stable life as a fire captain in Seattle, married to one of my best friends and raising two awesome kids. Now, my kids are grown, and my marriage is toast. I'm solidly past forty and back in my tiny hometown of Mount Hope, Oregon, filling in as a firefighter. My future is one big question mark keeping me up at night.

Also keeping me up? The short-order cook at Honey's Hotcake Hut.

Denver might be close to my age, but we're total opposites. The former rock roadie runs from stability, never puts down roots, and lives for the moment. Point in case, we barely speak before he invites me into his shower.

I've never been with a man, but my fresh start has me trying all sorts of new things—including Denver's shower.

Our future? Hopeless.

Denver doesn't do repeats, but I convince him to have a fling since we're both in Mount Hope short-term. The more time we spend together, the deeper our friendship and bond grows. Our time together outside of the bedroom, reveals a caring side to the grumpy cook. Even better, my sunshine-y optimism softens him like butter.

Should a fling give me these deep feelings? Nope.

Worse, the feelings are mutual. Big decisions loom for both our futures, and our time together grows short. I might have Denver's heart, but his trust is far harder to win. He's the answer to all my question marks, and I need him to believe in us. Can I convince him to give our love a chance?

UP ALL NIGHT features a grumpy/sunshine pairing for a forty-something firefighter on a path of self-discovery with an UP ALL NIGHT short-order cook. It contains loads of first-time feels with sexual awakening and exploration with a heaping helping of personal growth and deep connection for this opposites-attract couple.

Join Annabeth Albert's Ream

Find short stories, bonus scenes, subscribe for free ebooks, signed paperbacks, exclusive swag, and more by checking out and following me on Ream! Scan the QR code below to check out Annabeth Albert on Ream.

Author Note/Reader Advisory

UP ALL NIGHT is a low-angst, high-feels, small-town romance, but it does touch very gently on issues of loss, divorce, starting over, substance abuse, and neglectful parenting, all in the past. A happy ending is guaranteed!

Mount Hope is a made-up small town somewhere west of Portland, Oregon, in the beautiful Columbia River Gorge area. This series takes place in the same universe as my other novels, but it is entirely a standalone. Any resemblance to real towns, persons, places, businesses, and situations is entirely coincidental.

To fresh starts after forty. It's never too late, and you're not too old to conquer your dreams and change your destiny.

Prologue

One Month Ago

Sean

My tie itched and tugged against my neck, a combo of a too-close shave and a lack of familiarity with tie-wearing. I didn't attend a ton of events that called for a suit. Like my twenty-year marriage, my days of escorting Maxine to faculty functions were long past, and even as a fire captain, occasions for suits were few and far between.

But Doctor Montgomery Wallace's funeral was one of those nonnegotiable suit occasions, so here I was, best suit I owned and uncomfortable as hell.

"What's with your tie?" My dad frowned as he reached out to straighten my gray tie, which featured little DNA helixes. Like me, he was in a dark suit, hair tamed, clean-shaven. Other than how his red hair had far more white than mine, we could have been brothers. We could have worn our dress blues, but we'd decided on our civilian best to pay our respects.

Shrugging, I let Dad fuss with my tie and lapels. "I bought it to wear when Maxine received that big fellowship and research grant. Seemed appropriate for today, what with Montgomery having been a doctor. Better than most of my other ties, which are firehouse themed."

"Fair enough." Dad nodded sharply. The large reception hall at the Mount Hope Episcopal Church was crowded with a who's who of Mount Hope residents, and ordinarily, my fire chief father would be making the rounds and greeting folks. He knew everyone. However, he'd stuck close to me all morning and narrowed his eyes as he scrutinized my face. "You need to stop acting married. Get back out there. Meet someone wonderful."

"I'm aware I'm single." *And how.* I suppressed a groan at my parents' favorite topic for the last three years. Undoubtedly, Dad had glued himself to my side for the chance to resume the lecture he'd started as soon as I'd arrived back in town two days ago. "The house sale closes in two weeks."

Maxine had kindly let me stay in our marital home while we hammered out the terms of our amicable divorce. No way could I afford to buy her out without emptying my entire pension, so selling had been inevitable, much as I pretended otherwise. And when Maxine was given the opportunity for a once-in-a-lifetime Antarctic research trip, all I could do was cheer her on and watch as our—*my*— beloved historic Seattle craftsman sold for a staggering figure.

In two weeks, I'd have an unprecedented sum of money and no clue what to do with it. Or my life.

"And you still don't have an apartment. Or a job." Dad wasn't one to shy away from stating the obvious. I'd taken leave to finish getting the house ready for sale and to free myself to move to a less pricey part of Seattle. "Come home, Sean."

Up All Night

As soon as my folks had heard I was open to moving, they'd put their bid in for me to return to Mount Hope.

"That's a wonderful idea." My mother bustled over to lay a hand on Dad's elbow. Like Montgomery and Eric, they were relationship goals, the sort of couple that invited envy even from those who barely knew them. "Your old room could be ready in a jiffy."

Only she could get away with words like *jiffy*. Smiling, I gentled my tone. "Thanks, Mom."

I wasn't about to point out that my old room, like the rest of the house, had been taken over by her obsession with Disney collectibles. No way was I moving into a room dominated by Minnie Mouse memorabilia. Same twin bed, but my desk was covered with boxes of pins, and my bookshelves held box after box of other collectibles in pristine condition.

"Evelyn Rodriguez is going out on maternity leave for a few months. We'll be short-handed. We could work together." Dad pitched his voice extra hearty. He knew full well that I'd burned out on admin work as captain. The chance to be out in the field more was tempting as hell, even before he added, "One last time before I retire."

"Gee, lay it on thick, Dad." Groaning, I rolled my neck side to side. As I returned to normal posture, I considered my parents more closely. When had they become senior citizens on the brink of retirement? Dad's shoulders were as wide as mine, but he was more stooped these days, years of hard work taking its toll on his back. This was his last year as fire chief. He'd been a captain when I'd been a rookie, the last time we'd been able to work together before Maxine's schooling and later work had taken us away from Mount Hope for two decades. Glancing beyond my folks, I saw many familiar but aging faces, the small Oregon mountain town continuing to plod along in my absence. *Maybe...*

However, I knew better than to admit to either of my folks that I was wavering. Instead, I looked toward the front of the room. After the memorial service ended, the crowd around Montgomery's family's table had been so deep that I'd hung back with Dad to wait our turn.

"There's Eric." I gestured to where one of my oldest friends sat slumped in a folding chair. He looked far leaner than the last time I'd seen him, closely cropped hair thinner and eyes haunted. Hardly surprising, yet my gut twisted. "Crowd's finally moved on."

"Yes, we should pay our respects." My mom, bless her heart, dropped the subject of my moving home and led the way to where Eric sat.

Following Mom's charge, I almost collided with a giant of a guy in a white dress shirt and gray pants. Okay, not a *giant*, but a big dude nonetheless. Tall and beefy with big biceps and thick shoulders that contrasted with a softer belly and midsection. He also had a well-groomed beard and a mass of dark curly hair caught up in a haphazard ponytail.

"Sorry, friend." Voice as California casual as the sun streaks in his brown hair, the guy stepped out of the way.

"No worries." I forbid my gaze from following as he strode away toward one of the exits. He could have been anyone, yet something about him intrigued me. Another addition to Mount Hope in my absence? The drumbeat of *maybe* grew louder in my brain.

As we reached Eric, he started to stand, but my dad was having none of that as he clapped him on the shoulder.

"We're so sorry for your loss." Dad and Mom said all the usual things one said at times like this, then drifted to the buffet set up along the side of the reception space, leaving me alone with Eric. We'd known each other for almost twenty-five years, and I had zero clue what the right thing to say was.

"Hey, buddy." I took one of the nearby empty chairs, so I didn't loom over him. Standing, Eric was taller and a little broader in the shoulders but narrower in the waist than my Irish spark-plug build. Today, though, there was little trace of Eric's swimmer build and usual take-charge personality. Weariness rolled off him in waves. "I figure you're sick of the question, so I'm not gonna ask how you're holding up. Do you need anything though? Food?"

I gestured at the buffet table, but Eric merely shook his head.

"Time machine?" He gave a harsh laugh before returning to an impassive expression. "Sorry. I'm good. Haven't been able to eat much."

"You need to try." Eric and Montgomery's oldest kid, Maren, drifted over, toting a large piece of cake. She'd arrived home from college in time for the service, and I'd yet to see her sit for more than five minutes. She reminded me so much of my Bridget with her similar age and efficient mannerisms. "Here." Maren pressed the plate into Eric's hands. "It's carrot cake. Your favorite."

"Thanks, sweetie." Eric stared down at the generous square of cake. "It was Monty's favorite too. We had it at the wedding."

"I remember." I tried for a warm rather than wistful tone. "It was a great day."

"Great weekend," our mutual friend Jonas added as he snagged another nearby chair. An ER nurse supervisor, he had a naturally reassuring voice. "Even Tony came."

"Might have been the last time the four of us were

together." Eric sighed as Tony himself wandered over. I hadn't been aware he'd been able to come, and I smiled broadly at our old friend. Tony had worn his army dress uniform. His longer hair and beard said he'd come off a recent deployment for the hush-hush work he did for the Rangers.

"We're here now, buddy. And here for you." Tony clapped Eric on the shoulder before taking a seat next to me. "What needs doing at the house? Laundry? Kitchen? Bathrooms? I'm your man. Put me to work."

"We're fine—" Eric started to reply, but Jonas held up a hand.

"Thanks, Tony. The house has plenty of work to go around." Unlike Tony and me, Jonas had only briefly left Mount Hope for school. He'd stayed with Eric and Montgomery during Montgomery's hospice care to help keep the household running. "I've caught up with the laundry, but if you want to come by later and help me put the kitchen to rights, that would be great."

Eric opened and shut his mouth before swallowing hard. "Thank you." He scrubbed at his hair. "God, I hate needing help."

"You'd tell any of us to take the help offered," I pointed out. Taking a clue from Tony's and Jonas's refusals to take no for an answer, I added, "I'll be by too. See if there's some yard work."

"Plenty of that." Eric slumped farther in his chair. "More if—when—I put the place on the market."

"You need to sell?" I couldn't keep the dismay out of my voice. If anyone loved their house as much as I'd loved mine, it was Eric and Montgomery, who owned one of Mount Hope's largest, most historic homes. Their purchase a few years back and remodeling efforts had been a time of much joy. "Oh, dude."

"I've been over the numbers. And over them. Huge mortgage, one kid in college, three close behind, and me not pulling near enough hours." Eric shook his head. His eyes were red, and my chest ached for him. "I don't know what else to do."

"Dad." Maren had returned with a paper cup of coffee for Eric. "You can't sell."

"I know, baby girl." Eric reached out to pat her arm before taking the cup of coffee. "Breaks my heart too. And I hate the idea of moving you kids."

In addition to Maren, Eric and Montgomery had three other adopted kids, a rowdy crew of teens.

"Rent my room." Maren's voice brokered little argument. "I've barely slept there in well over a year. Heck, you've slept up there more than me. Or turn the old carriage house into a rental. Maybe both?"

"I'll start paying rent for the basement." Leaning forward, Jonas spoke up before Eric could reply. "Today."

"I thought you wanted your own place?" Eric frowned, but Jonas waved the concern off.

"Nah. Turns out the basement is more than enough space for me and Oz."

"Okay. I should say no, but that might help." Eric's tone was pained. "Give us a little breathing room."

Maybe... The drumbeat from earlier returned, loud and insistent, and before I could overthink things, I raised a hand.

"I can help too." I used my fire captain voice. Maren and Jonas weren't the only ones who could be forces to be reckoned with. "Let me fix up the carriage house. I could take Maren's room while I work."

"You're coming back to town?" Eric asked.

"Yeah. It's my dad's last year of work. Nothing tying me to Seattle anymore. Declan's in southern Oregon, and Bridget's in LA. I've been debating the move." I crossed my fingers, hoping the last fifteen minutes counted as *debate*. "And Dad's got a firefighter going out on maternity—"

"Rodriguez." Eric nodded sharply. He'd been on leave during Montgomery's time in hospice, but Eric was a lead paramedic for Mount Hope, and like my father, he knew all the area first responders. "He'd love having you around more, that's for sure."

"And no offense to my mom, but no way am I taking over my old room at forty-three." I made my eyes wide and horrified and added a smile as Tony and Jonas laughed.

"I suppose you and Jonas as renters isn't the worst idea." Eric sounded distinctly reluctant, but I could hardly fault the guy. He looked like he hadn't slept well in weeks and had enough on his plate even without facing a potential move. "I hate the idea of moving the younger kids. And more adults around would mean I could take more shifts."

"Let us help you, buddy." I reached out to quickly pat his knee.

"Get that carriage house done or free up another room by the time I process out this summer, and I'm in too." Tony nodded sharply, another done deal.

"Oh wow." Eric's gaze swept between the three of us.

"See, Dad?" Maren was the most enthusiastic of us all. "It will all work out."

"Yep." Tony grinned. "The four of us, together again."

"But not in a two-bedroom dump near the college." Jonas shuddered, and I had to agree. No way did I want to return to the community college lifestyle of our young adult years.

"Are you sure you want to upend your life to come back to Mount Hope?" Eric studied me closely, the only person besides my dad who could always spot the lie.

"Absolutely." I did my best to banish the doubt from my voice and expression, but in truth, I was anything other than certain. All four of us were too old to be starting over, yet as Tony had pointed out, here we were again.

Chapter One

Denver

The hot ginger firefighter was in for breakfast again. A little older than my thirty-nine and on the shorter side, but oh so easy on the eyes. Third time this week, but his first after a shift change. Knowing the shift schedule for the nearby firehouse was an occupational hazard, not the result of stalking any first responder eye candy.

I might look, but uniforms were far from my usual. Give me someone scruffy, a little feral, a lot wounded... Okay. Hot messes were my personal kryptonite, a habit I was trying hard to break. I'd given up smoking, partying, and I'd been working the overnight shift here at Honey's Hotcake Hut for over eighteen months now. I was almost a regular upstanding citizen. Almost.

Sizzle. Two eggs over easy joined the not-too-crispy bacon on my griddle as I finished the previous order while Tammy got the firefighters situated at the counter. Only three of them today, down from their usual full-shift crew looking for after-midnight chow. We were one of the very few twenty-four-hour options for food in Mount Hope, so I didn't kid myself that the new guy had been coming around to see me specifically.

I did, however, nod at all three of them as Tammy poured their coffee and doled out glasses of juice.

"No middle-of-the-night munchies run?" I teased the group as I plated the order for the only other patron at the counter, an old farmer named Ed who spoke little, tipped less, but came in like clockwork every Saturday. Near the window, a hungover group of twenty-somethings nursed coffee refills while picking at half-eaten plates of loaded hash browns.

"We were up all night babysitting the last of a warehouse fire out south of town." Ginger's younger friend, a blond firefighter I'd privately nicknamed Fireman Flirty, answered first. Flirty's real name was Caleb, and he'd demonstrated a willingness to banter with everyone from eight months to eighty.

"And now we're starving." Ginger groaned. He wore jeans and a blue pullover rather than his usual uniform. The look made him seem far more approachable, a quiet vulnerability in his eyes that did something for me. "I could murder a stack of pancakes."

"That's rather violent." Caleb laughed easily. "But I'd like to make out with some bacon about now."

"Your usual meat-lovers omelet with a side of bacon?" I asked, already prepping. Caleb was as predictable as he was flirty.

"You know it." Chuckling, Caleb jerked his head toward Ginger. "And whatever my friend here wants. I owe Sean big time after last night."

"Hey, I'm enjoying being out in the field." Ginger—*Sean*—held up his hands. The name suited him, a short, sharp, masculine nod to his Irish looks. And damn it, of course, he had dimples. Adults had no business with dimples. Too damn devastating and possibly as tempting as wounded eyes and pouty lips. "Saving Caleb's ass a mud bath was a bonus."

"And what a cute ass it is." Tammy smirked as she topped off the coffee. Like Caleb, she was an unrepentant flirt. Somewhere between fifty-five and seventy, not that she'd ever fess up to that many years, Tammy looked like Dolly Parton's redheaded half-sister. Like me, she'd had her share of hard-living years, but her smile and quick wit kept diners coming in. "Good thing you didn't get dirty. Might have had to offer you a sponge bath myself."

"Don't encourage him." The third firefighter grimaced. Tom Johnson had been coming in for as long as I'd been at Honey's, and he'd been grumpy the whole damn time. "And I'll take some of those loaded hash browns. Gotta recall my misspent single youth."

"Coming up." I nodded even before Tammy added the order. Johnson's unhappily married state was a frequent source of his complaints and his attempts at jokes.

"And you, sweetie?" Tammy asked Sean. Busy at the grill, I still managed to listen for his reply.

"Can't decide. I'm torn between an omelet and hash browns. Or a skillet. Decisions." Sean's tone wasn't nearly as flirty as Caleb's, but I liked his friendly yet strong voice. Made me feel a certain warmth I hadn't had much of this long damn winter.

I briefly turned back to the counter. "Want me to surprise you?"

"Take Denver up on it," Tammy urged with a cackle. "His surprises are usually worth it. Usually."

"Sure thing. Save me from myself." Sean offered a grin,

and those dimples were even better in high-definition. Made me want to make him smile more, an unfamiliar urge outside of the normal desire to make sure our diners left happy.

"Any allergies?"

"Only to good taste." Answering for Sean, Caleb pretended to shudder. "Pineapple does *not* belong on pizza."

"Hey, I ordered the usual suspects too." Sean rolled his eyes at the younger firefighter.

"I should take you to Pinball Pizza. Teach you what the good stuff tastes like," Caleb countered as I continued to work on their orders.

"You asking the newbie out?" Johnson didn't sound horrified as much as curious, which was about what I'd expect from this crew. Like me, Caleb seemed to have an equal opportunity dick, and I'd seen all manner of pairings among the area's first responders. Interestingly, Sean blushed but didn't do the straight-guy bluster thing.

"If I ask someone out, there's no doubt." Caleb gave a flirty wink that set Tammy to laughing.

"You're a heartbreaker, for sure." Tammy moved to the register to ring the college kids out, then seated an older couple in a booth and a trucker at the counter. We were starting to pick up, and I was happy to see Amos wander in for his shift about that time, followed by two more servers. Tammy was busy filling the day crew in on how the overnight went, so I delivered the firefighters' orders myself.

"Meat-lovers special. hash browns." I slid Caleb and Johnson their plates. "And for you, a Hawaiian omelet."

"I love it." Sean treated me to another dimple show, and the flex of his biceps as he reached for the hot sauce offered even more to like. "Thank you."

Amos had already fired up the second grill, so I took a breather to lean on the counter. "So, newbie, what brings you to town?"

"He thinks you're a rookie." Caleb made a sound between a cough and a laugh, which made me wish Sean had come in without the audience. "Tom was joking earlier. Sean's not really a newbie. Captain out of Seattle. But he's Chief Murphy's son. Mount Hope royalty."

"Hardly." Sean snorted. "But to answer the question, I'm helping out an old friend and making my folks happy at the same time."

"Ah." I'd had a vague sense of knowing the dude all week, and the pieces finally clicked into place. "Bumped into you at Doc Wallace's service, didn't I?"

I didn't know exactly why I'd gone to that funeral. Neighborly thing to do, but I was hardly known as the neighborly type. And while Dr. Wallace had been my doctor and someone who'd helped me, I wasn't sure I'd call him a friend. I'd run into Sean here on my way out of the church when my head had been a jumble of conflicting thoughts, and it was no wonder I'd needed time to place the connection.

"Yep." Sean's ready answer said he'd known who I was all along. "I'm staying with Eric and covering for a firefighter on maternity leave."

"Good for you." Tammy floated over to refill the coffee cups again. "I'm sure those Wallace-Davis kids need all the help they can get."

"Yep." I gave a last nod before turning to clean my grill and get ready to clock out. Figuring out where I knew Sean from had unsettled me some, but the cleaning routine cleared my head. Honey's Hotcake Hut was located in the same aging building it had occupied for fifty-something years. Not the fanciest or newest joint, but with so many nurses and first responders among the regulars, the place prided itself on cleanliness, something I appreciated too.

I heard Tammy ring up the firefighters shortly before we clocked out at seven. Already counting down to a hot shower, I headed for my ancient red Chevy. To my surprise, I found Sean standing next to a much shinier blue truck. A deep scowl had replaced his dimples.

"You still here?" I asked as I approached. "Truck problems?"

"Locked my dumbass out. Not even sure how." He made a sour face as he pointed at the keys laying on the passenger seat. "I've got a spare back at Eric's, but I don't want to wake him or the kids up early on a Saturday. And God knows I'm not calling the station."

"The teasing might do you in," I agreed. The firefighters were among my favorite customers, but they could be a rowdy bunch.

"Guess I might as well start walking."

"Nah." I shook my head and pointed at my truck. "Get in."

Chapter Two

Sean

Short on sleep, I blinked at the burly cook from Honey's Hotcake Hut. Was he serious about the offer of a ride? Tammy had referred to him as Denver, but I wasn't sure if it was a nickname or his actual name. I'd been surprised earlier in the week to discover the big guy from Montgomery's funeral behind the griddle at the longtime Mount Hope diner. Honey's had been there for weekend breakfasts with my dad and grandad, hungover college days, and meals with my crew, but this Denver person was new.

"You don't need to give me a ride." I kept my voice easy. No need for him to suspect I'd suggested Honey's for breakfast again in hopes of getting another look at him. No harm in looking. "It's my own dumb fault, and it's not that long of a walk."

"It's damn cold and a good two miles." Denver gave me a stern look, and perversely, heat gathered low in my belly. Fierce looked good on the dude, giving him the air of grumpy warrior king with the wild hair and broad build.

He'd shed his white chef coat in favor of a battered leather jacket over a plain T-shirt, which added to the vibe. And he wasn't wrong. It was only a hair over thirty degrees, and the historic Prospect Place street where Eric lived was clear on the other side of downtown, a decent hike from the fire station and Honey's. "And I live on the same street. Get in."

Denver motioned again at his truck, an older two-door Chevy.

"You live on Prospect Place?" Deciding it was easier and warmer to let the guy give me a ride, I climbed in. But I wasn't sure I bought the coincidence.

"I rent a studio in the old McGregor house down the street from your pal." Denver let his truck warm up while turning down the stereo set to a driving hard rock tune. "Doc Wallace hooked me up with the vacancy."

"You knew Montgomery?" Another shocker. Eric's late husband had been older than us by a few years, elegant in that East Coast elite way, and while friendly with everyone, a surgeon was hardly the type to pal around with a rough-around-the-edges guy like Denver.

"Sort of." Denver shrugged. "I picked up a job at Timberline winter before last. The idea was to spend the winter snowboarding and working in the lodge before figuring out my next move. One emergency appendectomy surgery later, though, and I was unable to do the job for a stretch and not snowboarding any time soon."

"Ah. Montgomery did your operation?" I asked as Denver put the truck in Drive and headed out of the Honey's parking lot.

"Yep. Doc convinced me to stay in town through my follow-up appointment. Said he had a lead on a neighbor with a rental and hooked me up with the month-to-month place."

"That sounds like Montgomery." Like my dad, Montgomery had known everyone of importance around town. Montgomery had been on the Prospect Place neighborhood board along with several hospital committees and charities. "So you decided to stay on in Mount Hope?"

"Yup. Nice enough place." Denver's voice made the decision to relocate sound as easy and uninvolved as what to have for dinner. Maybe for him, it was. "I got bored of lazing around recovering. Wandered into Honey's, and the rest is history. I'll move on eventually, but here works for now."

"Professional nomad?" My entire existence had been one of deep roots and complicated ties. What would it be like to have unlimited choices? To drift from job to job?

"Something like that." Denver's tone went from casual to ever so slightly cagey. "What about you? You been away awhile?"

"Twenty years, give or take." I gave him the change in topics as we approached downtown Mount Hope and the maze of one-way streets that slowed traffic. "My ex's graduate schooling and professorship took us out of the area. But no more ex, no more house, no more reason to stay in Seattle, so coming home for a bit seemed to make sense."

"Well, welcome home." Denver offered me a pragmatic smile. "Probably better off without the ex."

Of course the drifter who floated from temporary job to temporary job would think relationships weren't all that. "Not sure about that."

Maxine and I had been...comfortable. Not romantic, but a deep, three decades-long friendship. When we'd split, I'd been shocked at how much I missed her and hated coming home to an empty house.

"Take Caleb up on the dinner invite." Denver winked

before pulling forward to the next in a series of lights. "That'll change your tune."

"You're suggesting..." I trailed off. Despite Tom's teasing, Caleb hadn't been asking me out. At least, I didn't think so. He had been rather...attentive since I started at the station though. Hell. Now, I wasn't at all certain. "I can't hook up with a coworker."

"Ha." Denver grinned wide like he'd caught me in some lie.

"What?"

"Nothing." He continued to look like a collie who'd treed a squirrel. "Just what you didn't say there. No issues with Caleb's gender, just his uniform?"

"Something like that." I echoed Denver's earlier cagey tone. I wasn't about to unpack my sexuality with someone I'd known less than half an hour.

"Good to know." Denver smirked as the endless traffic lights downtown finally let us pass into the surrounding residential streets. "Should I pull in at the Wallace-Davis house or park on the street? You said you didn't want to wake the kids?"

"They're teenagers. Saturday is for sleeping in." I chuckled. "You don't need to drop me off right at the house. Park where you usually do. I'll walk over and have Eric or Jonas run me back to my truck later with my spare key."

"Sure thing." Denver pulled into the old McGregor house—a mint-green Edwardian with three stories that had been carved into several apartments. Well-kept exterior, though, and the long driveway led to a discreet parking area for residents behind the house. As he parked, he gave me a long, considering look. So long, in fact, that I started to shift around in my seat. I was known for my cool under pressure, but Denver seemed determined to test that.

"In a hurry to get your beauty rest?" he asked at last, a certain gravity to the question I couldn't quite place.

"Nah." I tried to hedge my bets in case Denver wanted some sort of favor, but his expression remained intense and unreadable. "I'm always super keyed up after a shift. I'll nap at some point, but right now, my priority is a shower. Didn't get one at the station."

He nodded sharply, like he'd come to some critical decision. "I have a shower."

Oh. It had been decades since I'd heard a come-on. Guys on my various crews were always teasing me about my inability to recognize flirtation, but oblivion had served me well during my married years. Now, however, I was single, and Denver was rather blatant as he added some heat to his stare, a lengthy once-over that left little doubt.

I swallowed hard. "You...do?"

"I do." He exited the truck with a surprising grace, given his height, and pointed at the house. "You should let your housemates sleep in. Come inside with me. Check my shower out."

Chapter Three

Sean

That I wasn't the kind of guy to say yes to an impulsive hookup with some dude I barely knew was the understatement of the millennium. And for all everyone kept urging me to "get back out there," this wasn't what they meant.

Or was it?

I exited the truck, intent on finding the backbone to turn Denver down. But my feet didn't listen, marching me around the truck to stand in front of Denver. He raised an eyebrow but stayed quiet. He wasn't going to make this easy.

I'd always done the responsible thing, the *right* thing. While my friends had been out spending their late teens and early twenties partying and having all the sex, I'd been married, helping Maxine through school, raising Declan and Bridget.

Not having sex.

Maybe I was overthinking things, as per my usual. Why not have a taste of the youth I'd never had? One little hookup. One bite of the thing I'd thought about for decades but had never had. One chance to answer that question in the back of my head once and for all.

Yes. As soon as I let myself have the thought, I nodded. Couldn't quite bring myself to speak, but Denver didn't seem troubled by my silent agreement.

"Come on. I'm on the first floor." He led the way to the front door of the large house. Once inside, a staircase dominated the entryway with a door on either side of the hall. Denver unlocked the door on the right before standing back so I could enter.

He'd called his apartment a studio, but it was far larger than most studios, especially those I'd seen in Seattle. A large living area flowed into a small nook for a kitchenette with a table and two wooden chairs. On the other side of the living room, French doors led to a narrow sun porch with windows all around. Likely original and not insulated, but a pretty space nonetheless, with two rocking chairs. In the living room, a queen bed with an iron frame was tucked into a bay window with wooden blinds for privacy. The main space featured an older couch with wood trim that suited the age of the house, a fireplace, and ample shelving.

"Nice place." I finally found my voice as Denver pulled off his jacket and tossed it on a coat tree in the corner near the kitchenette. "I love all the original built-ins."

"Yep." Denver gestured for me to add my coat to the rack. "It came furnished, though, so don't go giving me credit."

I shrugged off my coat. Slowly. Not as a tease, but more to quiet my racing brain, which lagged behind my ready-to-go body. Denver, on the other hand, seemed totally at ease. Maybe too comfortable.

"You...uh...do this a lot?"

"Nope." Denver's expression remained impassive, perhaps a little impatient. "I'm tested on the regular though. All negative."

Oh yeah. Safety first. In my readiness to reclaim my wild side, I'd forgotten a few details.

"Me too," I said quickly, trying to think what else I should know about. "No...uh...significant other?"

"I'm a lot of things, but not a cheater." He regarded me through a level gaze that made me feel already naked, exposed on a level I wasn't sure I'd been before.

"Good." I didn't try to hide my relief. "Me either. I'm single."

"I know. You said." A smile played around the edge of his mouth. He was large and imposing, but when he smiled, he had a gentleness that made him far more approachable. "Figure I can get your mind off your ex for an hour or so. Follow me."

"I...yeah." No sense in explaining I'd never been hung up on Maxine that way. I followed him past the kitchen area to a surprisingly large and airy bathroom with an absolute giant clawfoot tub under a window with a wraparound shower curtain. The old tub contrasted with a more modern showerhead, likely purchased during the same remodel that added the newer-style basin sink and recessed lighting. "That's a huge tub."

Denver smiled wider. "First I've had as an adult where I could take a real bath."

"Nice." The image of Denver reclined in the tub, all soapy, was almost more than I could take, but then he went and yanked off his T-shirt, easy as breathing. Turning, he shed his white chef pants and boxers next.

Denver was impressive, almost intimidating, when dressed, but naked took him to a breathtaking level. Big. All over. Wide chest. Less fuzzy than I'd expected given the wild hair on his head, but a decent smattering of chest hair. Dark nipples in keeping with his golden skin tone. He looked ready for an August surfing competition while I was still winter-pale, as always. He had muscular arms and powerful thighs, a soft belly, and a hard cock that bounced as he walked to the tub. His comfort level was almost as arousing as his physique.

"You planning on joining?" Pointing at my fully clothed self, he turned back to fully face me. I swallowed hard and flexed my hands as a tremor raced through me. Quaking like one of my mom's dubious gelatin salads was hardly in line with my twenty years of firefighting experience, but here I was, nervous and entirely out of my depth. A scowl replaced Denver's smile. "I'm good with you watching if that's your jam, but you're gonna have to find your words. Tell me what you like. I'm not here to talk you into anything."

I don't know wasn't an acceptable answer, but the idea of Denver calling a halt to the proceedings loosened my tongue.

"I like whatever you like." I tried for an impish grin, unsure if I actually pulled it off.

"Uh-huh." Denver didn't sound convinced, but he made a little go-ahead gesture. "I'd like your clothes on my floor."

"I can do that." An eagerness to please that I hadn't felt since my rookie days hastened my movements, stripping away some of my nerves along with my clothes. I was shorter than Denver, far more freckled, less hairy, and had a decidedly more average-sized dick than his porn-worthy cock. But he must have liked what he saw because he made an approving noise, heat returning to his gaze.

"That's better." His approval sent all my blood south,

making my already interested dick painfully hard. Giving a low chuckle, he flipped on the shower. "Come over here."

Only a fire alarm could get me moving faster as I crossed to stand next to him, awaiting his next command. Denver narrowed his eyes, more of that intense stare that saw far more than I wanted to reveal. "You like orders?"

His somber tone didn't leave much room for a flip response.

"Apparently." I glanced down at my aching erection. "You talking...it does something for me. I'm used to being in charge, but you telling me what to do feels good."

Good was far too tepid a word for the pounding of my pulse and rush of adrenaline coursing through me, but the guy was cocky enough without me heaping on the praise.

"I can roll with that." He stretched his neck from side to side, flexing like he was preparing for a workout. Which maybe he was. "You okay if I get a little...*bossy*?"

Only Denver could make the word *bossy* sound so sexy. All the air rushed out of my lungs. "Oh, fuck yes."

"That's what I like to hear." He gave me a feral grin before jerking a thumb at the tub. "Into the shower."

The water was bracingly hot, almost but not quite too much, not unlike Denver himself. On my own, I would have turned down the heat, but here, I was more than content to wait for Denver's next order.

And wait.

He took his damn time stepping into the tub, arranging the shower curtain, and pulling out his ponytail elastic from his hair. He shook his hair loose, and it was longer than I'd expected, falling in haphazard curls around his shoulders. Moving to stand in front of me, under the spray, he wet his hair before lathering it with a thick, creamy shampoo that made me think of other creamy white fluids. My dick pulsed hard, bobbing against my belly.

The effortless way Denver carried out the task transfixed me. His shampoo smelled like fruity coconuts and came in a lavender bottle that proclaimed its suitability for curly hair, yet Denver radiated masculine energy. Everything from the way his big fingers dug into his scalp to the delicate way he untangled the waves of hair while rinsing to the flex of his meaty biceps turned me on.

I hissed in a breath as he shuffled around so I had an equal amount of the water spray. He was close enough now that I could feel his warmth as well as the water's. Another centimeter in any direction and our bodies would touch, and my every nerve ending tingled with anticipation. But I stayed rooted to the spot, mere seconds away from begging for another command.

Denver chuckled knowingly. "Nice as your eyes are, we need to find a use for your hands."

"*Yes.*"

"Wash me." He handed me a thick slab of soap that smelled like nutty butter with undertones of coffee and spice. Happy, I accepted the soap and immediately reached for his impressive cock. Might as well start with the good parts. But all that earned me was a clucking noise and a head shake from Denver. "Nah-uh. Do it right."

The sternness in his tone made me want to earn his approval and praise, to not simply do it right, but do it the best he'd ever had.

"This?" Moving deliberately, I started with his neck, digging my fingers into the thick cords of muscle before moving to his shoulders, rubbing and soaping.

"Perfect." His praise felt warmer than the near-scalding water and made me spend that much more time on his chest, soaping, rinsing, repeating. He had more chest hair than it had seemed at first glance, and I loved how it crinkled against my palms. A rumble not unlike a purr escaped his lips and his eyes flickered shut. Emboldened, I washed lower, skating over his soft belly, all around his proud cock, but not touching it. Denver chuckled. "I see what you're doing."

"Sorr—"

"Did I say stop?" He gave me a pointed look, so I resumed my efforts, soaping his powerful thighs. "Keep going. Got more to wash."

I took that as permission to reach for his cock again, gently washing it and his heavy balls. A dick other than my own was a novelty, yet Denver felt *right* in my hand. I wrapped my fingers around his shaft, enjoying the way his plump cockhead poked out of my fist. I jacked him experimentally, using a looser grip than I would for myself.

"Mmmm." Head tipping back, he moaned low, and all I wanted in the world was to figure out how to coax more of those pleasured sounds from him. I swept my thumb across his tip, gathering a slick bead of precome, but the shower washed it away before I could lick my finger.

"Jesus, I want to taste you." The words came out in a breathless rush.

"Yeah?" Denver didn't seem nearly as surprised as I was at my request. "On your knees then."

He turned and spread his stance wider, allowing me to kneel on the anti-slip mat on the bottom of the tub.

"Thank you."

"No thanking me yet." Denver gave a wicked smile as he gripped his cock, waggling it in front of my face. "Open wide."

He traced my lips with his cockhead, and I greeted it

with enthusiastic licking. Denver made a noise of approval before releasing his shaft and letting me take over. Enthusiasm seemed to be working for me, so I set about mimicking my favorite porn blowjobs, going fast and deep.

I promptly choked as I encountered a heretofore undiscovered gag reflex. Not one to be defeated, I tried again, but going slower didn't make me more coordinated. I was overthinking this, and I made a frustrated noise.

"Easy, baby. You don't have to set any records here." Denver pitched his voice more soothing than stern, which hardly helped my irritation at my ineptitude. But then he fisted his cock again, lower this time, and resumed teasing my lips. "Here, let me drive."

"Yes." Oh, I liked this, not having to think or worry about choking. All I had to do was chase his cockhead with my tongue, sucking when he allowed, taking only what he gave me. "Yes. *Please.*"

I wasn't sure what I was begging for, only that I wanted more of this floaty sensation, adrenaline surging as anticipation replaced any fear over giving up control.

"You like this?" Denver fed me a bit more of his shaft, and amazingly, this time, I didn't choke. For all that Denver was a near-stranger, I trusted him. He wouldn't give me more than I could take, and he knew exactly what he wanted. No more guesswork on my part. "This what you want? Me to use your mouth?"

"Yes. Yes." Warm water sluiced over my back, and Denver's dirty talk further heated me, but a shudder raced through me, hands shaking from how badly I wanted more.

"Good. Keep those teeth back, and just let me fuck that gorgeous mouth of yours." Denver set a slow, easy tempo of shallow thrusts, dragging his cock against the flat of my tongue on every retreat. I loved the weight of his shaft and the way it pulsed, a vital energy to his cock I couldn't have anticipated but was quickly coming to crave. Feeling bold, I stroked his balls. "Nah-uh." Denver made a low warning noise. "Hands on my hips. Pinch me if I go too hard, but I think you can take it."

"I can." My voice was so husky I barely recognized it. Strangely, letting Denver stay in charge made me way more confident in my abilities. He knew what he wanted. He'd take exactly what he needed, but the gentleness in his approving smile reassured me he wouldn't claim more than I could give. Denver was stern and commanding without an ounce of cruelty, a combination that settled any of my remaining nervousness.

I gave myself over to his cock, living for each forward thrust, protesting every retreat with little moans and stronger suction until Denver was also groaning and breathing fast.

"Fuck. How am I this close?" The wonder in Denver's voice had me doubling down. More suction. More surrender. I leaned into his hand on my shoulder, letting him direct me how he wished. With his other hand, he let go of his cock to stroke my jaw. A small gesture that got a huge reaction from my own cock, which throbbed harder.

Without his hand to guide his cock, Denver was able to thrust more freely, and surprisingly, my gag reflex was nowhere to be found. I melted into the tub, losing all sense of time, surrounded by warm water and a hotter man, reduced to nothing more than vibrating nerve endings.

"You want it?" Denver's voice took on a more urgent note. "Want to swallow?"

"Swallow." I couldn't answer fast enough. No way had I come this far not to finish the job. Nice of him to give me a choice, but I wanted to get right back to that melty, brain-numbing space where I didn't have to think. *"Please."*

"Good choice." Denver went faster now, with deeper thrusts, but somehow, I kept up with him, relaxing my body and finding that place of surrender again. "Fuck, you're amazing." My breathing synced with his right down to the little hitches as he got closer. I was close too, the shower washing away what felt like a near-constant pulse of precome, more with every moan of Denver's. "Can't believe you're letting me... *God. God.* Keep sucking."

I sucked hard, harder than I knew was possible, as he came down my throat with a shout that echoed off the bathroom tile. As I swallowed the salty, slightly bitter load, he thrust in shallow motions, drawing out his pleasure in an erotic display that had my abs and thighs tensing, a white-hot rush racing through me.

I shuddered along with Denver, scarcely aware I was climaxing as well until another harsh wave hit me as he pulled back. My come hit the shower curtain and side of the tub. Yup. All those questions I'd had were answered with unmistakable clarity. I loved this. My body loved this. My knees and jaw ached, and my dick was spent, and still, I'd do it again right that moment if he asked. Between the lack of sleep and the absolute soul-snatching pleasure of the orgasm, I could do little more than chuckle helplessly between gasps.

"Fuck. That was fast." Denver offered me a hand up, eyes widening as his gaze swept over the streaks of my come clinging to the shower curtain along the side of the tub. "You came untouched?"

"Um. Yeah." Damn, my Irish skin. I was likely glowing pink at that point.

"Damn." He whistled as I clambered to my feet. "Guess it had been a long time for you too, huh?"

"Try ever." I was still dazed and more than a little wobbly, or I might have thought twice about the admission.

Denver blinked, then blinked again, voice going from impressed to downright horrified. "You're a virgin?"

Chapter Four

Denver

I hadn't lied to Sean. It had been years since I'd made a habit of hookups. Sure, I could be impulsive, but these days, I limited my questionable decision-making to a few times a year. Rarely customers, but something about the ginger firefighter had made me break that rule. And speaking of rules, one of the ones I clung tightest too was no virgins. No more curiosity-driven fucks turned into aching hearts. Nope. Been there, done that, got the T-shirt collection. Never again.

Sean's sheepish expression answered for him, even before he hedged. "Virgin is a rather broad term."

"Uh-huh." Playtime over, I flipped off the shower and hopped out of the tub to grab two towels. I handed one to Sean. "But that doesn't answer my question. That was your first time? Like, first time giving head? First time...ever? With anyone?"

Part of the attraction of the dude had been his mature age. He'd seemed settled, the sort of solidly responsible, no-drama dude who knew what he wanted. Sure, he'd seemed out of the hookup game, but so was I. When he'd needed the ride, the opportunity seemed to be knocking, with no need for a stupid app or a night at the bar. And he had to be over forty, a rarity on apps and at bars. But a virgin? *Fuck me.* And not in the good way.

"You don't have to sound so horrified." Sean dried off. He had the palest skin with acres of freckles. Not the most body hair, but what he had was red like his head. Intriguing, like the rest of him, and while I bore responsibility for inviting him in, his hotness wreaked havoc on my good judgment. Hell, even the way he bristled under my questioning was hot. "First time with a man if you need specifics."

"I do." I groaned. Why did I always seem to attract the curious-but-closeted crowd? Why? I scrubbed at my damp stomach with the towel. "I told you. I'm not a cheater. And that includes people cheating themselves. I'm not interested in being a walk on the wild side for closeted straight guys."

"I'm not..." Sean looked down as he shook his towel out like it might have more answers than he did. "I mean...it's complicated."

I'd heard that a time or twenty, but something in his expression gave me pause, the vulnerable cast to his eyes or maybe the way his pink tongue darted out to lick at his lower lip. I gentled my voice. "Want to explain?"

"So you can judge me harder?" He gave me the pointed look I surely deserved. He didn't know my history.

"Sorry." I moved behind him to lay a hand on his bare shoulder. "I came off harsher than intended there. Partly because I've been burned before. And partly because I was shocked. You let me fuck your face like a veteran porn star."

"Uh. Thanks." Sean made a choking sound that turned into a laugh of sorts. His shoulder was warm under my hand, and I took my sweet time moving away. Turning his head, he offered me an impish smile that played off his pink cheeks. "And I've watched enough porn. Maybe that's why I was good at it."

I guffawed loudly at that. "If porn watching could make people better at sex, there would be a lot less bad sex in this world."

"True." Sean shrugged. "Maybe the fact I liked it so much counted for something?"

"Definitely." I couldn't help but smile at the memory of how damn amazing that orgasm had been. Top ten of all time, for sure, but I wasn't liking the awkward afterglow nearly as much. "But if you liked it so much, why wait until you were...what? Forty-one?"

"Forty-three. And like you, I'm not a cheater. I was married to a woman for over two decades. I took our vows seriously." Sean's tone was conversational but firm. "She was one of my best friends. Even if she would have been okay with me screwing around on the side, I wasn't going to step out on her or the kids. That's not who I am."

My eyebrows lifted. "She wouldn't have minded?"

"She implied as much a few times. Maxine is an academic-minded climate scientist who'd rather be analyzing snow samples than making bedroom magic." Sean's tone was fond, and he gave an almost wistful shake of his head. "We were the classic high-school couple of valedictorian good girl and second-string football player. Our families went to the same church, and our dating felt predestined. Not many sparks, but a deep friendship. We always could talk about anything."

"Talking is good." I said the words, but I tended to go for sparks. I wasn't one for deep conversations. Sean's chatty nature was both infectious and unnerving, the way I wanted him to keep going rather than herding him out of my apartment. "So you were high-school sweethearts?"

"Yup. Predictably went all the way on senior prom night. Had sporadic sex over the next year. Got pregnant with Declan despite using protection."

"That happens." Not to me, but the way Sean's mouth twisted said he still had unresolved feelings about the decades-old surprise. "So you got married?"

"Tale as old as time." Done toweling off, he pulled back on his jeans. "Got married. Conceived Bridget in a sleep-deprived act neither of us remembered until the two pink lines showed up."

I blinked at that. "Can't say I've ever had sex while sleeping."

"Can't say I recommend it." Sean chuckled as he picked up his pullover from the bathroom floor and put it on. "We muddled through those early years together. Then Maxine discovered the queer community in graduate school and became comfortable with talking about her asexuality. It explained a lot of our bedroom friction."

"I'm sorry." As soon as I said it, I knew that probably wasn't the right reply, and predictably, Sean bristled.

"Don't be. It was a good life, and I had my right hand and porn for restless nights. We were both committed to raising the kids. Sex took a backseat, but we made a lot of great family memories. Then, she asked for a divorce. Said it was time. Kids are grown. Her career is global at this point. The marriage that had been so comfortable for us both had started to chafe, I guess."

"But not for you?" Not in any particular hurry to get dressed, I wrapped my towel around my waist as Sean found his socks.

"Maxine said it wasn't fair to me to keep it going. That I

needed to get out there, find what would make me happy. I wasn't so sure. I'm kind of a creature of habit. The marriage and lack of sex weren't ideal, but things were familiar. I liked our house, our neighborhood, our friends, and my job. Our life, really. I liked that life."

"Maxine's not wrong." I wasn't sure what to make of Sean pining for a domesticity I'd never known or craved. This Maxine seemed wiser and more logical than Sean. Move on. That's what I'd do, but then, that was what I'd always done. "So you took her advice finally? That's why you said yes to me? An experiment? See if dick does it for you before you find the next Mrs.?"

"Boy, you have a lot of bitterness for someone who had the bright idea to invite me in for a shower." Sean shook his head, tone more disappointed than censoring. "I'm not sure who wounded you, but it wasn't me."

"You're right." I blew out a harsh breath. This wasn't like me, the snappy, judgmental attitude. Unlike Sean, I wasn't good at the whole sharing my life history thing, but I owed him a piece of the truth.

"It's not your fault. I seem to be a magnet for straight dudes. I don't really do relationships, but the closest I had was a toxic on-again-off-again thing with a band member when I was a roadie for a number of years." Somehow, I managed to make the disaster that was getting involved with James sound like a mild cold, not the poison that almost did me in. "He wasn't ever coming out, and I knew it, but somehow, we kept ending up back in bed. I finally ended it. I wouldn't say wounded, but maybe there are a few scars."

Liar. My chest ached, the deep hole where others had hearts calling me out.

"Understandable. And I'll be honest with you. I'm not sure what this was." A muscle in Sean's jaw moved as he finished putting on his shoes. "When I was younger, before Maxine and I got serious, I had some inkling that certain guys did it for me. Never acted on it because there was a lot of pressure to do the all-American football player thing. Then later, my porn-watching habits became rather... diverse. And then gradually more and more oriented toward man-on-man action. I didn't want the divorce, but now that it's happened, exploring doesn't seem like the worst idea."

"It's not. Be safe out there, but sow those wild oats." I made my voice hearty but detached. "Sounds like you never got the chance earlier. Go forth and have all the hookups."

"But not with you?" Sean met my gaze, peering deeply into my eyes.

I glanced away. Didn't need him seeing how damn much I'd like seconds with him. But I couldn't. "Not with me."

"You're good with casual, but not repeats?" He sounded let down. Not only had he been a fire captain used to being in charge, but he was also charming enough that he probably didn't often hear the word *no*.

"I'm not opposed to repeats, but I can't be your introductory course in queer sex." I went for firm honesty, steering him out of the bathroom, out of temptation's range, and toward the door.

"Even if I asked nicely?" Yep. He was charming, all right. So charming I could way too easily picture him on his knees again, maybe this time on my bed...

Buzz. Buzz. Sean dug his phone out of his pocket before I could answer his question.

"Darn it. Eric's kids are awake." Frowning, he grabbed his jacket off the coat rack. "Some sort of pancake drama happening. I better go."

I swallowed a frustrated noise. I'd been way too close to

giving in and resented the reminder that Sean was a responsible guy. He was in town to help a friend, not drifting through, and for all he was eager to experience more, this wasn't a guy who did casual anything. Dangerous for us both.

I nodded sharply, gesturing at the door. "Yeah, you better."

"Well, uh... Thanks?" Sean offered me a crooked smile that quickly faded to a confused expression. He wasn't the only one who had no idea how to part, but I couldn't let him see that any more than I could let him see how tempted I was.

I nodded sharply but didn't speak as Sean lingered near the door.

"See you around?"

Not if I can help it. "See you around."

Chapter Five

Sean

Still reeling from my talk with Denver, I entered Eric's kitchen only to encounter a war zone. The spacious room had been extensively remodeled, but it kept true to its late-Victorian roots with white cabinetry, a large farmhouse sink, a butcher-block island, and white tile backsplash and flooring. The stainless steel appliances were usually gleaming, and even with four teens, Eric managed to keep the space pristine. When we'd roomed together with Jonas and Tony, Eric had always been the neatnik.

He would freak out if he saw his immaculate kitchen covered with what appeared to be pancake batter studded with chunks of unidentified matter. On the island, several sticks of butter had been roughly hacked into bits without the benefit of a cutting board, and a river of syrup meandered toward the tile floor. A nearby blender was partially full of the same batter the cabinets currently sported, and the hand mixer, the food processor, and no less than three skillets and four mixing bowls had also been employed.

And I didn't need to look farther than a stool at the island to spot the culprit.

"Wren." I shook my head at Eric's youngest kiddo. They'd nabbed a white lab coat from somewhere and thick goggles spattered with batter completed their mad scientist look. Short and stout, Wren's build was not unlike my own, and I'd always had a soft spot for them. But even my affection had limits, and my inner dad voice took over. "What did you do?"

"What do you mean what did *I* do?" Sliding off the stool, Wren pulled themselves up to their full unsubstantial height. They were undoubtedly one of the shortest seventh graders. And smartest, their high IQ getting them into endless pickles. Neither of my two kids had been nearly so disaster-prone at this age. Practically snorting smoke like a dragon, Wren glared at their brother, who was lounging in the doorway to the dining room. "John texted you, didn't he?"

For his part, John shrugged, causing his Mount Hope Football T-shirt to tug across his chest. Despite the fact that John also wasn't the tallest kid, I often forgot he and Wren were bio siblings. Where Wren was a hurricane and a force of nature, John was a placid lake, calm and cool, unruffled by Wren's indignation.

"It was that or wake Dad."

"And I'm glad you didn't do that. Eric needs rest," I said quickly, already moving to right the syrup bottle. "Jonas is at work?"

Jonas's rangy cattle dog, Oz, lurked near John's leg, a clear sign Jonas wasn't in the house or his basement room. He'd continued to work his shifts as an ER supervisor even through his own divorce and Montgomery's illness. But he did enough around the house and with the kids that Wren likely wouldn't have attempted whatever the heck this mess was had he been home.

"Yep." John nodded before pointing at the stairs. "Rowan and Dad are both still asleep." Rowan was Eric's fourth teen and a notorious night owl. I wasn't shocked he'd slept through this disaster. Eric was still sleeping in Maren's room on the third floor, so he likely hadn't heard the commotion, thankfully.

"They both need their sleep." I gave Wren a pointed look.

"Agreed." John sounded far older than almost sixteen, weary tone more parental than brotherly. "But Wren had the bright idea to make popping pancakes."

"Popping pancakes?" I studied the splatters all over the kitchen cabinets for clues. Upon closer examination, what I'd initially assumed to be lumps of batter looked closer to round butter pellets.

"Exactly. Pancakes that pop." Wren bobbed their head, wild hair shaking from their obvious enthusiasm. "Like those candies that explode in your mouth? But breakfast. And the explosions in your mouth would be syrup and butter."

I blinked. Wren's delight in the word *explosions* was more than a little disconcerting.

"Sounds more violent than most breakfasts." I was joking, but Wren predictably didn't laugh. A sense of humor wasn't among their many gifts, so I backtracked. "I mean, brilliant invention. But slightly dangerous?"

"It's science." Wren gave me a withering look. "I know what I'm doing."

That made one of us. I still didn't know what I was doing back in Mount Hope, what I was doing with my life, or how to effectively help Eric and the kids. Heck, I didn't even know what I'd been doing earlier with Denver. I'd practically begged for a repeat despite Denver's disgust at my lack of experience. He might be reluctant to go for another round, but my body had no such reservations. That had been the single best sex act of my life, confirming decades of suspicion, and something I was desperate to have more of. But first, I had to broker teen peace and supervise kitchen cleaning.

"Bad science. Maybe your calculations were wrong?" John made the suggestion with an offhand tone, but Wren made an indignant noise even as he continued, "And now we have a huge mess and no breakfast."

"Let's remedy that." I slipped into my familiar in-charge role. Both as a dad and fire captain, I was comfortable leading unruly teams past conflict and toward a common goal. Like breakfast. "Is there more pancake mix?"

"Of course. Dad buys in bulk." John pointed at the well-stocked pantry at the rear of the kitchen.

"Let's clean up, and then I'll whip up a fresh batch. No popping." I made the executive decision that we'd had enough science experiments for the morning. I might not have a ton of experience in parenting genius mad scientists, but raising Declan and Bridget, as well as all my years in fire stations, had made me an A-plus pancake flipper.

Naturally, Wren groaned in defeat. "But—"

"I'll make bacon as well." I retrieved a large package from the fridge, grateful Eric kept Wren's favorite food in stock. As a huffy Wren and John started scrubbing cabinets, I readied a cast iron skillet, the sizzle reminding me of the diner.

And Denver. Unlike Wren's dubious experiments, Denver's innovation of the Hawaiian omelet had been delicious. The dish had been the perfect pairing of spicy sauce, creamy cheese, soft eggs, salty ham, and just enough pineapple to keep it interesting. He'd made it especially for me, riffing on my love of pineapple on pizza. Sweet-but-spicy was apparently my jam in men as well as food because I'd loved Denver's filthy mouth, demanding hands, and kind eyes.

I couldn't fully get the man off my mind, even as I prepared a mountain of pancakes and bacon for the kids. A bleary-eyed Rowan with messy hair wandered into the kitchen in time to grab a plate, and Eric followed him down the back stairs a short time later.

"Pancakes? And bacon?" Eric managed a small smile at the platters of food I'd arranged on the now-sparkling kitchen island, along with clean containers of syrup and butter. He plucked up one of the last pieces of bacon and bit it in half. "Thought you'd be sacked out by now."

"Nah." I stretched my neck from side to side, trying to look less tired. Twenty-odd hours of alertness was starting to take its toll, but no way was I complaining around Eric. "And the kids helped."

"Well, actually," Wren started at the same time that John said, "Wren—"

I shot both of them a warning look, which made John quickly add, "The bacon was Wren's idea."

"Good idea, bug." Eric ruffled Wren's wild hair before peering out the kitchen window. "Hey, where's your truck?"

Eric might be grieving, but he was as observant as ever. I plastered on my best easy smile, keeping my tone casual. "Long story, but I locked my keys in the truck while parked at Honey's Hotcake Hut. Any chance you could give me a ride back?"

"Sure." Eric glanced down at his baggy workout pants

and yellow T-shirt. "Guess I'm presentable enough. Let's do it now, get the errand over with."

"I could take him," John piped up, returning to the kitchen for seconds.

"You could not." Eric's stern dad voice was as good as mine, if not better. John had had his permit for a while now, but Eric seemed unusually reluctant to meet John's eager demands for driving practice.

"We need to get you more practice hours before your test." I aimed for a peace-making tone, but John continued to huff as he loaded more pancakes onto his plate.

"Do any of you know the statistics on teen drivers?" Not at all helpful, Wren looked all-too-ready to launch into gory detail.

"We do," Eric said grimly, resignation clear from the slump in his shoulders and the set of his chin. "I'll take you out later, John, promise."

"I can take him out practicing too. If you're not—"

"I'm fine." Eric poured himself a travel mug of black coffee from the pot I'd made while juggling pancakes. I didn't want to contradict him in front of the kids, so I waited until we were walking out to Eric's SUV to pick the conversation back up.

"Let me help more with the kids," I said as Eric unlocked the large SUV. He also had Montgomery's smaller compact parked near the detached carriage house garage, as well as an older truck. I pointed over at both vehicles. "I'm happy to take John out driving later in one of the older cars after I get some sleep."

"I should do it." Eric cast a guilty look in the direction of Montgomery's car. *Ah.* That was undoubtedly part of the issue. "I haven't spent enough time with him. He's had the permit for months now."

"Don't beat yourself up. You're doing the best you can." I handed out advice I needed to take too. I'd been adrift for months now with the sale of the house, the sabbatical from work, the return to Mount Hope, and settling into my new roles at the fire station and in Eric's house. The most alive and energized I'd felt had been in Denver's shower. There, I'd had a clear purpose, directions to follow, and none of this second-guessing my every move. "We all are. You. The kids. Rest of us."

"I guess." Eric didn't sound any more sure than I was about how well either of us was coping. As he pulled out of the driveway onto Prospect Place, he gave me a quick glance. "How'd you get home anyway? Don't tell me you walked. I would have come for you."

"I know you would have." I worried the inside of my cheek with my teeth, not sure how much of my morning to reveal. "I...uh...I caught a ride."

"Ha." Eric released a rusty laugh. "Bet the guys at the station had a field day drawing straws to see who got to come to your rescue."

"God, no." I shifted in the passenger seat. "The overnight cook at Honey's. He lives on your street."

"Oh, that's right." Eric took on a thoughtful tone as we headed out of the neighborhood. "Montgomery helped him find that studio apartment down the street. He was always helpful like that." He paused for a fond sigh. "Meddling almost, but his patients loved him."

"We all did." I gave him a quick pat on the shoulder as he stopped for a red light. "And he loved you and the kids so much."

"I know." He looked far off into the distance, down the hill from the historic neighborhood, past the start of the downtown buildings, past the river, into that tunnel of grief where none of us could follow. "And I'm grateful. But sometimes…it's hard."

"That's love." I wished either of my parents was with us because they'd know far better what to say. "Love isn't easy, but it's worth it. Better to have loved, right?"

"I suppose." Eric gave a subtle shake of his head that said I'd missed the mark with my platitudes. "But don't let my…stuff deter *you*. You should get back out there while you're in town."

I let him have the clear bid to change the topic. "You sound like my dad."

"He's not wrong." Eric offered me a brittle smile. "Date. Have fun. Have a fling while you decide your next move."

"Huh." Despite all the urging me to start dating again, no one else had encouraged me to think short-term or casual. "Maybe."

This would be an ideal moment to tell Eric about my encounter with Denver, but I kept my mouth shut for reasons I didn't entirely understand. It wasn't that I feared Eric's judgment. Indeed, I could use a friend's help figuring out what it all meant in terms of who I was, who I'd always been. *Oh.* That was likely it. I wasn't ready for the conversation, and as much as I could use Eric's steady advice, I didn't want to burden him with my rather trivial shit.

Instead, I continued to think quietly about the fling idea after Eric dropped me at my truck. I took a long moment considering Honey's before pulling out of the parking lot. Denver was likely home sleeping like I should be as well. But hell if I could get him off my mind. Like almost everyone else, he'd assumed I was in the market for another spouse sooner rather than later. I wasn't. And not because Maxine and our cozy companionship were irreplaceable, but because, like Eric said, it was hard. Loss of any kind sucked, and I wasn't eager to do it again.

But a fling...

That had possibilities. I was already jonesing for a repeat with Denver. Maybe if I tried his ultra-casual approach, I'd have better luck. I took the turn onto Prospect Place slowly, driving by Denver's place like some lovesick teen. His blinds were drawn. I didn't want to wake him, but we did need to talk. And soon.

Chapter Six

Denver

I'd been a night owl as long as I could remember, so working nights at Honey's Hotcake Hut wasn't ordinarily much of a challenge. However, squeezing in enough hours of daytime sleep while trying my damnedest not to think about Sean? That was a feat on par with reaching the top of Mount Hood. And forget thinking—simply trying not to give into the temptation to jerk off thinking about our shower sex had taken major willpower, something I wasn't exactly known for. Not surprisingly, I cut it close to the start of my Saturday-night shift at Honey's. Tammy was already there, rolling silverware, a fresh apron in place, and reddish hair towering over her heart-shaped face.

"What are you doing beating me here?" I aimed for a joking tone to distract from my own near-tardiness. "Gonna make me look bad."

"Eh. Not much to do at home." Tammy shrugged, ample bosom rising under her black apron. "Nothing good on TV tonight. Saturday night's not what it used to be."

"I hear that. You could always try one of the streaming services." I tended to avoid all the recurring monthly bills I possibly could, but an older woman like Tammy, living alone with three cats and working graveyards, seemed like an ideal candidate for shows on demand. Also, I didn't like the touch of loneliness in her voice or the way her chin sagged. "You okay though? Taking care of yourself? Sleeping?"

Earlier in the winter, during a slow shift, Tammy had mentioned being proud of a particular twelve-step milestone. I wasn't much on meetings, but we'd bonded over similar decisions to leave hard living behind us. Over the past few years, I'd reached a point where I seldom dwelled on my younger years of wild parties and rock group tours. I didn't know Tammy's full story, but I was fond of her and would miss her when I inevitably drifted on.

"Yes. Worrywart." She patted my upper arm, then my chin, ruffling my short beard. "You're sweet."

I wasn't, but it was nice of her to pretend. "Nah, I just don't want to have to cover all by my lonesome."

"What? Raking in all the tips for your handsome self?" She laughed lightly as I secured my hair and beard nets and headed to my grill station. During the day, Honey's operated two grill stations, both ringed by countertop stools. Overnight, though, we only needed the one. We also likely wouldn't need the mountain of silverware Tammy had rolled. "You'd love it."

"Ha." I shook my head because while the kitchen got a percentage of the tips, I was only too happy for Tammy to get the biggest share, as it was her hustle that earned the dollars. "It's you they come to see, Tammy."

"True." Arching her neck, she gave a regal nod before moving the silverware to a bus tub and grabbing a rag for the already-shining countertop. "And here's to hoping for a good night. Might be the last truly cold one for a while, but we'll have to see if the cold keeps the young folks from Saturday-night fun."

"As long as they treat you right." Our regulars—truckers, first responders, shift workers—were usually decent folks and good about tipping. However, the rowdy, semi-drunken weekend party crowd could be a mixed bag of big checks and bigger headaches.

"See? You're a sweet one. I don't care what anyone else says. You're a good one."

"What?" I whirled around from the grill I'd been prepping. I wasn't aware that I had a reputation in town—good, bad, or otherwise. I generally flew under the radar and preferred it that way. "What does—"

"Howdy, gals." Tammy waved as two women in nursing scrubs came through the front doors. "Pick a booth."

The next few hours were steady. Not crazy busy, but enough to keep us moving. At least Tammy was happy with all the fresh faces to chat with, her earlier somber mood giving way to her trademark cheer.

"Ah. Here comes the eye candy," she crowed as the door opened on a gust of cold air to admit a crew of firefighters in uniform. I spied their engine in the parking lot as I took stock of the crew. Not that I was looking for Sean. First, the dude had finished a shift earlier that day and was unlikely to be on again so soon. Second, and more importantly, I was *not* eager to see those twinkling blue eyes again. I had zero clue what I'd say, a feeling I didn't much care for. I should have been relieved, but I couldn't stop the slump of my shoulders as the Sean-less crew filed in to take seats around the counter.

"How goes it for my favorite crew?" Tammy asked as she handed out menus.

"You say that to all the boys, Tammy." Luther, an older firefighter with a bit of a belly and fading hairline loved to flirt back with Tammy. He was a predictable chili omelet, extra hash browns customer who was usually good for a laugh or two. However, his coworker, a younger woman seated next to him, gave him a withering look.

"Ahem."

"Sorry, Suzy." Luther offered an appropriately apologetic smile. "All the crews? Crew members? All of us?"

"I can't wait for Rodriguez to make it back so I'm not the only mom on the crew trying to keep you doofuses in line." Suzy gave a long-suffering sigh as I pulled out the egg substitute for the veggie lover's special she never deviated from.

"Aw, Suz. You know we love you," the firefighter on Suzy's other side piped up. He was a skinny dude who always ordered the lumberjack breakfast, extra crispy bacon, jam not syrup for the pancakes. "And Murphy—Sean, not the chief—is fitting in great. Doesn't quite have Rodriguez's takeout ordering skills down yet, but he's a good dude."

"He is. But don't count on him sticking around." Suzy gave an arch look, tossing her brown ponytail over one shoulder.

"How do you figure?" Luther frowned. Trying not to follow suit, I busied myself with the orders.

"Even if there's a position open once Evelyn comes back, Sean's used to being captain. He's not going to be happy on the line long-term." Suzy was known for being opinionated, but in this case, she was wrong. Sean had been plenty happy accepting orders in my shower. And I needed to stop thinking about Sean, orders, and showers while cooking.

"Maybe he puts in for chief," Luther suggested. Apparently, the universe wasn't done making me think about Sean because now the question of whether he was in town for the long haul kept poking at my brain.

"Nepotism much?" Suzy rolled her eyes. "Nah. Sean likes the field too much to be behind a desk full-time, but he needs to be captain somewhere."

"Like you." The firefighter on her other side piped up, and from the way Suzy bristled, he'd hit a nerve.

"Hey, now." Turning toward the guy, she gave him a harsh stare before lightening her voice. "Plus, Chief Murphy is retiring to California. Some sort of Disney retirement village down there." She did a pretend shudder. "Doubt Sean sticks around without his folks here. He's a short-termer."

Huh. If he was short-term and I was short-term...

Nope. Couldn't go thinking like that. I'd been a cook too long to let myself play with fire.

"Someone better tell Caleb." Luther chortled.

"Oh, Lord." Suzy cast a dramatic glance heavenward. "Is he crushing already?"

Better not be. But, of course, I couldn't say that. Shouldn't even think it. If Sean wanted to take up with the younger firefighter, so be it.

"That boy is trouble," the skinny firefighter added as I slid plates in front of the three.

Tammy arrived to refill their coffees in time to add, "I like trouble."

"We know." Everyone, including me, laughed, and thankfully, the conversation shifted to ribbing Tammy. No more distracting mentions of Sean, although he kept showing up in my thoughts. Damn it. I needed to put the hookup behind me.

The rest of the night after the firefighters headed out was rather slow. Not too many Saturday partiers out braving the cold. We were almost empty and approaching the last dragging hour of our shift when the front door jangled.

"Hey, Irish!" Tammy brightened as Sean walked in. He, not Caleb or Tammy, was the real trouble. I forced myself to stare at the grill, not join Tammy in greeting him. "Whatcha doing in on your off day, hon?"

"Eh. My old bones are still adjusting to working twenty-four on, forty-eight off again. Back in Seattle, they had my crew on twelves. Woke up starving this morning but didn't want to wake the household."

He lied well. Had to give him that. Still wasn't going to give him the satisfaction of acknowledging his presence, but his smooth delivery sure made it seem like he wasn't there to see me.

"Well, we're happy to have you." Tammy seated him at the counter, shooting me a questioning look. I supposed I deserved it as I was being grumpier than usual, so I gave Sean a curt nod.

"What'll it be?"

"Well..." Sean's sharp gaze gave me a long perusal. I stood firm, resisting any urge to squirm like a middle schooler at a dance. "I guess a second chef's surprise is out of the question."

"I'm sure not." Tammy smiled broadly. "Denver loves being in charge."

If she only knew... I didn't do blushing or stammering, but I sure as hell glanced away. "I'll come up with something for you."

"I'm sure it'll be memorable." Sean managed to make the praise sound offhand, but the heat in his eyes said he hadn't forgotten one second of our steamy encounter. Hmm. If it was heat he wanted, it was heat he'd get. I went off-menu again, this time devising a spicy meat-lovers pizza omelet with sausage, pepperoni, and ham blanketed in spicy marinara and smothered with three kinds of cheese. Instead of hash browns, I split one of our famous giant biscuits and spread it with garlic butter.

"This is amazing," Sean said between bites and happy noises that went straight to my dick. If he sighed happily again, I was going to need a quick five minutes in the restroom. "Thank you."

"No problem." My voice came out too gruff, and Sean's smile widened. He had me, and he knew it. And even though I largely ignored him for the rest of his meal, I wasn't surprised to find him outside the diner after my shift, lurking near my truck.

The smart call would have been to shut him down firmly and send him on his way. But I'd never been accused of brilliance.

"Need another ride?"

Chapter Seven

Sean

The early morning air was crisp, the last gasp of winter with a frosty wind and gray-toned dawn. However, Denver's considering look and question made my chilly wait for him to emerge worth it. I did love it when a plan worked out. And yeah, I could have simply marched over to his apartment after his shift, but I'd woken before dawn craving both the man and his cooking.

"I do need a ride." I grinned because a repeat of the day before was exactly what I wanted, and Denver offering was a great first step.

"Where's your truck?" He narrowed his eyes. Damn. The man sure did stern well, making all sorts of blood rush south to my cock.

"Back at Eric's." I widened my smile, not trying to hide my deviousness. I wasn't going to put Eric out a second day in a row, no matter what I had a hankering for.

"You walked in this cold?" Denver wrapped his jacket

more securely around his wide torso before unlocking the truck.

"Yep." I glanced meaningfully at the passenger side door, waiting for him to formally invite me along. "Wasn't too bad. Had some warm thoughts to keep me company."

"I bet." His gaze went from suspicious to heated, every dirty, delicious memory right there in his dark eyes. "What are you after, Sean?"

"A ride?" I made my tone all innocent.

Denver shook his head like he wasn't buying my act but jerked a thumb at the truck. "Get in."

Happily vindicated, I hopped into the passenger seat. Mercifully, Denver cranked the heat before silently turning out of Honey's lot. I wasn't sure what to say as my plan and bravado had only carried me so far. But when Denver turned away from downtown onto one of the country roads leading northeast out of Mount Hope, I had to speak up.

"You're not heading toward Prospect Place."

"Very smart, hometown boy." For the first time since exiting Honey's, Denver smiled. "Thought you wanted a ride."

"I do." My voice turned all husky. If he wanted to drive or, better yet, park, I wouldn't object. "I've got time before the household wakes up."

"Good to know." His smile turned feral as he picked up speed on the lonely road, heading away from the gentle hills of Mount Hope into more mountainous terrain. He was a damn good driver, handling the truck with admirable skill on the curvy road. I'd never found watching someone drive or being the passenger to be particular turn-ons, but there was a first time for everything. Apparently, my body liked the relative freedom of sitting back and letting Denver navigate the back roads. I trusted Denver, a strange sensation, but the feeling went beyond the driving. A low thrum of arousal pulsed through my veins, gathering strength with every passing mile.

"I've never had a fling before." I kept my tone conversational. Outside, the rising sun cast a golden glow over the forest at the edge of the road, contributing to my loose mood. Further, the lack of traffic made it seem like we were the only two awake in the world. "Might be fun."

"I have." Denver matched my tone before hardening his voice. "Not looking to be your first."

I raised a finger but kept right on smiling. "But you were."

"And you're some sort of duckling?" Denver raised his bushy brows. He laughed, which softened the tease. "Imprinted on me after one blowjob?"

"Maybe." I gave him a toothy grin he didn't return. Sighing, I sobered. "No, seriously. I'm not looking to take advantage of you like that other guy you mentioned yesterday." I did appreciate Denver being honest, and I felt bad for the guy, having been through the wringer with his chickenshit rock star. "I'm upfront about being inexperienced and looking to explore, but I'm not a user, and I'm not looking to break hearts."

"Appreciated." Denver pursed his lips as he turned onto an old logging road. Surprisingly, I didn't feel even a flutter of nerves. For all his sarcasm, Denver gave off gentle giant vibes, no hint of malice. He wasn't out to hurt me, and that he'd sought out a private spot gave me and my raging lust hope.

"Would a repeat really be that bad?" I asked as he parked out of view of the main road.

"Or that good." His dire tone was at odds with his words.

"Or that good." I waggled my eyebrows at him, which earned me a resigned chuckle from Denver.

"You're the near-virgin after a long dry spell. Everything is gonna be good for you."

Now it was my turn to sound glum. "And this is where you sing the benefits of hookups again."

"I'm not wrong." Denver held up his hands. "You should get the queer youth you never had. Go into Portland, check out the clubs, download a few apps, have some fun."

"I'm not a hookup person." Following an impulse I didn't fully understand, I captured one of his hands. My chest went warm and tight when Denver didn't pull away. "I know that much. I don't have club-worthy game and my phone gets most of its use on weather, sports scores, and takeout. I'm not interested in learning the rules of swiping this way and that."

"Hookups are a mixed bag for sure." Denver squeezed my hand, swinging it lightly. "But so are casual flings."

"I'm no expert, but most skills get better with practice and repetition, right? I would think that would be an argument in favor of repeats versus one-offs."

Denver made a frustrated noise. "Are you always in a good mood?"

"Pretty much. I try." I gave him my friendliest smile, fueled by how damn good his hand felt against mine, warm and big and secure.

"I can tell." Denver shook his head. "Wear them down with niceness?"

"Is it working?"

"You tell me." Holding my gaze, Denver leaned in. I sucked in a breath. For all we'd done earlier, we hadn't kissed, an oversight I was suddenly desperate to remedy. Rather than wait for him to close the gap, I moved in first.

He met my kiss easily, lips parting on a smile. His lips were as soft as his beard was bristly. My first first kiss in well over twenty years, my first time meeting a male mouth ever. No wonder my hands shook and my abs trembled. My kiss went clumsy, my mouth no longer taking directions from my brain, and my teeth grazed his lower lip in a distinctly non-sexy way.

"Hey. Careful." Denver moved his free hand to the back of my neck, anchoring me in place. But not pushing me away, a fact my cock took careful note of.

"See? I clearly need all the tips I can get."

"You need something all right." Denver leaned in again, and I eagerly met him, only to bump noses when I tried to tilt in the same direction. "Easy," he chuckled against my mouth. "Let me."

Third time was indeed the charm as I let go of the need to initiate and choreograph the kiss. And as it turned out, not thinking was utterly blissful. In my limited past experience, I'd always been the one to drive, so to speak. Similar to being a passenger in Denver's truck, letting go of control and simply hanging on was the path to the best kiss of my life.

His lips were soft but firm as he took command of my mouth. Heat flooded my body as he coaxed new sensations with each pass of his lips. He licked and nibbled and sipped until I was a puddle of warm goo—no more brain power than a bowl of oatmeal.

"Oh." A dazed sound escaped my lips, and Denver swallowed the moan that followed. I didn't have to kiss him back as much as simply give myself over to the experience. My body knew what to do even if my brain was solidly offline. I clutched at Denver's meaty shoulder and reveled in how his grip tightened on my neck and back. "This is good."

Denver chuckled at my vast understatement. "Yeah, it is."

Still laughing, he kissed me again, no false starts this time, a smooth yet devastating claiming. Joy mingled with the heat coursing through me. Fun. This was fun, something I hadn't at all expected. I made a happy noise, and Denver shuddered as if this were all new to him as well. My lips parted, and Denver delved deeply, the slide of his tongue against mine a heavenly friction. My eyes shut, senses reduced to Denver's warmth, scent, and touch. My heart pounded, and as unlikely as it was, I swore it was in unison with Denver's heartbeat. I'd never felt more in sync with another person.

"Want more." I dropped my hand to his chest, tracing a line down as I unzipped his jacket. He let me explore his torso, but as soon as I reached for his waistband, he stayed my hand.

"Nuh-uh. We're too old to go home with wet pants."

"But I have a mouth." I did an exaggerated pout, a light, bouncy energy surging through me. I'd been the mature one for so very long. The first friend married, first to have kids, and being demanding, almost bratty, was as freeing as a bottle of bubbly. "And I wanna use it."

"I know you do." Denver chucked me lightly under the chin. "And you're too damn tempting."

Releasing me, he put the truck in gear, and I made a disappointed noise on par with a fumbled football in a playoff game.

"You're taking me home?"

"For now."

Oh, there was a world of potential in those words, and I chortled. "So that's a yes on a repeat?"

"That's me saying the next time I have your mouth is gonna be in a bed, and I might not let you out for a week." His tone was a stern warning, but I merely laughed again.

"Don't threaten me with a good time."

"You're trouble." He shook his head as we headed back down the logging road.

"God, I hope so." I couldn't wait to be all the trouble Denver could handle, and soon.

Chapter Eight

Denver

For now. Sean ending up in my bed was rather clearly a matter of when not if. Memories of our heated Sunday kiss lingered as the week started, and my willpower waned, but the opportunity didn't materialize. I had Monday off, but Sean was on duty, and Tuesday and Wednesday went by without a Sean sighting. Undoubtedly, he was waiting for a summons. Privately, I'd been hoping for another dawn request for a ride to allow my logic to take a backseat to my want.

By Thursday, I was kicking myself for turning down car sex and hoping Sean turned up soon to save me from composing a text message. He'd insisted on exchanging numbers, so I didn't have that excuse. What I did have was something unfamiliar: fear. Our kiss had rattled me to my core. Whether it was Sean's enthusiasm or some weird chemistry between us, I'd never been so moved by a kiss. That unprecedented reaction, not any noble impulses, was why I'd pulled back. I needed to steel my nerves before a repeat of the sex.

Of course the smarter move would be no repeat at all, but that same damn chemistry kept me craving more, and I'd never been great at self-denial.

I had a few chores before work on Thursday, including stocking up on coffee and other essential groceries. As I unloaded bags at the house where I rented the studio, smoke billowed out of the Wallace-Davis backyard.

Uh-oh. *Sean.* Dropping my groceries on the porch, I broke into a run. Turned out my fear of emotional connection was nothing compared to fear for the dude's physical safety. I raced up the big house's wide driveway and rounded into the backyard. Three Wallace-Davis kids surrounded a smoldering grill on the back deck, which was covered with fire extinguisher spray.

"John!" The smallest of the teens stamped their foot. I'd heard the others refer to them as Wren, and they were red in the face, with wild blond curly hair flying around their elfin face. "Why did you call 911? Why? Dad's gonna kill me."

"John did the right thing." Another teen gestured with a large fire extinguisher. He was a skinny dark-haired kid who looked ready to audition for the lead in a boy band in a slim-fitting gray button-down, perfectly fitted tight jeans, and clunky boots. "The fire's still not completely out. Geez, Wren. Cut it out with the cooking experiments."

"I called because I didn't want to lose the house." The third teen, who had to be John, was on the shorter side but muscular. He had a garden hose and was watering the lawn and house itself. Smart thinker.

"What's on the grill?" I asked as sirens sounded in the distance. "Where are your...adults?"

"Oh, hey. We're fine." John turned toward me, all bravado. "Help's on the way."

A fresh round of sparks erupted from the grill.

"Get off the deck," I shouted before bodily removing the small one who turned toward the grill with a large pair of tongs in hand instead of following orders.

"I need to check my meat," Wren said urgently as I tucked them under one arm. "The laws of thermodynamics say—"

"Rowan! Get the dog!" John called out to the other teen as he joined me in hauling Wren off the deck. Rowan, the boy band wannabe, scooped up a medium-sized dog waiting near the kitchen door and followed us down the steps to the sloping yard. The grill made an ominous hiss.

"Down. Get down." I shielded the three and the shaking dog as best I could as the sirens became louder. And right as a host of fire trucks pulled up, the grill blew. The explosion echoed through the neighborhood.

I kept the kids down as a group of firefighters raced into the yard, only letting them up once the grill had been thoroughly doused and the risk of any more flaming debris had passed. Firefighters swarmed the yard, a carefully calculated response. Sean was there in the thick of it. Suzy had been right—he was a natural leader, calling out orders and directing his fellow firefighters. Not to mention, he made a rather impressive sight in uniform. His ease at being in charge made the way he'd given up control to me in the shower and with kissing that much sweeter.

Trying not to think too much about kissing, I hung back with the kids. Once the grill was no longer a hazard, Sean hurried over to us, eyes only for the kids.

"Wren, what did you do?" he asked as he turned Wren

this way and that, undoubtedly checking for injuries beyond teen pride.

Pursing their lips, Wren made a series of grumpy noises. "Why is it always, 'Wren, what did you do?' And never 'who did this?' It might not have been my fault."

"But it was," John inserted quickly as Sean moved on to inspecting him and Rowan.

"Not helping, John." Rowan rolled his eyes as he let Sean look him over as well. His nice shirt was ripped, and all three kids were damp and sooty, but thankfully none seemed injured. "Jonas got called in for an emergency at the hospital. You and Dad were already on duty, and rather than heat up pizza like Dad directed, Wren had the bright idea of using science to cook frozen chicken."

"It wasn't a terrible idea." Wren puffed up like an angry rooster.

"How about next time you want to try cooking, you call me?" I had no idea what prompted my offer. I didn't much know what to do with kids and couldn't say as I particularly liked them, but something in the last ten minutes had softened me toward this trio. "Keep the house in one piece?"

"Who are you anyway?" Head tilting, Wren gave me a suspicious glare.

"I'm...a neighbor." I had no clue why I hesitated over a purely factual response.

"And a friend," Sean added, seemingly only now noticing me. "I'm sure Wren would benefit from some actual cooking lessons."

"Science—" Wren started another academic point only to be met with groans from both siblings.

"*Wren.*"

"Uh-oh. Here's Dad," Rowan said as an ambulance joined the firetrucks and Eric Davis hopped out, along with two other paramedics. The other two kids followed Rowan in marching toward Eric, leaving me alone with Sean. Or rather, as alone as we were likely to get in a yard crawling with firefighters, kids, and concerned neighbors.

"You okay?" Sean raised a hand like he was tempted to touch my shoulder, then quickly lowered it. "Thank God you were here to help."

"I'm fine." I waved off the concern. "And the older kids had the situation largely under control. John even thought to hose down the house."

"First responder kid." Sean nodded with obvious approval. "Eric will be proud once he gets over being scared to death."

Over by the ambulance, Eric seemed to be alternating between handing out hugs and lectures, with Wren gesturing wildly, undoubtedly continuing to proclaim their innocence.

"Yep." I chuckled, adrenaline making my laugh shaky. "I meant it about the cooking lessons."

"Thanks." A sheepish expression crossed Sean's face as he glanced over at Eric and the kids. "We don't usually leave dinner to the kids. We've tried to stagger our schedules so there's always an adult here, but tonight was a bit of a perfect storm all around."

"Those kids are more than old enough to help out though. Everyone should know the basics of cooking." I kept my voice practical. Sean didn't need any additional guilt.

"I hear that. My mom gave me a crash course the summer before I got married. She made sure all three of us kids could hold our own in the kitchen."

"Good mom." I stared off at the freestanding garage that had old-fashioned carriage house styling. "I picked up skills here and there from various foster homes, but mainly from working restaurant gigs from fifteen on."

"I'm... That must have sucked for you." Sean had evidently thought better of the tired "I'm sorry" response that so many folks liked to trot out. "All four of Eric's kids came from the foster-to-adopt program. Two sibling groups."

"Lucky kids. Not everyone gets adopted. Some of us age out." I shrugged and looked away when Sean's face creased with concern.

"Your whole childhood was in foster care?" he said softly. "Wait. You don't have to tell me. Of course I'm curious, but you don't owe me your story."

"It's okay." I appreciated that he was trying not to push, but the curiosity was natural. "And it's a pretty short, common story. My parents were young and in and out of trouble even before I came along. Dad stuck around long enough to be on the birth certificate and to give me this name, but he was nowhere to be found when the state got involved a few years later. Mom made multiple attempts at sobriety, none of which stuck. I don't remember much about either of them, but by the time the state finally terminated parental rights, I was at that hard-to-adopt elementary school age. School wasn't my jam, and all the fights I wound up in didn't exactly help my adoption prospects."

"It wasn't your fault." Sean's voice was firm and loyal. "The system failed you. And that sucks. I hate how many kids have stories like yours, bouncing from home to home, eventually aging out. There aren't enough families like Eric and Montgomery's."

"Yeah. These kids are lucky." I glanced over at the trio with Eric again. He was clearly in dad mode and upset, but the love he had for the kids also came through loud and

Up All Night

clear. "And I turned out okay," I lied to reassure myself as much as Sean. "After I aged out, I had a lot of good years, bumming around the country, and food service work was always something I could fall back on."

"Still had to be hard—hey, you have a cut." Abruptly changing topics, Sean pointed at a thin line running the length of my palm onto my forearm.

Damn it. That would smart under a glove all night at the diner. "It's a scratch. Nothing—"

"Tate!" Sean cut me off to yell over to the ambulance crew. "Bring your kit over here."

"Coming." A younger EMT with closely cropped black hair standing near Eric started digging around in their rig.

"Seriously. I don't need patching up," I said, only to get a stern look from Sean. More of that leadership potential others saw so easily. He was darn near commanding as he pushed me to sit on a nearby bench.

"You're going to let Tate look you over."

"Thought I gave the orders around here." I kept my voice low but meaningful.

"Using what? Telepathy?" Sean's reply was equally pointed. And warranted.

"Guess I deserve that." I met his harsh gaze. "I'm sorry I didn't text."

"It's... It is what it is." Sean quirked his mouth. Something twisted in my gut. Gone was the happy-go-lucky guy with a counter for my every objection. And, perversely, I missed that guy and his determination. "If you've changed your mind..."

"Nope," I said quickly as the younger EMT headed our way. My fear morphed again, fear of missing out on more of Sean and his sunshine personality and those world-shattering kisses making me reckless. "Tomorrow morning. After our shifts. Kids will be at school?"

"I'll be there." He nodded sharply. No chance of a no-show there, no playing hard to get after my failure to get in touch. Sean would be there, and all I could do was hope I wouldn't regret it too much.

Chapter Nine

Denver

Sean was exactly on time as predicted, going so far as to send me a text as he left the station that Eric and the other roommate, Jonas, were handling getting the teens off to school. No surprise that Sean also included a precise ETA. I narrowly beat him to my place and had just enough time to shower and pull on a pair of baggy lounge pants. I didn't bother with a shirt. We both knew what he was coming for.

Accordingly, I opened the door to usher him in with a dry, "You came."

"Well, not yet." Sean's infectious grin was firmly in place despite the early hour. He also looked awfully fresh with damp slightly curly hair and a clean green pullover and jeans. "But here's to hoping."

He held out a white paper bag for me to take before hanging up his own coat on my coat tree.

"What's this?" My mouth twisted as I studied the bag. Sean didn't seem the type to so obviously bring the lube. "Supplies?"

"Muffins." His pale cheeks flushed pink. "I passed that new spot on my way back from the station. An offer of coffee seemed dicey, coming on the heels of a shift. Ditto beer at seven in the morning." His good cheer flagged a little at my lack of reply. "Hookup no-no to bring food?"

Actually, I'd never had a hookup bring snacks and couldn't say as I'd had many dates of the food-and-activity variety. But I didn't want Sean to feel bad for making the effort.

"Nah. Appreciated." I opened the bag and spied two large cinnamon streusel muffins. Their sugary, spicy scent was almost enough to make me want to delay the sex. Almost. "And I don't do beer. No alcohol these days."

"Noted." Thankfully, Sean didn't make a big deal out of my non-drinking or ask for my whole story like some might. Instead, he kicked off his shoes, lining them up next to mine by the shoe tree before stalking toward the nook with my queen-size bed.

After setting the muffins on the counter, I followed him, shaking a playful finger at his eagerness. "You're awfully cocky for a guy who likes following orders."

"You said I needed to be in a bed to get my mouth on your dick again." He stepped away from the bed to place both hands on my shoulders, smiling at me. "I'm just expediting the process."

"Are you?" Spinning us, I pinned him against the nearby wall. I enjoyed how easily he let me move him because he undoubtedly had the training and skill to resist me despite our size difference. "And did I say that?"

"You did." He tilted his head accommodatingly, clearly angling for a kiss. And I should have kept him waiting, but I wanted it too. Sean had far more power over me than he realized, and I used the kiss to reassert my dominance.

Or at least that was my aim, but our combustible connection mocked my attempts to keep control. Heat licked up my spine, more sparks than Wren's ill-fated barbecue experiment, each meeting of our mouths a fresh explosion of pleasure. I'd started off wanting to show him who was in control, but I ended up merely hanging on, a happy prisoner to Sean. I might be the one leading, tongue delving deep, but he had all the power, a fact made clear as he pulled back to wink at me.

"Bed seems awfully far away."

"It does." I held his gaze, slightly gratified by how glassy and pleasure-drunk his blue eyes seemed. Other than his eyes and flushed skin, he was amazingly cocky for someone with so little experience. "You have a solution, Captain?"

"Eh. I'm not captain here. But I might have an idea." He smiled wider as he reversed our position with the sort of skill I'd suspected he might have. Before I had a chance to make a wisecrack about it, he sank to his knees far smoother than any forty-something had a right to.

"You're in a bold mood."

"Complaining?"

"You get me off first, and I'm gonna make you wait for yours until I can go again." I made my tone as stern as I could, given that Sean was busy pulling my dick out. "Prepare to beg. Fair warning: I'm not as young as I used to be."

"Neither of us are." He gave me a devilish wink. If anyone was going to be begging, chances were alarmingly high it might be me. "And that sounds more like a promise than a threat."

"You're asking for it."

"Yep." Sean didn't waste any more time before sucking my cockhead into his waiting mouth. Whatever he lacked in experience, he more than made up for with enthusiasm and willingness to experiment. In fact, it was almost...*fun*. A word I didn't generally associate with getting blown. Hot, erotic, pleasurable, sure, but fun was something new. But accurate as Sean tried out different tricks—licking the tip, teasing with different grips, and varying his rhythm and depth, all with undeniable glee. Fun.

And then he discovered how to go deep and milk the shaft with the flat of his tongue.

"Oh, hell yes." My breath practically sizzled out of me, my entire body a fucking inferno. And the only firefighter in sight seemed determined to make it worse, not better. He upped the tempo but kept the tongue action going, and my vision fucking blurred. "Damn. Your mouth is something else."

He paused, but his smile was surprisingly shy as he gazed at me. "Do it like last time?"

"Last time?" *Fuck.* The only thing better than Sean in playful mode was Sean wanting, *craving*, me in charge. Heady damn stuff. "You want me to own your mouth again?"

I dropped a hand to his jaw, and he hummed his agreement.

"Open wider," I commanded, more to assert control than because Sean needed tips. Using my hand, I guided him into a deeper, faster fuck, but he stayed far tenser than last time. "Relax, baby. I've got you."

"Not nervous," he gritted out the words. "Trying not to come."

I pursed my lips to avoid chuckling, instead going for a stern, "Try harder."

That must have been the response he needed because he visibly relaxed, brow creasing with concentration as he gave himself over to following my lead, going pliant in my grip. Damn. Nothing better than a powerful man willingly turning himself to putty for our mutual pleasure. And devious, devious man, he quickly figured out how to let me fuck his face while doing more of that tongue action.

"*Fuck.*" I drew the word out, low and urgent. "More. More of that."

I barely had the order out before he doubled down on the suction and friction, meeting my every thrust with the absolutely perfect marriage of submission and active effort to get me off. And said efforts were working even faster than I'd predicted, my balls lifting and hamstrings burning.

"Good. So good." I pressed my shoulders hard against the wall. No use. My body kept climbing, every muscle tensing, and any attempt by my brain to slow this down was overridden by my cock. *Faster. Faster.* And the faster I went, the more Sean seemed to love it, need it, moaning his enjoyment, moving in concert with me until only one thing mattered. "Fuck. Fuck. Gonna."

Inevitable infinity. Bad poetry spiraled through my head, snippets of lyrics from my years on rock tours. My ears rang from the roar of an invisible crowd, and my vision shorted like a strobe light. I felt like a fucking rock god for an instant that dragged on and on, a rush unlike anything I'd ever experienced.

"Mmm." Sean moaned louder than me, drinking down my come with an eagerness that coaxed a few more spurts loose from my cock.

"God. Fucking. Damn." I whistled as I offered Sean a hand up. "That was spectacular."

"Yeah, it was." He smiled wide enough to power a stadium with the wattage before wiping his mouth.

"Still cocky." I shook my head in pretend disappointment.

"Yep." He didn't even give me the grace of fake chuckling.

"Let's see what we can do about that." I spun him in the direction of my bed and pointed. "On the bed."

Chapter Ten

Sean

I'd never wanted to be anywhere as much as I wanted to be in Denver's bed. The blowjob had only made me hungrier for him and everything he offered. I loved being on my knees for him with a ferocity I'd never expected. I'd known I'd like the sex, but it was the freedom of giving him control that I had a bottomless hunger for.

"Strip." He made a little go-ahead gesture as I approached the bed. I didn't know the first thing about sexy striptease moves and had zero patience for learning, so I wrenched off my clothes with no finesse but lots of speed before launching myself onto the bed.

"You're something." Denver shook his head, but there was a fondness in his tone that made my muscles warm and loose. I'd always felt the need to rein myself in with Maxine, save my most authentic goofy moments. With Denver, there was no need to pretend or hold myself in check. Not only did I trust him to push back against whatever I dished out, but he seemed to enjoy all of me.

"Coming?" I waggled my eyebrows at him before patting the bed. Denver removed his pants with deliberate slowness before ambling over to the bed. His cock still glistened with traces of my spit, and that, combined with the rest of his naked appeal, had me throbbing that much more.

"You're not coming any time soon." He grinned, a wicked promise that transformed his whole face, brown eyes gaining golden specks, mouth wide and generous, chiseled jaw and nose softening, and little lines emerging around his eyes and mouth.

"Whoa." I didn't have to fake my appreciation. "You do smile sometimes."

"I smile lots." He offered me a cheesy smile more suited to a slithery salesperson before stretching out next to me.

"Not nearly enough." I was already making lists of things I could try to earn more genuine Denver grins.

"Says you." He rolled his eyes even as he gathered me close, inhaling deeply with his face in my hair. The intimacy of the gesture surprised me, given how hard I'd had to work to sell him on the idea of a repeat. But I liked it. A lot. I stretched into the contact, which had the desired result of him holding me that much tighter and nuzzling my neck. "Tell me what's on your list."

"My list?" My voice came out raspy and more than a little confused. Throat well-used, I was pleasantly buzzed on his nearness and the earlier sex.

"All the sex you want to try." Denver gave me a patient look. "I'm sure you've got quite the list."

Oh. Right. When I'd brought up the idea of a repeat, I'd had some vague notion of Denver giving me sex lessons, but now that I was actually here in his bed, a curriculum was the last thing on my mind. I wanted experience. No note-taking allowed.

"It's a pretty short list." I sounded more self-conscious than I liked, but it was the truth. "I like sucking you. I'd like anything that includes more kissing. I think I'd like getting fucked. But what I really like is the whole not thinking and you giving me orders thing. I make a million tiny decisions a day, many of them with big consequences. Not thinking... that's a gift."

"I like being able to give you that." A thoughtful expression crossed Denver's face, a different softness than the grin but equally appealing. "I can work with being in charge, but you gotta speak up if you don't like something."

"What if I like everything?" I grinned precisely to earn his stern stare and head shake. "Seriously, though, I'll tell you if something's not working for me."

"Good." His smile turned more purposeful, almost scary in its intensity. "And I like everything on your shortlist. You think you'd like getting fucked? Have you played around on your own with penetration?"

"Um. Some." My cheeks heated. Funny how I could be naked with the dude and still be embarrassed to discuss jerking off. "Not a ton, but when I watch porn or fantasize, I'm almost always the one getting fucked. I want to try."

"Fair enough. And we'll get there, but you gotta trust me to set the pace."

I made a face because his speed was likely snail-holding-up-traffic slow. Nevertheless, I nodded. "I trust you."

"Good." Denver sat up to loom over me. "Hands up. Touch the bedframe."

The old-fashioned metal headboard was perfect for grabbing, and as soon as I wrapped my hands around the bars, a sense of total relief washed over me. I was safe here, and Denver was fully in charge. I didn't have to think.

Didn't need to plan or anticipate. All I needed to do was hold on.

He started by dancing his fingers down my jaw and neck, across my collarbones, and over my sternum. I shivered, trying not to moan from the light contact.

"Ticklish?"

"Not..." I trailed off as he indeed found a ticklish spot at the base of my ribs and another under my left arm. "Hey!"

"Objections, Captain?" He raised a thick eyebrow.

"No." I'd put up with his teasing if it meant not having to think.

"Right answer." Denver rewarded me with a leisurely lick down the center of my chest before capturing a nipple in his mouth. My nipples were small, pink, and, up until that exact second, an afterthought when it came to pleasure zones.

"Oh wow." I sucked in a breath and arched my chest to invite more of the warm, wet heat. Mercifully not calling me on my attempts to direct him, Denver upped the ante, alternately sucking and scraping lightly with his teeth.

"Jesus, you're responsive." His tone was full of approval and a bit of awe. "Try not to come."

"I'm not *that* close," I protested, only to whimper when a warm breath gusted across my straining cock, which had already painted a wet stripe on my belly. "Okay. Point taken."

I'd said many prayers in my life, for serious and trivial matters both, but none more fervent than the plea to the heavens that Denver suck my cock next.

And he did, mouth skillfully descending over my cock, making my whole body bow upward. "Holy shit."

"No coming." He paused to give me an authoritative

glare. Damn, but I wanted to please this man. Not merely following his directions but earning his praise and approval. If that meant clamping back on my rising need to come, then so be it.

"I won't." My hamstrings burned and my heels dug into the mattress. But no way did I want to miss a second of this delicious torture. His mouth was warmer and softer than I'd expected, and the friction of his tongue provided electric sparks I felt everywhere, from my balls to the back of my neck. "More."

"I decide." And just like that, the amazing pleasure retreated as Denver raised his head. He trailed his hands down my legs and back up, ruffling my leg hair and sending more electricity throughout my already-revved body. Holding my gaze, he repositioned himself between my legs.

"Uh..." My abs tensed despite my deep breaths.

"Relax. I set the pace, remember?" Denver stroked my legs again, softer this time.

"Yeah." Closing my eyes, I released another deliberate exhale. *Trust.* I trusted Denver, and whatever was coming next would be good. He might be big and powerful and excellent at taking charge, but he wouldn't push me too far, too fast.

Hands remaining on my legs, Denver gently pushed them up and back. I opened my eyes as he arranged himself on his stomach, my legs on his shoulders, his face and mouth level with—

"Oh Jesus." One would think with all the rimming I'd seen in porn that I would have been more prepared. Wrong. It was sexy to watch, but more often than not, I fast-forwarded to the good stuff. "I had no idea..."

"We're just getting started." Denver chuckled, breath

warm against my ass before he licked a broad stripe down the seam of my ass. Turned out, this was the good stuff, his strong hands holding my ass, a hint of stretch that made everything more intense, his agile tongue exploring my rim, which apparently had far more nerve endings than my nipples.

What a day for discoveries. A laugh escaped my chest, more glee than nerves, but Denver glanced up anyway. "This okay?"

"More than." My laughter turned to moans as he rimmed me with unexpected gusto. Thank goodness for my post-shift shower. One less thing to worry about. And the newness of having someone's mouth *there* quickly morphed into a cascade of sensations. Denver licked and teased and used the barest hint of teeth in ways that had me near keening. "God. God."

Thinking became optional and then impossible as all I could do was try to ride the waves of pleasure. I was a tiny boat with a tsunami approaching. Hell, if I wanted to stop. Even when Denver added a finger to his teasing, all I wanted was more. Curiosity about penetration became an undeniable need. His little circles and glancing touches were nowhere near enough.

"More," I demanded roughly. Thankfully, Denver didn't take the opportunity to rebuke me, instead sitting up to root around in a nearby wicker nightstand with decorative bins for drawers.

"I've got you." He pulled out a tube of lube. Holding my gaze, he slicked his fingers, making a show of rubbing the clear liquid around. Undoubtedly, he was also giving me a chance to object, but rather than nerves, all I felt was desire. I'd never been more turned on in my life, even before he started teasing my rim. When he slowly pressed a finger in, I made an almost inhuman noise.

"Oh." I drew the word out so long my throat strained. His finger retreated, then pushed in again, deeper this time. My cock pulsed, breath coming far too rapidly. "Wait—"

"Breathe." Denver immediately went still, gentling his tone and going so far as to inhale and exhale as if to show me what to do. "It gets easier."

He'd stayed kneeling after grabbing the lube, and his tense crouch made the big guy look ready to leap into battle. On my behalf, which was damn humbling.

"Not painful." I bit out the words because even without movement, the pressure made every nerve ending between my ass and cock sing. "Too much. Too close."

"Damn." Denver whistled before resuming finger-fucking me with slow, deliberate passes. "You are *fun* with that quick trigger of yours."

Fun was hardly the word I'd use, but he seemed almost gleeful about getting me to detonate early again. In fact, he picked up speed, going deeper with each thrust until he was firmly nudging my prostate. My ab muscles went from tense to quivering and my breath came in little gasps. My cock ached, but I didn't dare let go of the headboard to reach for it. But even without a hand on my dick, my lungs burned from forcing myself away from the urge to race toward climax.

"I might come." My voice was thready, and I flexed my hands against the metal bars of the headboard, seeking something, anything to root myself.

"It's a risk I'm willing to take." Denver chuckled, magical finger retreating, only to return joined by a second. More fullness, more pressure, more of the burn I craved.

And when he thrust deep, the increased contact with my prostate made my back arch.

"Fuck. Denver. That's..." I trailed off, no longer capable of stringing together a complete sentence.

"Yeah, say my name." His eyes were glassy, and his face shone with a thin layer of sweat. Knowing he was turned on pushed me that much higher.

"Denver." My voice was a broken plea. Here came the begging he'd threatened. "More."

"Greedy, aren't you?" His tone was so pleased that I almost wept. As it was, I exhaled, years' worth of relief rolling off my shoulders. With Denver, it was totally okay to need, to want, to beg, even to whine and whimper.

"Please." For the first time ever, I let myself enjoy fully letting go, finding freedom not only in Denver's control but also in pushing against him, finding solace in his strength. "I need it."

"I know you do, baby." He fucked me harder with his fingers, scissoring them to intensify the stretch.

"Oh, that's it. That's it," I chanted, already lost even before Denver readjusted his position so he could lean over my cock, warm breath followed by an even warmer tongue. "Don't." My moan was highly unconvincing, but I had to try. "If you even breathe on my cock again, I'll come."

"Then come." Denver sounded unconcerned and, indeed, redoubled his efforts, thrusting his fingers in short, hard bursts that nailed my prostate in the most perfect way possible while lazily licking my cockhead. He didn't even need to suck before my balls tightened. My heels pressed into the bed so hard that I was surely leaving permanent dents, not that I had time to worry about that. My body bowed, ass riding Denver's fingers with some newly discovered instinct.

"Yes." Figuring out how to move in concert with him, how to become an active participant in the fuck while still giving him control, was a heady rush that tipped me right over the edge. "Denver. I'm coming. Coming."

I came on a roar, vaguely aware of Denver chuckling, raising his head to smile at me as I spurted all over my belly. A stray line of come ended up on his cheek, above the line of his beard, and he used his free hand to wipe it away.

"Yum." Winking at me, he licked his finger before carefully withdrawing his other hand from my ass and wiping both hands with a washcloth he retrieved from the nightstand. "One less item on the list?"

"Fuck." I licked my dry lips. "I'm pretty sure I'm dead, but I still want it. You can fuck me now."

"Ha. Hardly." He lowered my wobbly legs to the bed before straddling my midsection. He dragged his hard cock through my come, using it as lube to stroke himself. I whimpered. The blatant sexiness of his actions was too much, too soon after my orgasm. My dick pulsed against my belly, valiantly attempting to rejoin the party.

"I can take it." I made a hopeful face. I hoped I wasn't lying. My ass kept clenching with aftershocks, and my skin felt hypersensitive everywhere, but damn, I wanted Denver.

"I'm in charge," he said sternly, continuing to jack himself. "And I say when."

"Okay." I didn't have enough brain cells online to argue. And watching him was its own kind of pleasure. "Damn, you're hot."

I sighed, jaw falling open, as he stretched and flexed, stroking himself harder and faster, big cock moving in and out of his tight fist.

"That's right," Denver urged, rising. "Open your mouth."

"Come on me. God, I want that." I trembled with fresh want.

"I am. Gonna come all over you." He grunted softly between strokes, hips moving in time with his fist. "And don't you worry, I'm gonna fuck that hot ass eventually too."

"Yes." The word flew out of me, a too-loud declaration of approval. *Eventually* had almost giddy levels of potential.

"Fuck." Luckily, Denver was too busy coming to laugh. He groaned, eyes falling shut, dick pulsing. Ropes of come painted my stomach and chest, a single drop landing on my lower lip.

I licked it up, moaning along with him. "God, I love your taste."

That earned me a chuckle, but a fond one. "You're a mess."

He hefted himself off the bed with surprising grace, loping across the room, naked but totally at ease.

Now what was I supposed to do? Go shower? Clean up with the washcloth he'd used on his hands and get dressed? Was I being dismissed now? Was this how casual flings worked? Fuck and flee?

But before I could decide, Denver returned with a warm, wet washcloth and a small towel. I reached for the cloth, but he waved away my hand in favor of sponging me off himself, then drying me with the same care he might show a pristine '57 Chevy.

"There." Seemingly satisfied, he tossed the washcloth and towel aside before stretching out next to me. "Not perfect, but it'll do for now."

The same could be said for whatever the heck this thing was between us. No idea what it was, but the right now was too damn terrific to protest as Denver gathered me close.

"Fuck. I'm sleepy." Yawning, he spooned around me,

breath ruffling my hair. *Huh.* I'd never been the little spoon before, never thought about this particular position in all my many vivid fantasies. But damn if I didn't love it. I exhaled, and he gave my hip an approving pat. "Sleep now. Muffins later."

Well, I guessed that answered the question of whether I was staying. It would do for now, indeed.

Chapter Eleven

Denver

Was it possible to wear out a cheap phone by checking the messages again? As I parked at Honey's Sunday night, I had a sneaking suspicion I was well on my way to finding out. Friday's sex-fest had turned into a long, lazy sleep broken by Sean's alarm reminding him about the time school ended for the teens. Because, of course, Captain Punctual had an alarm for that. He'd dashed off, but later that evening, he'd texted.

Today was fun. Sorry I didn't get to stay for muffins. Do it again some time?

I hadn't kept him waiting, but I had kept my reply brief. *Sure thing.*

Knowing Sean, he was dying for a specific date and time to put in his phone calendar and set up three reminders for, but that wasn't how I rolled. I'd figured he'd show up at the dinner Saturday morning, but he hadn't. And when I'd driven home, he'd been outside doing yard work with his

Up All Night

friend Eric and the jock kid, John. Not the time to stop and work out details for another hookup.

Before falling into bed, I texted:

> Take your shirt off next time you trim the hedges.

> Ha. It's barely April in Oregon. I might not freeze, but I'd be damn chilly.

> I'd warm you up.

Sleep had claimed me, and when I'd woken, Sean had taken a page from my book.

> Good

And now it was Sunday, and he was back on duty, and so was I. According to the handwritten schedule posted near the walk-in fridge, I was supposed to have Sunday and Monday nights off. In theory. Between trading shifts, covering for others, and dealing with high employee turnover outside of Tammy and me, I ended up working well over forty hours most weeks. Somewhere, my twenty-something self was cackling over me putting in this kind of work for relatively low reward. Not that we'd slacked off during the various rock tours I'd been a part of, but I sure as hell hadn't been punching a clock.

"Manager was just in," Tammy reported as I prepped my station to start my shift.

"Fuck." Working overnights, we didn't often have to deal with management. This was a good thing. The original Honey's had been founded by Loretta and Lionel Honey in the early 1970s. However, the pair had died within weeks of each other a few years back, leaving their kids and grandkids bickering over the business.

"Watch your mouth, sugar." Tammy came around the counter to pat my jaw. "And the visit wasn't that bad."

"Which one was it this time?" As part of the squabbling over what to do with the business, various relatives played the part of manager, usually whoever was down on their luck and between other employment.

"The grandson. Dean. The kid with big ears. He's nice enough." Tammy was rather fond of the rotating crew of third-generation Honeys, many of whom were my age with kids of their own.

"Pretty sure that kid is pushing forty."

"Hush. You're all babies to me." Tammy bustled away to wipe the long countertop. "Anyway, he was mainly in to check on a late dairy delivery, but he mentioned that the older kids—"

"You mean his sixty-something mother and her siblings?" I had to laugh, but Tammy made a ruffled hen noise.

"Do you want the gossip or not?"

"Go ahead." I made a little gesture with my hand. She'd tell me anyway, but I didn't want to spoil her fun.

"Honey's kids are yammering about selling again."

"Running out of relatives to pass jobs on to?" I tried another joke, knowing how Tammy tended to fret over the diner's future.

"Be nice." She waved her dish towel at me. "And I'm serious here. What will we do if this place closes?"

"Who says it will close?" I stepped away from the grill to pat her slim shoulder. "Even if they sell, the new folks might keep the staff around."

I didn't tell her I'd likely move on before then. It

wouldn't help her worries any. But the stability of the business was one more reason why my stay in town was limited. And why I couldn't go dwelling on messages or lack thereof from Sean. No matter how good sleeping next to him had felt, anything between us would be short-lived.

"Land, Denver. Land. Property values." Tammy shook her head, making me feel every hour of the GED classes I'd managed a few years back. "This place is worth far more as developable land than this old building with a too-big parking lot. They could likely get six townhomes or more here. If the kids opt to fold, we'll all be out on our ears."

"I doubt it will come to that." I pitched my voice low and soothing. "They threatened to sell six months ago, remember? And that went nowhere."

"True." Tammy's lips stayed pursed and her forehead crinkled. Despite her agreement, she was sadder than a piece of old aluminum foil. Luckily, we were nearly empty, only a pair of older truckers nursing the last of their coffees over empty platters. I fetched Tammy a piece of her favorite cheesecake from the dessert cooler.

"Here. Eat this. You'll feel better."

"You're a sweet one." Her face finally relaxed into her usual smile, but I was careful not to mention the fate of Honey's again. Sunday nights were almost always slow, and this one was more painful than most. I was nursing yet another cup of coffee and counting down the hour or so until I could put my feet up when the door jangled.

"My favorite fellows!" Tammy was first to greet Sean and Caleb, who were both fresh-faced and in street clothes. Instead of heading right to the counter like always, they grabbed a booth near the door.

Shit. Was this a date? Had I missed my chance by not being more direct? Or maybe Sean was more ready to sow some of those wild oats than he'd thought. Whatever it was, I didn't like it one bit. I scraped the already-clean grill with a vengeance as Tammy brought them their coffee and menus.

"What'll it be, bright eyes?" Tammy asked Sean. He didn't look especially bright to me though. His shoulders had a pronounced slump, and his mouth was bracketed by deep lines. He was undoubtedly short on sleep but seemed more weary than usual.

"Just a cheese omelet with a side of hash browns, extra crispy." No cheerful request for a surprise. He didn't even glance in my direction. Damn. Cold. Either this was a date, or he was that exhausted, and either way, my hand flexed with the urge to touch him.

"You got it, love." Tammy did what I couldn't and briefly patted Sean's shoulder before turning to Caleb. "And, Mr. Meat?"

"Hey, what can I say? I like my life spicy...and meaty." He winked, whether at Tammy or Sean, I wasn't sure. His usual flirty antics grated like sand on a sunburn. "My usual plus a cinnamon roll. Damn hungry after that shift."

"Yeah." Nodding, Sean stared off into space. If this was a date, it wasn't a very cheerful one, a fact that brought me unwarranted relief. I wasn't a petty or possessive dude. As long as Sean played safe, I had no reason to stake a claim, but hell if I didn't want to hang a big *Hands Off* sign around his neck.

And the more he sat and sighed and stewed, the more I simply wanted to hold him like I had after the sex Friday morning. Falling asleep with him in my arms had been unexpectedly wonderful, and I wanted that bliss again, wanted to see him that relaxed and happy, wanted to give him whatever it would take to get his cheerful self back.

Up All Night

"Here, sugar. You look like you need a refill." Tammy brought Sean a fresh cup of coffee as I worked on their orders. I tried to keep from staring, but when Caleb touched Sean's hand and murmured something, I damn near saw red.

Hell. This was a date. And maybe Sean felt guilty to be having it in my presence. A better guy than me would undoubtedly smile at him, give the ol' thumbs-up, let him know it was no biggie.

But it was, and I damn near torched my first effort at his hash browns. Extra crispy went to extra burned went to the garbage as I fought the urge to march over there. As I was redoing the hash browns, the door jangled again, and the younger dark-haired EMT who'd patched me up the other day strode in, going right to the booth and sliding in next to Sean.

"Hey, I'm late. Sorry."

Not a date. The EMT had been in a couple of times with his long-haired hippie lawyer boyfriend. No way was he signing up for a three-way with Sean and Caleb. My hand finally relaxed on the spatula, and my movements became free and easy again. No more feeling like I was cutting through concrete and making stupid mistakes.

"Drinking anything other than black coffee? How about some water? Gotta keep hydrated after your night." The EMT motioned Tammy over. She handed out water glasses to all three guys as my gut churned. I'd been so busy being jealous that I'd forgotten who Sean was.

He was many things, but he was a firefighter first, down to his DNA. He could have seen any number of tragedies on his shift, and his exhaustion was likely emotional as well as physical, but me being a dumbass, I hadn't let myself see it. I put extra care into plating his food as the EMT rubbed Sean's tense shoulder.

"You did everything you could."

"Yeah." Sean shook his head, clearly not in agreement but without the energy to argue. I'd been there. He stretched away from the EMT guy before asking, "Any updates?"

"Yep." The EMT nodded. No smile. I braced for Sean to get some sort of bad news. "Lifeflight landed in Portland. The trauma team and burn team both met the chopper, and the dude is in surgery now. It's the best news we can hope for, really."

"Young guy." Even the usually jokey Caleb was somber.

"Yeah." Sean stared off into space. "About the same age as Declan."

Oh. That had to be the kid he'd mentioned a couple of times. Twenty-something and some kind of motocross racer. Damn. Bad night on duty and likely a bad night to be a dad. My feet twitched as I watched Tammy bring Sean and Caleb their plates. I wanted to go to him, a strange but undeniable need.

However, I managed to bide my time until Tate disappeared to the restroom right as Caleb's phone rang.

"I better take this." Caleb stepped outside the diner.

The sun was barely peeking over the horizon. The day shift would be here soon, and I couldn't waste this chance. Tammy was busy taking orders from a trio of construction workers, so I scooped up the coffee pot and headed to the booth on the slimmest of pretexts.

"Hey." I slowly refilled all three coffee cups.

"Hey, yourself." For the first time all morning, Sean met my gaze, and yeah, the dude was hurting, exactly as I'd suspected. The pain and vulnerability in his expression made me want to offer him everything I had. I wasn't a caretaker. I didn't have siblings or family. I'd been a lone wolf for so long that I had no clue how to exist in a pack. But even knowing all that, I wanted to fix things for Sean so badly that my hand clenched on the coffee pot.

"Gonna need a ride?" I asked in a low whisper. *Please say yes. Let me help.* I tried to beam the message directly into his eyeballs.

Teeth digging into that lower lip of his I liked so much, he took his sweet time nodding. "Yeah. That might be nice."

I'd give him better than nice. Ride. Sex. Talking. Whatever he needed. Hell, I'd give him the whole damn world if only to see him smile again.

Chapter Twelve

Sean

I stood near Denver's truck in the cool morning breeze, feeling a little foolish and a lot needy. My own perfectly serviceable truck sat only a few spots away. But as Denver emerged from the diner, I exhaled for the first time in what felt like days.

"You waited." His tone was solemn, matching my mood just fine.

"You asked." I waited while he unlocked the truck, and then I climbed into the passenger seat.

"I did." Denver ambled over to the driver's side, taking his time turning the truck on and letting it warm without peppering me with questions, which I appreciated more than he'd ever know. "Want to drive a bit?" he asked at last before putting the truck in gear. "Clear your head?"

"Sure." My voice was so flat even I was sick of my own presence. Denver didn't need me being a sad sack on his day off. "I mean, that, or you pound me through your mattress. Both might work."

Denver didn't laugh, nor did he head toward Prospect Place. "I'm not fucking you with you all kinds of twisted up."

"But I'm flexible." I offered him a grin I really didn't feel.

"I'm not." Denver drove steadily out of town, away from the houses and stoplights and neighbors taking advantage of a sunny spring morning to jog or garden or breakfast on their decks. Ordinary lives on a morning when nothing felt ordinary and everything seemed to be closing in. My skin was tight and dry, nasal passages burning, eyes bleary, and despite the multiple glasses of water Tate had forced on me, I was parched. But as we fled town for the green hills covered in evergreen trees and familiar rocky terrain, I exhaled, reaching for the window controller.

"Everything okay?" Denver's tone was wary like I might be about to hurl in his truck.

"Sorry. Just wanted to smell the fresh air."

"Smell away." He rolled his own window down, creating a marvelous cross breeze. "We can get out and walk at some point if you want."

"Why are you being so nice to me?" I wasn't at all sure I'd earned his concern. I hadn't told him a thing about my shift, and our few short text messages had been casual, a pronounced gap between hookup buddies and friends. Yet, this, taking me on a drive instead of fucking, was definitely a friend gesture.

Denver shrugged. "You brought me muffins. I owe you."

"Now who's not being serious?"

"Honestly, I don't know either." His tone turned thoughtful. "You're hurting. I want to fix it. I don't know how, and I'm probably doing a crap job, but I'd like to help."

"Wow." I didn't have a better reply than that. I couldn't

say as anyone, even Maxine, had been that direct with me before.

A dusky flush spread up Denver's neck. "Should have stuck with the muffins."

"No, I like honesty." I managed a small smile just for him. I relaxed in my seat more, letting myself enjoy the scenery and the breeze whipping through the truck. "And this is helping. The smell of the trees and sunshine."

"Good." Denver turned onto another curving back road, not forcing conversation, letting me soak up the sun and clean smells. As he navigated another bend in the road, I spotted a familiar-looking logging road.

"Hey, is that our spot?" I pointed.

"We have a spot?" Despite sounding confused, Denver indulgently slowed before turning onto the bumpy, unpaved road.

"The one where we first kissed?" I gestured around us. Yeah, this was the place. My attention had been all on Denver, but the hidden cove of trees was seared into my memory, right along with the taste of his lips.

"Ah. I guess it is." Denver flushed deeper, like I'd called him out on some sentimental secret. But he knew. He was remembering too. A fact made clear by how he glanced at my mouth before looking out the window. "There's a neat view of a creek a way up the hill. Thought maybe you might want to sniff some more air."

"I do." Surprisingly, I was eager to exit the truck. Bone tired, every muscle hurting and joints creaking, yet there was nowhere I'd rather be than following Denver up the faint little trail leading away from the logging road. The more we walked, the looser my whole body felt, lips included. "The nose is a funny thing. I can wash off gasoline, oil, antifreeze, blood, guts. A little soap and some scrubbing, and it's all good as new."

"Is it?" Denver paused near a huge stump, weathered and beaten.

"Maybe." Bending, I ran a hand over the rough wood. Once upon a time, the whole forest had been full of trees wider than my mom's dining room table with all the leaves added in. "Okay, no. It's not." Denver's quiet steadiness and us being the only humans for miles around made me way more truthful. "Because I can still smell it. See it. Hear it."

Denver didn't say anything, only nodded as he regarded me with watchful eyes.

"And usually, I'm good at washing it all down the drain, leaving it behind after a hard shift." I tried to sound resigned, maybe echo a bit of Denver's steadiness. But then he touched me. A hand on my upper arm. And I broke. "I did my best, like the guys said at breakfast. I did my best, and that used to be good enough for me to sleep. Move on to the next call."

"But something changed." Denver didn't ask as much as deduced the truth, which made it far easier to continue.

"Declan got a motorbike." I closed my eyes, seeing my kid back in the tween years, all gangly elbows and knees and unbridled enthusiasm. He had my red hair and Maxine's intelligent eyes and long limbs. "We took him to a motocross race up north of Seattle the year he turned ten. Day trip. Buddy from the firehouse knew someone racing. Never thought Declan would come away with his passion in life, but that's kids for you."

"Yep." Denver moved to sit on the stump. "And now he races?"

"He does." I sat beside Denver, feeling like I'd removed

two hundred and fifty pounds of gear. "And he's damn good at it. Turned pro a little after he was seventeen, racked up the points, made it into the big races in record time."

"But you worry."

"Of course I do." I bit my lip, intending to leave it at that, but the words tumbled out anyway. "But not so much about Declan racing—they've often got medics standing by, and he's got all the latest safety gear. No, I worry about the after-parties, the hard living, the collection of motorcycles, and his fearless disregard for the laws of physics and speed limits."

"A lot of people party hard in their early twenties and make it through." Denver's tone was pragmatic but not unkind. "I'm sure that's not what a dad wants to hear though. You want him safe."

"Exactly. And the thing is, he's a great rider." Despite the heaviness of the topic, I smiled as I often did when Declan's name came up. In my head, he was three, racing cars across the carpet, then eleven on his first dirt bike, then fourteen, hoisting an amateur trophy, and now, old enough to share a beer and a laugh with, and still my kid. "Declan is a total natural like all the press says about him. But even the best riders in the world don't stand a chance against motor vehicles that don't care about sharing the road."

"Nope. Lost a good friend in high school to a collision like that." Denver put his hand on my thigh. Not a pat precisely, but there, holding on. "A drummer on one of our tours lost a brother to a motorcycle crash, and I worked a few seasons at a resort with a dude who barely survived an accident of his own. Scary stuff."

"You don't ride?" Given Denver's freewheeling nature, I might have assumed he'd have a Harley or two in his past, but he shook his head.

"I love adrenaline, but I don't have..." He trailed off, mouth twisting.

"A death wish. It's okay. That's the opinion a lot of people have." Hell, I'd had it myself for years. I stared off down the valley toward the creek Denver had mentioned. "But riders like Declan love it. The risk is worth it to him. Not to me, his dad, but he gets something out of riding that I've come to accept I'm not going to understand."

"That's a good perspective." Denver squeezed my leg. "We're not always going to understand what another person needs and why." He said the words matter-of-fact, like he wasn't already damn good at knowing what I needed, like this drive and walk. "Hell, most of us don't understand that about ourselves."

My chest filled with too much oxygen, too fast, too many feelings to hold, too much of a perfect moment to last. But it was here, and so were we, and I wasn't going to let the moment pass. I leaned in, pressed a soft kiss to Denver's surprised mouth, swallowing his gasp, then clinging to his shoulder when he deepened the kiss. Long and lingering, but not precisely sexual. Or rather, not only sexual. More soothing, a layer of affection I hadn't expected. I returned his gasp as a shudder raced through me.

"What was that?" Denver pulled away slightly but kept an arm slung around my shoulders.

"I needed it," I said simply.

"Good." Denver gave a sharp nod like that was ample reason. I inhaled deeply, tasting not only the spring air but also acceptance. As with the sex, it was okay to be a little needy and clingy with him, to ask for things I might not with others.

"Most days, I accept that Declan's going to take risks I don't agree with. And then, last night, we got called to a crash. A pickup truck and a biker tangoed on the interstate. Both lost, but the biker got the worst of it."

"Fuck." Denver whistled low and squeezed my shoulder.

"We were first on the scene before the ambulance unit. We did what we could. *I* did what I could." I tried to stick to the facts, not share too many gory details, but it was all too easy to relive the scene, fresh adrenaline surging through me. But Denver held me close, steadying me.

"And you kept seeing your boy."

"Yeah." My breath whooshed out of me. Denver got it. "And now that John, Eric's kid, is learning to drive, I saw him in the kid in the pickup too. It's so damn easy to get distracted as a young driver. And yeah, the whole time we were working on the motorcycle rider, I kept seeing Declan. Hearing him. Similar age. Similar build. Similar fearlessness."

"Did you call him?" Denver asked.

"Who? The patient?"

"No, your son. Declan." Denver kept his voice calm amid my confusion. "Did you call him after?"

"Why would I?" I wasn't being flip or defensive. It had honestly never occurred to me to call anyone after a hard shift. Maxine had preferred not to hear about it, and I had my first responder buddies to vent to. Declan might be an adult now, but he was still my kid, and I wanted to protect him from the ugly side of my job. "He doesn't need to hear all my worries or that I had a bad shift or any of that. He's young and living his best life."

"But it would make you feel better."

I pursed my lips, about to issue a denial, then shook my head. "You're right. How'd you get so wise?"

"I've got a stack of numbers I can't dial." He stared into the distance, beyond the valley and the creek, into a past I couldn't follow.

"I'm sorry." I shifted so I could lean into his embrace.

"And maybe your kid is like me. Maybe he'd want to help."

"He would. He's got a good heart." I squinted at the sun, rethinking all sorts of things I'd thought I'd known. "So do you."

"Eh. Don't go spreading rumors of my niceness."

"I'll keep it between us." I patted his thick thigh before digging out my phone. Declan was likely still asleep, phone on silent. I could simply leave a short message. But my phone stubbornly refused to find even a roaming signal. "Damn. No signal out here."

"Not surprising." Denver gestured around us at the relative remoteness. Standing, he brushed off his chef pants before offering me a hand. "Let's head back so you can make that call."

"No outdoor sex?" I didn't drop his hand. Silly little thing, but it felt right, letting him lead me back to the truck.

"Not this morning," he said lightly.

"Tonight?" I knew from things he'd said in passing that Mondays were his usual day off. "Wait. Not tonight. I volunteered to work on Eric's carriage house after dinner. The space has great potential for another roommate, but it needs cleaning."

"I'm not afraid of getting dirty." Denver climbed back into the truck, expression placid as ever.

"That you offering to help?"

"I guess it is." He sounded as surprised at his agreement as I was. And it was another step toward friendship, two

103

activities in one day with limited potential for sex. Although the carriage house did have a locking door, a thought that kept me warm all the way back to town.

Chapter Thirteen

Denver

Dusk settled over the neighborhood as I arrived at Sean's place after dinner, ready to work in old clothes and toting the small toolbox I kept in the back of the truck. I wasn't sure what we'd need, but I wanted to be prepared. I used the same justification for the lube packets and condom in my pocket. I wasn't truly expecting sex, especially after Sean's last twenty-four hours, but I wouldn't turn it down either.

I could hear voices and laughter filtering in from the backyard, so I didn't bother with the doorbell. I trudged around the house and was pleased to note that the barbecue explosion didn't seem to have done any lasting damage. The middle kid, Rowan, lounged on the deck in pink running shorts and a gray sweatshirt advertising a theater camp. No surprise there. The dog sprawled at his feet. The youngest teen, Wren, was crouched over a small glass aquarium.

I smiled to myself. It might be deadly bugs or reptiles, but at least it wasn't fire tonight. On the grass, Sean was throwing a football for John. Nowhere near fall, but John seemed the kind of jock to be focused year-round.

"Throw it higher. Make me work," John called to Sean, who was wearing a faded T-shirt for a firefighter pancake breakfast fundraiser and loose shorts.

"Remember, I wasn't a quarterback. That was Tony, not me." Sean laughed as he threw it again, a perfect pass right to John's waiting hands. John caught the ball and launched into a sprint, dodging lawn chairs and a mower as Sean called out tips. "Stay low, don't get ahead of your feet."

Thinking of our earlier conversation, I wondered if Sean missed his kids being high-school age. He would have been a good dad, involved and supportive. Everything I hadn't had, but I wasn't jealous as much as grateful people like Sean existed. Kids needed people like him, and it was clear from how he'd talked about Declan earlier that he loved his kid deeply. What would affection like that feel like? I had no clue.

In no hurry to announce my presence, I leaned against Sean's truck, which was parked near the carriage house. Given the age of the house, the older, freestanding structure that was a cross between a cottage and a garage could easily predate the automobile era. The whole scene felt like a throwback, something out of a movie or idyllic memory.

"Hey, you." Sean smiled widely when he finally noticed me in between throws to John. "You play any sports?"

"Nah." I shook my head. "Wasn't that big on school, let alone team sports."

Not to mention, sports cost money foster families didn't often have. And being on a team and developing athletic skills were benefits of being in one place for a decent amount of time, a luxury I'd seldom had.

"You probably could have been on the offensive line."

John jogged over next to Sean. "Or defense. Wanna try to tackle me?"

"Uh..."

"It's getting late." Sean saved me by gesturing back at the house. "Homework. Showers. You know the drill."

"Homework." John made a disgusted noise.

"I can do your geometry," Wren called out. "Since it's so hard for you."

John made a face, but Sean held up a hand before sibling bickering could break out.

"Why don't you work on that human geography project? Jonas should be done eating by now, and I bet he'd be happy to look over it for you."

"Maybe."

"Well, the three of you need to at least make an attempt at homework. Jonas will be around to say goodnight at nine-thirty. Be sure to have showered."

"Don't have to tell me twice." Rowan stood and stretched, the dog following him in. John groaned again before jogging toward the back door himself.

Which left Wren eyeing me suspiciously from the deck. "Why are you here?"

"Wren." Sean's tone was patient. "I told you. I'm working on the carriage house tonight. Denver's helping."

"Pretty weird date."

"It's not a date." Sean flushed, looking far too guilty. "Now, head inside with your siblings, and for God's sake, take the turtle with you."

"Turtle?" I asked Sean in a low voice.

"Found in the yard. Wren wants to monitor its eating habits. Maybe find a second turtle and conduct dietary experiments."

"Of course." I blinked. Funny kid, but I liked how indulgent Sean was of their quirks.

"Come on, let me show you the mess we're dealing with." Sean led the way to the carriage house. "Sorry to keep you waiting."

"You didn't. It was fun watching you with the kids." I rather enjoyed Sean's wide eyes. I was surprised at me too. "How are they doing with...everything?"

"It's okay. You can say Montgomery's name. It's not an off-limits topic around here." Sean kept his tone upbeat as he opened the wooden door for the carriage house, which was stuck and took a bit of rattling. "And kids are amazingly resilient creatures. Maren's back at college, finishing up the spring term. Rowan's got a big part in the school production. Wren's up to their usual experiments and research. John is the quietest one. I worry about him the most, but they're all hanging in there."

"Good." I wasn't sure what else to say. It wasn't a loss I had a deep familiarity with. Having never had something was different from having had that bond and then losing it. "And Eric?"

"Good days and not-so-good days." Pausing his efforts to open the stubborn door, Sean shrugged, but the lines around his eyes and mouth tightened. "He's still sleeping on the third floor in Maren's old room. He let me have the first-floor primary bedroom, and that's part of why I want to get the carriage house fixed up. Give us more options as far as space. Another friend is due to arrive this summer after he processes out of the army."

"It's kind of cool how your whole friend group has pulled together." Another thing I didn't have experience with. I'd always been mystified by people with decades of connection, especially with friendships versus family.

"Yeah, that's just how we roll." Sean exhaled as the door finally swung open. "We've known each other since community college right after high school. Eric had an ad up for roommates for an apartment he'd found near the college. I wanted out of my parents' house in the worst way, and the rest was history."

"I've had roommates here and there. Can't say as I've stayed in touch." My mouth twisted, an odd sense of guilt or perhaps shame slithering up my spine, making my saliva turn bitter. I swallowed hard, but the taste remained.

Sean hesitated partway inside the darkened building. "Well, friendships can be hard to keep going for sure."

Afraid he might be about to offer me friendship tips next, I waited while he fumbled for a light switch. Our different life experiences only underscored our lack of a future—Sean was a ride-or-die type, always one of a tight-knit crew, while I rode alone. I wouldn't know the first thing about being the sort of friend Sean needed. Sure, I could try, like the drive earlier, but sooner or later, Sean would need something I couldn't give.

"Lights!" Sean crowed as an ancient ceiling fixture flickered to life. The interior was less garage-like than I'd expected, with finished walls and ceiling. The tons of boxes, trash, and layers of dust, though, said it had been years since the space had been anything more than storage.

"This is an...interesting space." On the far wall, a whimsical set of stairs led to a small loft area where more boxes lurked. To the left of the door where we'd entered, a single line of old-fashioned wood cabinets created what was presumably a kitchenette. A wood stove lurked on the other side of the door, another unexpected homey touch, not that I'd advise firing the thing up.

"Yep. Under years of dirt and oddball items, there are

some neat features." Sean flipped another light on before gesturing to a door near the stairs. "Some previous owner even put a bathroom in the back in the seventies."

"Nice." I wasn't someone with a remodeling gene. I could be handy with a toolset, but I lacked the vision for transforming spaces. Out of necessity, along with preference, I usually rented furnished spaces, but the gleam in Sean's eyes said he was the type to crave DIY projects. He'd mentioned his Seattle house a few times with obvious pride. He'd undoubtedly be a homeowner again someday, a thought which made my stomach give a weird flip.

Not wanting to analyze my reaction, I quickly set my toolbox near the front door.

"Put me to work."

"You're letting me give orders?" Sean sounded utterly delighted.

"Cute." I spared a glance at the nearby grimy front window. No one was in the backyard, so I stole a fast, hard kiss. "Sure, you can order me around. But you'll remember who's in charge when it counts."

"Uh-huh." Sean gulped, cheeks going scarlet. "Don't tempt me into fast-forwarding to that part."

"Work first." I smiled, gaze dropping to his groin. One kiss, and he was already raring to go. Did my ego—and other parts—good. "Gotta earn your distractions."

"Yes, s—. I mean, indeed." Still blushing, Sean handed me a large black trash bag. "Let's see if we can clear out enough junk and trash to make cleaning possible."

"You got it." We worked in companionable comfort for a time, Sean chatty as ever, sharing stories about when Declan and his other kid, Bridget, had been little. I enjoyed listening to him talk, especially since he seemed to require minimal input from me. Too many folks assumed good conversation meant taking turns and ensuring everyone had an equal opportunity to contribute. I preferred the casual nature of hanging out with Sean, where I could interject as I wished, yet I didn't feel any pressure to reciprocate.

"You're good at this." Sean gestured as I added another bag of trash to the pile by the door. The sun had set some time prior, but I wasn't at all tired of the work or Sean's cheery presence.

"What? Sorting trash?" I chuckled. "At least let me show you some skills with a drill or a crowbar before you go handing out compliments."

"Trust me. After recently clearing out a twenty-year marriage, I'll take demolishing a kitchen over sorting through an attic, basement, or a space like this." He sighed as he turned a plastic kid-sized shovel over in his hands, thumb catching on a crack in the handle. "You don't get as caught up in sentimentality or what to keep."

"It's easy when it's not your stuff." I plucked the broken shovel from his grasp and added it to the trash pile. Moving on, I opened a box to find musty gardening magazines from long-gone decades. An ominous-looking spiderweb occupied one corner, so I quickly shut the box and tossed it near the door. "Not that I've ever owned much. I like to travel light."

Sean continued to paw through a box of old beach toys. "Having kids, I didn't have the luxury of backpacking around in my twenties or anything like that, but downsizing everything after the divorce was rather freeing. I can see the appeal of the open road."

"It's fun." I whistled the opening lines from an oldie about wild road trips. Sean laughed, and a warm feeling settled over me. Maybe he'd like an adventure. Head out together if we could manage a string of mutual days off. Or maybe—

"I'm probably too old for that kind of fun." Sean laughed again, more self-consciously. "I say I'd like to travel, but I'd likely miss having roots too much to be a permanent nomad."

"Probably so." I nodded, ignoring the sudden ache in my chest. Sean might have a bit of post-divorce fun, but he was a family guy at his core. I gestured at the now much-emptier carriage house. "After you get this place all fixed up, you'll want to stay awhile."

It was clear he was already attached to Eric's kids. Sean was the type to love easily, giving his heart away freely. I needed to remember that and tread carefully. I didn't want to hurt him, but I also didn't want to get used to all his easy affection, forget that caring was in his genes and not something personal.

"Sweat equity?" Sean finally added the box of beach toys to the trash pile, pausing to move a serviceable pail to the smaller collection of items to donate. He paused to wipe his forehead with the hem of his T-shirt. "There's something to that. When you put in work, you feel more invested in a thing."

"Hmm." I wasn't so sure I agreed, but I also didn't want to derail Sean's good mood with my own grumpy logic. In Sean's world, a person did work, got rewarded for it, and built up capital they could count on. In my experience, life was seldom that kind.

"Oh, hey, I took your advice." Sean looked up from opening a box of what appeared to be more boxes—small empty shoe boxes and other packing materials.

"Yeah?" The way he was smiling made me shuffle my feet, find something new to do with my hands. I gathered up big handfuls of old newspapers. What advice had I given him? The bit about needing to explore his sexuality? My back stiffened. "I mean good for you, play safe and all—"

"Not about sowing my wild oats. You're about all I can handle right now, but thanks for the vote of support." Sean rolled his eyes at me, seeing right through my efforts to not seem jealous. "No, I meant I called Declan."

"Oh." I guess that suggestion did count as advice. A strange sensation spread through my chest. I'd told him to do something outside the bedroom, and he'd actually done the thing. "How'd that go?"

"Declan answered instead of letting the call go to voicemail. Early for him, but he sounded happy enough to hear from his old man." Sean finished making a neat stack of the empty boxes, gaze darting between the donate and trash piles. I gave him a stern look until he gently added the stack to the trash. "He told me about Saturday night's race. I told him not to party too hard after a good finish. He groaned, but then he said not to worry."

Knowing Sean, he'd worry about the kid till Sean's own final breath, but I liked how much lighter and happier Sean seemed now as opposed to earlier. "So it helped? Hearing from him?"

"Yeah." Sean's smile took on a sappy edge, eyes going soft as he crossed to where I was rinsing the newsprint off my hands in the sink of the old kitchenette. "You're pretty smart."

"Nah." I never did know what to do with a compliment. I looked everywhere but at Sean until my gaze landed on the furniture we'd uncovered under all the boxes. A little Formica dining set right out of the 1950s, along with some random wooden chairs. Over in the corner, away from the window, was a mammoth leather chair that was somewhere between a recliner and a loveseat. Ugly as sin and twice as lumpy. "Now that's a chair."

"It's huge." Sean grinned before touching my arm. "It could fit both of us."

"Could indeed." Suddenly, kissing seemed like the best idea on the planet, a great way to avoid more compliments and my own pesky stray thoughts. I nodded over at the carriage house's front door. "Lock the door."

Chapter Fourteen

Sean

I'd never locked a door so fast in my life. I scurried over to the front door of the carriage house, leaping over the piles for trash and recycling, and quickly flipped the lock, double-checking the handle for good measure.

"Come here." Denver was already sprawled in the oversized chair, taking up far more real estate than I'd thought possible. I wasn't sure where I was supposed to fit, but then Denver patted his thigh.

Huh. I didn't know what I thought about that suggestion, but an invisible magnet pulled me to the chair nonetheless. Denver had already shed his shirt, revealing that wide chest I liked so much and leaving him only in faded jeans with the top button undone. I reached for the hem of my own T-shirt, but when my fingers encountered the damp flesh of my side, I let the shirt fall back down.

"Should we shower?" I glanced back at the doorway to the small bathroom. It had a stall shower, a far cry from

Denver's huge tub. Might be a tight squeeze and not the fun kind. "Or at least me? I'm—"

"Perfect." Denver patted his thigh again, legs falling open invitingly. "I'm not afraid of a little sweat, but I am afraid of that scary-looking shower back there."

The bathroom was in rougher shape than the living space of the carriage house, with a cracked mirror, a pedestal sink with separate hot and cold taps, mismatched flooring, and a bent shower door stained with some sort of rust. The vinyl of the shower stall itself had at least one crack, so Denver's reluctance made sense. God only knew when the water had last been turned on in there.

"Point taken. We'll make cleaning the bathroom up and possibly replacing the shower a priority."

"Replacing. Some things can't be saved." Denver's tone was pragmatic, as it had been while sorting through boxes. He was unburdened by the sentimentality that could paralyze me, and I'd enjoyed working with him a great deal. We'd gotten far more done than I would have alone. Denver jerked a thumb over at the bathroom. "I'll help."

"You will?" My eyes went wide, and Denver's mouth pursed. Crap. Maybe he hadn't meant to offer. I spoke fast before he could rethink. "That's great. Looking forward to it."

I was all-in on any chance to see more of Denver, in or out of bed. And the carriage house work did need doing, and the less I needed Eric's help, the better. The kids and his return to his paramedic job had him busy enough.

"I'm looking forward to you in fewer clothes," Denver drawled, and I finally went ahead and pulled off my T-shirt. Moving closer to him, I let him pull me into his lap. I ended up half on him and half on the chair, but this definitely qualified as in someone's lap, which was an odd and entirely new sensation. Denver wrapped his arms around me, and despite the newness of the position, my whole body relaxed.

"This is weird."

"The chair?" Denver moved a hand from me to the arm of the chair, squeezing as if testing the strength of the structure.

"The position." I yanked his hand back to where he'd had it, resting against my stomach. He tried to move to give me more room in the chair, but I hooked a leg around his to prevent him from going anywhere. "No, don't move. I meant it's weird how much I like this."

Denver chuckled and held me closer. "You're funny. You're completely cool with how much you love sucking cock and getting rimmed, but you're all shy about a little cuddling."

"Is that what this is?" I couldn't say as I had a ton of experience with cuddling, certainly not with another guy.

"For starters." Giving me an exaggerated leer, Denver pulled me in for a fast kiss. Or rather, he tried to make it fast, but I wouldn't let him escape, deepening the kiss until he gave in with a groan. So far, he'd kissed me in a number of circumstances—sexy, friendly, comforting. However, this was the first I could say was *sweet*. Like a perfect slice of birthday cake, sweet with a depth of emotion as opposed to other sweets like a candy bar in the checkout line.

I might not be well-versed in the rules of flings and hookups, but I was fairly certain I wasn't supposed to be feeling half the things Denver inspired in me. But hell if I was going to let him go. I kissed him with fierce intensity, grateful when he responded in kind. He sucked hard on my tongue, and I shivered. He gathered me against his chest, and my shudder turned into a happy sigh.

"Okay, maybe this is more nice than weird." I offered him a dopey smile.

"Nice?" He chuckled before nipping at my neck. "I think we can do better than *nice*."

Denver kissed my neck with delicious thoroughness, finding every last nerve ending from below my ear to my Adam's apple to the line where my neck and shoulder met. I moved restlessly in his lap, both loving the position and also desperate for some friction for my aching cock. Denver swept his hands up and down my sides, but the light touches were far from enough.

"Damn. I need..."

"Straddle me." Denver's tone didn't offer room for objections, and I scrambled around, more concerned with meeting his order than any awkwardness. I shifted until my knees were on either side of him, and we could kiss face to face, bare chests rubbing together. Straddling him made it easier to rock against him, absorbing all his strength and solidness. But with each kiss and touch, my body heated further. I broke away with a groan.

"More."

Denver slumped farther in the chair, creating space between us. "Take my dick out."

"Are we gonna fuck?" My voice was more hopeful than nervous. With each encounter, I trusted Denver more and wanted everything he had to offer.

"Nah." Denver laughed. "That's the one activity that might benefit from showering first."

"Oh. Yeah." Hygiene. I should have thought of that, but this was all so new.

"But I've got you." Denver captured my hands and led them to his fly. His dick was as rock hard as mine, eager to escape the confines of his zipper, and its heavy length fell into my grasp as soon as I worked his zipper down. "Jack me."

Denver didn't have to ask me twice. I loved how he felt in my hand, weighty, substantial yet delicate, with soft skin and a perfectly round cockhead.

"I like touching you." I stroked his chest with my free hand, enjoying the faint rasp of fuzz.

"You'll like this even better." Denver winked at me before gesturing at my shorts. "Get your cock out too."

I liked how he ordered me instead of simply doing it himself. Felt sexier, somehow, him merely lounging there while I stroked each of us, one in each hand. I pushed any thoughts of our difference in size out of my head. Not everyone could be porn-star big like Denver, and given our height difference, my cock was...proportionate. And Denver seemed to like it fine, gaze riveted on my fist, watching my cock slide in and out.

"Try both of us together." Denver made it more demand than suggestion which meant my cock pulsed that much harder. I hurried to comply, shifting so our cocks aligned. Took me a few tries to figure out a good angle and grip.

"Ungh." I made a noise halfway between pleasure and discomfort. The press of his cock against mine was almost too much friction. But then Denver revealed a lube packet from his pocket and drizzled it over my fist.

"You travel with lube?" I watched the lube drip over both of our cocks.

"You don't?" Denver laughed. "No, not usually. Figured it might pay to be prepared tonight."

"Thank you." I gasped as I started stroking again, each movement slippery and perfect. "Oh, this is amazing."

"Don't you dare come yet." Denver gave me a stern glare.

"I won't," I said a little too hopefully. The slick lube and warm weight of Denver's cock combined to have me close in record time. Not that I needed much encouragement in that area. I'd be embarrassed at how fast Denver revved me up if it weren't for how much pleasure he seemed to take in my hair trigger.

"Liar." Denver tweaked one of my nipples. He placed his other hand over mine, guiding my rhythm.

"Well, when you do that..."

"No coming." Denver's voice worked like an invisible rope, holding me back from the edge. However, there was fun to be had in pushing against that rope, testing Denver's control.

"But I want—"

"And I want you to wait," Denver ordered exactly as firmly as I'd hoped. He was in control. I could tease and taunt, but he had the power. Warmth spread outward from the center of my chest. I was still all kinds of turned on but more relaxed now. Denver wouldn't let me down. Proving that point, he used a broad thumb to drag my chin closer. "Kiss me."

I did, little kisses that turned into longer ones, deeper, until we were kissing and stroking, and I was gasping like I was scaling a mountain up into thin air. My need to climax returned in full force.

"Not sure how this is supposed to help me wait."

"It's not." Denver gave a wicked laugh.

"You're mean." I pretended to pout, joy joining all the other emotions racing through me. *Fun.* Being with Denver was simply so much fun, even when I thought I'd die from needing to come.

"Yep." Denver captured my mouth again, tongue rubbing against mine in a way that had my hips rocking into our combined grips. Denver set the rhythm, though, guiding and directing my hand until I made a keening noise.

"Denver. I want..." I didn't recognize my own voice. Thready. Needy. Raspy from moaning so much, lips swollen from kissing. "Can't wait..."

"You want something?" Denver offered another devilish grin as he stilled our hands. He managed to seem totally casual, which only made me feel that much more crazed.

"Please. Please. I need to come."

"You sure do beg pretty." Denver sped up our strokes again. I was close, so close, but the urge to please Denver continued to narrowly beat out the need to climax. I wanted him to be proud of me. Wanted to earn my pleasure.

"Please. I'm trying..."

"I know you are, baby." Denver's voice was as soothing as his hand on my back. "You're doing amazing. So good for me."

Some switch tripped inside me, a lever I hadn't known about, and I went pliant. I stopped fighting my orgasm, stopped thinking about anything other than letting Denver use me. It was the same amazing, floaty place I went to when I let him fuck my face. Being a vessel for his pleasure, letting him take what he wanted from me, was the most freedom I'd ever known. My brain quieted and my restless fidgeting ceased as I let Denver set the pace of our strokes and guide my hip with his other hand.

"That's perfect." Denver's praise landed like a warm blanket around my shoulders. "Damn. When you listen, you listen."

"Yes." My eyes shut, all my focus on being what he needed. I silently encouraged him to use me however he wanted to get closer to climax himself. When his breathing stuttered, triumph rushed through me with his every moan. He sped up our strokes, thrusting into our fists.

"Need." My voice sounded far away, coming from a distant planet where I was dimly aware of how close my orgasm was, yet determined to hold it off until Denver gave the word. "Please."

"Go ahead, baby. Take what you need." His voice was as rough as his movements. I shuddered, brain unsure, but my body knew exactly what it wanted. My hips bucked, and I fucked into our joined fists, hard and fast. Denver made a pleased noise that pushed me that much higher.

"Fuck. Fuck. You're going to get me off too." He urged me faster, and pleasure spiraled through me, a cyclone sweeping up from my feet.

"Yes, yes. Please. Come with me." My back arched as I came in huge spurts, all over his chest and stomach. I felt utterly wrung out, like every neuron had given everything to my climax, leaving me boneless and hollow. But not alone. Denver shouted as his come joined mine.

"Oh damn. Damn. You are fucking perfect." More praise. Perfect indeed. The effort of waiting had almost done me in, yet it had been totally worth it to earn that praise and his soft kisses as we slipped back to earth.

A nearby box held a stack of old dish towels, and I stretched to grab one, dabbing the mess on Denver's stomach and cleaning both of our hands.

Back to myself, uncertainty rushed in as Denver took the towel from me and finished cleaning up. I supposed playtime was over, and I moved to climb off Denver's lap, but he held me tightly.

"Where do you think you're going?" His curly hair had escaped his ponytail at some point, and the long strands fluttered around his face. He looked as spent as I felt but far more content.

"I figured…"

"You figured you'd stay right here until I can feel my legs again," he said sternly. The order relaxed me, made me slump against him and simply breathe for long moments as he rubbed my back. Neither of us spoke. I wanted to ask him what the hell we were doing because I was pretty sure we'd left hooking up in the dust, but I didn't want to ruin this quiet perfection.

"What else needs doing tonight?" Eventually, when I was almost but not quite asleep, Denver's voice rumbled me back awake. "Did you have a goal?"

"We're talking cleaning?" Mouth and brain fuzzy, I stretched.

"Well, yeah. I didn't come over only to fuck around." He patted me like I should have known. "Doubt either of us is tired enough for sleep yet. Not gonna leave you to work when I could help."

I smiled slowly, trying not to look too surprised. "I'd like that."

I liked Denver too, probably more than I should, but right then, I refused to worry about anything other than making this happen again as often as possible.

Chapter Fifteen

Sean

As I snuck down Eric's back stairs on a warm April Saturday morning, the sun was barely poking out of the grayish-blue dawn. I felt almost like one of the teens. Not only was I carrying my shoes to make less noise, but I'd been giddy for over two weeks now, the secret of carrying on with Denver not unlike a teen crush. Not that I'd ever tell Denver I was crushing on him, but I was up early yet again, hoping to catch him at the end of his shift, sneak in a little time at his place before—

"You're up early."

I nearly missed the last stair and narrowly avoided crashing into Eric standing at the counter, adding grounds and water to the coffee maker. *Shit. Play it cool. Play it cool.* I pasted on a casual smile.

"So are you."

"Eh. I'm trying. Day off, so I figured if I was up early enough, I might be able to prevent more cooking experiments from Wren."

"What Wren needs is lessons." I'd been waiting for the chance to bring up this subject with Eric. "I've been thinking. The kids are all old enough to help with meal planning and prep, but they need supervision and instruction. What if we made a rotating chart for meal duty?"

"That's not a bad idea. I do like a good chart." Eric rubbed his bristly chin. He didn't wear a beard, but like me, he sometimes skipped shaving on his days off. "I used to have the household on a really tight schedule. Chores. Meals. School. It's been hard finding our footing again."

"I know." I waited until Eric hit the On button for the coffee maker to pat his shoulder. "And you need to let all of us help. Jonas is good at baking. I'm okay at breakfast food and firehouse meal basics like chili and spaghetti. And Denver offered to teach—"

"The short-order cook across the street?" Eyes brightening, Eric seemed far too interested in who Denver was. *Danger. Danger.*

"Yeah. He...uh...came by the day of the explosion."

"Which one?" Eric groaned and shook his head before chuckling. "And I've been waiting for you to tell me about him."

"What do you mean?" My voice was far higher pitched than necessary, and I had to brace a hand on the counter.

"You've sure been eating a lot of Honey's hotcakes despite the house here having four boxes of pancake mix, five dozen eggs at any given moment, and at least three pounds of bacon."

"Um. Yeah." I cast a guilty glance out the back window to where my truck was parked. *Change of plans.* "Guess I keep forgetting. Sorry. Bad post-divorce habit of eating out. How about I help you put some of that bacon to use? Do up a big breakfast for the kids?"

"Sean, go get your breakfast out. This is my morning to do the dad thing, maybe get a run in with John, watch Rowan rehearse for the play, listen to Wren's plans for world domination." Eric's tone was all-too-patient. "You'll tell me about the short-order cook when you're ready."

"I...uh..." If there was anyone who would likely understand, it would be Eric, my oldest friend. Heck, he'd encouraged me to have a casual fling. Denver's gender might be a shock. Or not. Perhaps Eric had guessed years ago when we'd lived together the first time and I still hadn't known myself. Maybe that was why I paused. Eric wouldn't judge me, but he might say something I wasn't ready to hear. Also, this thing with Denver felt too new, too precious, too fragile to hold up to the light. We hadn't agreed to secrecy, but my chest went tight at the thought of telling Eric, only to have the fling with Denver evaporate.

I'm not ready. Eric knew it, his blue-green eyes soft and patient. "It's okay. Truly. Go get breakfast. Bring him around to teach Wren how to flip burgers."

"Yeah." I nodded, clinging to the last edges of my sanity. "We're friends. I could do that. Ask him to dinner."

Maybe if I went public with a friendship with Denver, eased us into things, he wouldn't balk at keeping our fling going, and I wouldn't freak out at the thought of coming out.

"You could." A small smile danced across Eric's face, a ghost of the man he'd been before losing Montgomery, serious but always happy and smiling. "You could ask him to dinner even without kids involved."

"I could. Let someone else cook for the man." *Dating.* We could date, let the fling morph into something without an end point. It was a tantalizing prospect, and I nodded. Baby steps.

"You should. Now, go on with you." He waved me

toward the back door. Perhaps it wasn't a bad thing that Eric had guessed. I liked having Denver as my secret, but I didn't like lying to my oldest friend.

As I drove to the diner, my mind kept mulling over the delicate dance of keeping the fling going while also trying to nurture it into something more without spooking Denver or myself. Maxine had dragged me to the ballet in Seattle a number of times with fellow academic types. I hadn't had a lot of patience for teasing out the nuance of the storylines, but the impossible lightness with which the dancers moved had stuck with me. I felt like that now, all my weight balanced on a few tiny joints, about to soar. Or fall.

Didn't want to fall. Yet, when I entered the diner, and Denver looked up and smiled, wide and true, the risk of leaping didn't seem quite so scary. I headed for the counter, already anticipating our banter and what he might surprise me with this time.

"Sean!" Talk about a surprise. Right as I was about to grab a stool at the counter, my dad's booming voice made me stop, heels digging into the scratched linoleum floors, lungs turning icy and stiff. "My boy! Come join the new mayor and me. Didn't expect to see you this morning."

That makes two of us. I turned away from the counter, away from Denver, and made my way to the booth where my dad was sitting with a woman in her early fifties. Short ash-colored hair, blue glasses, pink sweater. I vaguely recognized her as someone from my parents' church who had been big into community service, then city council, and now mayor.

"Mayor." I gave her a nod as I slid in next to my dad.

"Oh, call me Rosalynn." She smiled warmly. "My wife is off at a library association conference this weekend, so your father was kind enough to indulge me in an early breakfast meeting to catch me up on all the fire and rescue news."

"That's great." I forced myself to smile and not glance at the counter area. "And I'm here because Eric wanted some one-on-one time with the kids."

The partial lie tasted sour. Eric was the one doing me a favor, not the other way around. But my pulse hadn't slowed since hearing my dad's voice, and sitting next to him made me feel even more like a guilty teen with a secret than I had earlier.

"There's my blue eyes." Tammy came over with a cup of coffee and a menu for me. Her eyes were tired, but her voice was a little too friendly and familiar. I *had* been making a habit of coming to the diner, and she was a smart lady who probably suspected more than she let on. She gave me a conspiratorial grin. "Figured you might be in."

My dad's mouth pursed like he was trying to reconcile my explanation for my appearance with Tammy treating me like one of the family.

"We've been coming in on shift a fair bit." I made my voice casual as if I wasn't the one to frequently suggest Honey's over other options.

"And off-duty too," Tammy teased. I tried to catch her gaze for a warning look. I didn't need my dad to be too curious about my presence here.

"Some." I waved my hand, adding a chuckle. "I'm kind of addicted to...the coffee." And okay, that reason was thinner than a paper filter. Honey's coffee was pretty much standard diner fare—strong and aromatic but nothing special. "And the hash browns. The one breakfast food I haven't mastered cooking yet."

"Remind me to assign you to the bacon at the annual firefighter's breakfast in May." My dad's voice was hearty as

Up All Night

ever. Not suspicious. Thank God, but my back was stiffer than an axe handle.

"Are you enjoying your term as mayor?" I asked Rosalynn, hoping she'd take pity on me and make small talk to distract my dad from any questions about my life.

My ploy worked long enough for the three of us to order. After Tammy collected our menus, though, Rosalynn returned the conversation to the fire department. Asking my dad about fire department news inevitably led to him bragging about my return. I stifled a groan.

"Your folks seem awfully pleased to have you back in town. Are you planning to make the move permanent?" Rosalynn asked as I desperately looked around to see where our food was. Ordering off the menu had felt weird. Wrong. I'd come to love not having to pick, enjoying whatever Denver dreamed up for me. I'd ordered loaded hash browns, but I'd rather have one of his surprises. My gaze landed on Denver's broad back. I loved holding on to his shoulders and... *Nope. Can't go there.*

"I...I'm not sure. A lot depends on what happens with the firefighter on maternity leave I'm covering for and where my folks end up after Dad retires." Staying certainly had a lot more appeal these days, with Eric and the kids keeping me busy and my secret fling with Denver giving me life. I couldn't imagine being anywhere else at the moment. Each day I worked on the carriage house was another step closer to staying as well. I couldn't help but picture myself there, but that image included Denver, which was dangerous thinking, indeed.

"If we let your dad go. He's the best fire chief Mount Hope has ever had." Rosalynn laughed lightly, but this was an unanticipated wrinkle. The longer my dad was in town, the more likely he was to guess about my private life.

Perhaps it was naive of me, but until this morning, I honestly hadn't given much thought to my parents finding out about what I'd been up to with Denver.

"Oh, I'm retiring. The wife will have a fit if I put it off again." My exhale of relief was short-lived as my dad turned his shrewd gaze in my direction. "Of course I'll need an amazing replacement."

"Dad."

"What? You were a decorated captain. You'd be perfect—"

"On my crew." Huh. At some point in the last month, I'd gone from feeling like an outsider to feeling like part of the crew. And I liked it. No matter what happened in the future, I'd miss this time. "With all due respect, I'm not ready for a desk."

"Fair enough." Dad nodded, voice pleasant, but his level gaze said the subject wasn't closed. I glanced over at the mayor. The first lesbian mayor in town history. Could the town handle a gay fire chief? Not that I was at all interested in the job, but the consequences of coming out kept seeming more and more real. This casual fling with Denver had led to several uncomfortable truths.

"I'll be right back." Rosalynn excused herself to the restroom, which gave my dad ample chance to return to his favorite topic: me.

"You know we only want you happy. Fire chief, captain, part of the crew, whatever you want. Just be happy."

He said those words, but how would he react if I told him I was happier with Denver than I'd been in a long, long time. This might be the right moment to test the waters...

"You being happy is why your mother wants you to come to dinner sometime soon. She's met the most lovely single mother at church. Mom will tell you all about her, but if you make it to church tomorrow—"

"On duty." My voice was clipped right along with my hopes. Nope. No water testing, not right now, at least. "And I can find my own dates."

Like Denver. My earlier thoughts in Eric's kitchen about dating Denver returned in full force. Why couldn't this all be easy? We were already sleeping together. We got along great. Why not date? Why did things have to be so complicated?

"Then find one. Bring your date around for dinner and make your mother happy. Or bring someone to the pancake breakfast. Be happy, Sean."

I had a brief flash of Denver eating my mom's mac-n-cheese with ham and green beans on the side, her Sunday special. He'd make her laugh. My sisters and their kids would be there, running around. Maybe Bridget or Declan would be in town. And Denver...

Would likely hate it. Image gone. He was a nomad at heart, allergic to domesticity, and the big Murphy clan might give him hives. But now that I'd had the thought... Oh, how I wanted. I glanced at the grill area, watching Denver flip an omelet onto a plate.

Complicated indeed. And the wise thing would be to follow my dad to my parents' home, get some good-son points by helping with yard work, but the second Denver subtly glanced toward the parking lot, I nodded. I wasn't giving this up, not yet.

Chapter Sixteen

Denver

"Fancy seeing you here." I opened my apartment door to let Sean in. I didn't bother faking surprise. I'd known he'd show up eventually. All it had taken was a momentary meeting of our eyes, and I'd known. Exactly how I'd known when he'd first walked into the diner that he'd come to see me, not his old man.

"Is this okay?" Sean twisted his mouth this way and that, giving his jaw muscles quite the workout. I wasn't sure how to answer. Was it okay? My body was sure as shit happy enough to see him, but it also felt like something had shifted between us. I stayed silent as I shut the door behind Sean. He was in jeans and a fire department polo. "I'm sorry I didn't talk to you more at the diner."

"Eh." I shrugged and adjusted the waistband of my low-riding workout shorts. I hadn't bothered putting anything else on after my shower. "We both know what this thing is."

"Do we?" Following me toward the kitchen area, Sean

sounded as confused as I felt, which was no help. This was sex. A fling, as Sean himself kept calling it. But the time I'd spent helping him with the carriage house wasn't sex. Nor was all the time Sean spent at the diner or the way we tended to linger after sex. I'd had purely sexual arrangements before, and this wasn't it. Friends with benefits?

I wasn't sure I liked that either. Leaning against my narrow stretch of kitchen counter, I pursed my lips. "Whatever it is, I'm hardly expecting to meet the folks."

Sean exhaled hard as his eyes narrowed. He was thinking way too hard. "I know you don't want any sort of family thing. But I still feel bad. I wish—"

I pushed away from the counter, closing the distance between us to silence Sean with a kiss. I didn't want to hear his wishes. I'd heard a million pretty speeches before.

I wish you could meet my mom. You'd love her.
I wish we could be together for real.
I wish we could take a vacation together.
I wish I could take you out on a real date.
I wish, I wish, I wish.

Wishes counted for less than nothing. Empty air. But this, what happened when our mouths met, was real. The chemistry between us was a living creature, large and more than a little scary but undeniably alive and potent. I kissed Sean to shut up the voices in my head, but as always, the beast had a mind of its own. The kiss went from hard and rough to deep and intoxicating passes of lips and tongues.

Sean clung to me, hands digging hard into my shoulders. He always grabbed me like I might be about to make a run for it.

And I probably should.

But I was powerless to do anything other than steer

Sean to one of the nearby dining chairs. Still kissing him, I shoved his jeans and briefs down to his knees and pushed him to sit in the chair. He opened his mouth like he might be about to talk again.

Couldn't have that. This time I silenced him by sinking to my knees in front of him and swallowing his cock in a single motion. Pretty nifty, if I did say so myself, and his gasp went straight to my own aching erection.

"Wow. Um. Quite the welcome." Sean gave a wobbly laugh, his hand coming to my shoulder. He flexed his fingers like he was deciding between pushing me away or pulling me closer. I made it an easy choice, sliding back up his shaft, sucking hard the whole upstroke, then slowly sinking back down, millimeter by millimeter, with all the tongue action I could muster.

I might not be great at talking things out, but sucking cock hadn't failed me yet. Each of Sean's moans was more gratifying than the last. I loved reducing him to needy sounds and clutching hands. Closer. He was definitely dragging me closer. My pulse pounded like a drum circle at Burning Man.

"I'm not going to last." Speaking of burning, my firefighter had a short fuse, as always, and I gave his thigh a fond pat as I pulled back enough to speak.

"Surprise, surprise."

"I'm serious." Chuckling self-consciously, Sean shoved at my shoulder. I gave his cockhead a leisurely lick, loving how his shove turned to a caress. I sucked him into my mouth again, and he gave a pained groan. "We could fuck."

"We could." I tried to sound indifferent. He'd only mentioned fucking a time or twenty. We had a steady oral and frot diet going, but Sean was plenty eager for more ass play. I'd made him come from fingering several times, but I'd been ridiculously reluctant to fuck. Stupid, really, but I figured if I held off on the top thing on Sean's sex bucket list, he'd keep me around longer. He wasn't the only one with wishes. "Or I could keep going, see if going for a second round is a possibility..."

"With you? Anything is possible." Sean offered a dopey, sex-drunk smile. I could only wish that were the case. Not liking that line of thinking, I redoubled my efforts on Sean's cock, sucking in a hard, fast rhythm and using my tongue all along the underside of the shaft.

"Damn." Sean gave a lusty moan. "I wanna learn all your tricks."

"Hush. Your mouth is plenty amazing. And right now, all I want to hear out of it is please, Denver. Yes, Denver. More, Denver."

"Yes, Denver." His chuckle turned straight to another moan as I went deep, breaking out a little tongue action for the top of his balls too. "Oh fuck, please."

His cock pulsed against my tongue, not coming, but pretty darn close.

"Love your hair trigger," I murmured before getting back to sucking. I shouldn't have used the L-word there, not that Sean seemed to have noticed, but I needed to guard against how affectionate he made me. And I needed him to come, needed the distraction and power rush of him flying apart. Dropping my right hand, I gently cradled his balls.

As I'd hoped, he moaned. "Seriously. Not gonna... wait..." He slumped lower in the chair, spreading his legs wide. I wasn't one to ignore such an invitation, so I skated my fingers even lower to flick his rim while I sucked him hard and fast. "Oh God, yes, that. More, Denver."

I gave him everything I had, sucking him deep, milking the shaft with my tongue, tracing circles around his rim, drinking in his every delicious response. For all my reluctance to fuck, I'd never had such a responsive partner before, and I couldn't wait to watch him go nuts on my cock.

"Denver. I'm coming," Sean moaned like I didn't already know that. His whole body shuddered, balls lifting against my hand. I tried not to chuckle as his salty taste filled my mouth and I swallowed him down. I softened my mouth but kept right on sucking until he pushed at my shoulder. "Too much."

"Or just enough." Winking at him, I stood. He was a rumpled mess, hair every which way, polo shirt rucked up around his chest, pants at his ankles, dick damp and waving in the breeze. Adorable. I gave into the temptation to ruffle his hair, and he gave a tired chuckle.

"Okay, what the hell was that? I mean, good hell, but damn."

"You never heard of a quickie?" I'd meant to tease him with the hair ruffling, but my hand had a mind of its own, smoothing out his hair, stroking the silky red strands.

"Yeah, but you didn't..." His gaze dropped meaningfully to my groin.

"Don't always have to." I rolled my shoulders, trying to ignore my insistent cock's disagreement. Shrugging free of my touch, Sean stood. Rather than getting dressed as I'd expected, he pulled off the rest of his clothes before grabbing my hand. "What are you doing?"

"Returning the favor." Pulling me over near my bed, he shoved my shorts down. "In a civilized fashion."

With that, he pushed me onto the bed before stretching out next to me.

"Not sure I'm in the mood." It was as close as I was

going to get to admitting how messed up my brain was where he was concerned. But Sean being Sean, he didn't leap off the bed and hurry home. Instead, he propped himself up on one elbow to peer deeply into my eyes.

"But you were in the mood to suck the chrome off my trailer hitch?" He laughed, then sobered, still holding my gaze. "What gives? Are you mad I ignored you at the diner?"

"Of course not." I sounded like a petty fifteen-year-old. How could I be jealous of Sean eating with his father? From all I'd heard, they had a great relationship. It wasn't surprising that he'd chosen to join his father. Nor was it a shocker that he'd spent ninety-nine percent of the time avoiding looking my way. And he'd sounded tense in the bit of conversation I'd overheard. "I'm no expert in family relationships, but I get it. You don't want your father knowing where you stick your—"

Sean cut me off with a frustrated noise. "Eric knows."

"What?" I rolled to my side. I stretched my neck, reconsidering my assumption that Sean truly was simply exploring and wouldn't want word of us being anything other than neighborly acquaintances getting around.

"I mean, he suspects." Sean's pale face was redder than a cherry tomato, and he seemed equally likely to burst. Words aside, he wasn't doing great at convincing me he wasn't like all the other "straight" dudes out there. "And Eric's not wrong. You and I do have something going. We didn't have the whole coming-out conversation, but I didn't correct Eric either."

"Are you wanting a medal?"

"Look, I know you were hurt before by someone who wouldn't come out. That's not me."

He sounded earnest, but I wasn't sure. I stayed silent

even as Sean's eyes went wide, the sort of pleading that usually had me giving in under other circumstances.

"It's not. I want to date you."

A loud, sputtery noise escaped my chest.

"Date isn't a four-letter word, Denver." Sean poked me lightly in the chest.

"Actually, it is." I poked him right back.

"Be serious. I'm serious," said the guy who was still tomato red. But earnest. So earnest. "I want to date you. And I'm not an idiot. I know that means coming out."

"Does it?" I propped my head on my hand.

"It does. And I'm going to."

"Don't come out for me." I sat all the way up. His insistence had gone from cute to terrifying. He was serious. He wanted to date. Date me. Gulp. "I'm a bad bet. I can't promise you—"

"Your turn to hush." Sitting as well, he laid a finger across my lips. "Even if you don't want anything more than sex, this thing has changed me. Wait. That's not it. It's *revealed* me. I see myself clearly now after forty-three years. I feel foolish that I didn't know—or rather, let myself know—earlier in life. Coming out? Over forty? When I have two kids and had a twenty-year marriage? It's a bit daunting."

His voice echoed some of my own terror, so I captured his hand. "You don't have to."

"You're not listening." Sean was back to that stubborn tone. "I do have to. For me. In my own time and my own way. But I do have to come out, and I want you to trust me that it's going to happen."

"I'm sure you intend—"

Sean cut me off with one of those deft first responder moves of his, getting me flat on my back and him straddling me in half a second. "Swear to God, if you give me the you're-a-nice-guy speech right now, we will have words."

"Aren't we having words right now?"

"You drive me crazy."

"And that's why—" I didn't get to finish that thought either. Sean kissed me hard and fast, and I almost forgot my own name, let alone why dating would be a bad idea.

Sean pulled away with a satisfied grin. "We should give this thing a shot. I can't get you out of my head. And even when you're annoying the ever-loving fuck out of me, I still want you more than I've ever wanted anything."

"More than my hash browns?" I tried to tease, but my voice came out far too somber.

"More than hash browns. More than pineapple. More than chocolate. More than bacon." Sean grinned down at me, the tenderness in his eyes the scariest thing I'd ever seen.

"Whoa there. More than bacon? You are serious."

"I am." Sean wouldn't let me look away, wouldn't let me hide behind another joke. "Trust me. Please? I don't want to keep you a secret forever. I need time, but I'm not out to fuck you over."

"Nah, you're out to get fucked." I waggled my eyebrows at him, loving his frustrated laugh almost as much as the kiss he gave me.

"True."

I pulled him down for another kiss and then another. Hoping we'd left this dating topic for now, I rocked my hips up to meet him, shifting until our cocks aligned. He gave in with a groan, grinding against me. I kissed him harder, swallowing his moans. For once, I didn't feel the need to direct or give orders.

Instead, I simply rode the perfect wave of kissing and

grinding, letting go of all my worries until my biggest question was whether to reach for the lube or not. My heels dug into the mattress. No way was I going to come before Sean. I grabbed his hips, pulling him—

"Wait." Sean held up a hand.

"Yes?" I blinked, eyes decidedly bleary. "You want to stop. Now?"

"You're going to get me off again."

"And?"

"I want to ask you to dinner." He spoke quickly, but his tone was decisive, the sort I'd heard him use with his fire crew. "With Eric's kids and me. Your next night off. We're going to do a new thing with a whole schedule for meals, and you promised Wren cooking lessons."

"I did." I nodded, hips still pushing up at Sean. My cock was already over this pause. "You really want to talk dinner date logistics right now?"

"You called it a date." Sean beamed at me. Gone was his blush, replaced by a golden glow. Even his freckles seemed happy.

"I guess I did." I groaned, knowing full well I'd been had. And that I'd regret letting Sean think we were dating. Dating meant a future, and I didn't have that to offer him or anyone else. But then he kissed me, sweet and slow, and I'd promise him a thousand dates.

"Thank you." He started rocking again, grin firmly in place.

"Thank me after I make you scream my name again." I matched his every movement until the friction became a bit much. I grabbed the lube and slicked us both.

He shuddered. "How am I so close again? It's too easy with you."

"I know. I love it."

There was that word again. Harmless and deathly terrifying at once. Sean's gaze went soft, voice dropping to a whisper. "Denver, I like this."

"I like it too," I whispered back. Some things were easier to share in a whisper, like a secret. Yeah, we liked each other, but maybe we didn't have to talk about it. I pulled him in for another long kiss, moving against him, cocks sliding past each other as we thrust harder and faster.

"We've...got...a good thing...here," Sean panted against my lips. I was way, way too far gone to argue. Not that I would. We did have something good here. I didn't want to hurt him, but I couldn't deny how good this felt. How good it was, full stop.

"Gonna." Sean moved frantically, losing control in the way most guaranteed to take me with him. I held him tightly, thrusting against his abs, letting his moans take me higher and higher until we were both coming.

"Denver." He said my name like a final prayer, head falling back, hands braced on my chest. I'd never seen anything so magnificent in my life. It was a cheesy name from a father I had no memory of, but it had never sounded better than that moment. "Denver."

He collapsed on me, and we lay together in a sticky heap. I was beyond blissed out and almost asleep as Sean fetched a towel and cleaned us. But instead of returning to my embrace, he sat next to me on the edge of the bed.

"Guess I should leave you to your sleep."

"Nap with me a while." I tugged his arm. "Unless Eric or the kids need you?"

"Nah. He wanted some one-on-one time with the kids. I could stay awhile." Sean smiled shyly.

"Then lie your ass back down." I gave him a fake glare until he stretched out, head on my chest.

"Yes, sir." Sean gave a sleepy sigh as his hand found mine and held tight. Well, maybe this dating thing wasn't all bad. And yeah, apparently, I'd agreed to dinner with a bunch of teen chaperones, but if it meant getting to hold Sean like this, I could deal.

Chapter Seventeen

Sean

"What's with the goggles?" I asked Wren as I came into the kitchen. Denver was due any second for our long-awaited cooking lesson date. It had taken longer than expected for our schedules to align. In the meantime, the rotating chart of meal duty had brought a lot more order to the household. But Wren was still Wren, as evidenced by the white lab coat and goggles with a graphing notebook and tablet at the ready on the kitchen island.

"Safety first." Wren waved a hand dismissively as if everyone sported lab wear for weeknight dinner prep. "Burgers are notorious for splattering. And I want to experiment—"

"No experimenting." I groaned. "Patty melts. Home fries. A salad. Let's stick to the basics."

"Do you know where the world would be without science?" Wren's tone turned scornful. "My dad always said —sorry. My other dad." Wren sucked their lips in, then pushed them out in a pout, eyes going from mocking to sad. "Guess it doesn't matter now."

"Of course it matters." I stepped closer to the island. Wren could be funny about touch, so I didn't offer a pat, but I tried to pitch my voice as sympathetic as possible. "Wren, it's okay to say your dad's name. You kids called him Dr. Dad, right?"

"Yeah." Wren's pouting expression made them look far younger than thirteen. Because they were so smart, it was all too easy to forget they were still a kid. A kid grieving an enormous loss. In my opinion, Wren needed a hug, but their stiff body language said otherwise.

Instead, I leaned into Wren's favorite subject. "Dr. Dad would be proud of your commitment to scientific inquiry."

"Then why isn't he here?" Wren practically spit out the words, the most emotion I'd seen from them. "Why'd he have to die?"

"I don't know. I don't have all the answers." In my own parenting experience, I'd learned that admitting when I didn't know something was even more important than sharing things I did know or having the perfect explanation. I kept my voice soothing, hoping that helped. "All I know is that it's okay to miss Dr. Dad. It's okay to be sad and angry and upset all at the same time. And it's okay to talk about him, to remember things he said."

"I don't want to make my other dad any more sad," Wren whispered, their guilty tone breaking my heart. "And I keep screwing up my experiments, which isn't helping, but it's like...I'm missing something, and I can't find it."

Oh. I'd felt exactly like that for years and years. I'd lived with that feeling for so long that I hadn't noticed its absence until that second. Or, more accurately, until Denver. I'd been missing something, and now, I'd found it, but whether

I'd get to keep it was the real question. However, Wren needed me to be focused on them, not my personal life.

"I get it. We're all a little off as we figure out how to move forward." I included myself in that because I was also in a new phase, still finding my footing, but surer every day. "And Eric is going to grieve regardless. It's okay to grieve. That's what the missing something feeling is. You sharing happy memories is a good thing. Tell me what he said about science."

"Dr. Dad always said not to guess at an answer. He said to trust science over hunches. And that science pushes the world to change by providing facts. I like facts." Wren exhaled hard. Facts and science were a security blanket for them, and I hated that these particular facts had to be so grim. "Why couldn't science fix him?"

"I wish I had an answer for that too. Maybe the science isn't there yet. Maybe it will take more research. Maybe someone in your generation will come up with new treatments for pancreatic cancer."

"Maybe me." Wren nodded, chin taking on a stubborn tilt.

"Maybe you." I smiled. "Dr. Dad would be proud of you regardless, but if you discover new cancer treatments? That would be super cool."

"No if. I will." Wren sounded not unlike a certain big-eared green Jedi.

"Good. Keep experimenting. Safely. And keep believing in science."

"Okay." Wren smiled for the first time since I'd entered the kitchen. Right as I returned the smile, the doorbell rang. Wren leaped ahead of me as the dog charged up from the basement. "Denver's here."

Between the dog and Wren, I was the last to greet

Denver as he came into the foyer. And as it turned out, I had zero idea how to handle said greeting.

"Hey."

"Hey, yourself."

We stood there staring at each other. The warm light of the entryway made Denver's skin even more golden than usual, and his hair was more tamed, slicked back into a neat bun. He wore a short-sleeve black-and-white patterned shirt with buttons and cargo pants, which gave him an air of heading out for a nice meal in Hawaii. Nicer clothes than I'd seen him wear, and perversely, his looking date-ready had me shuffling my feet and clearing my throat.

"Oh, just kiss already." Wren rolled their eyes before scampering back to the kitchen, dog at their heels.

"That sounded like an order." Denver's smile was tight, but his gaze dropped to my mouth.

"Yup." I stretched up for a fast peck, but then Denver pulled me in for a longer kiss. Better. My awkwardness drained away, replaced by desire.

"Whoa." John came bounding down the stairs only to stop halfway as Denver and I jumped apart. "Sorry."

"It's okay." I wiped my mouth and tried not to look as guilty as I felt. "Dinner will be ready in a bit. We're making patty melts with Wren, but you're welcome to help."

"Nah." John waved away the offer, gesture making him look that much more like Wren. "I wanted to see if you might want to take me driving after dinner, but it looks like you'll be busy."

"Go." Denver mouthed the word at me. I'd been planning on sneaking in some more kissing, either here or at Denver's place, but some things had to take priority.

"Not too busy for driving practice." I made my voice

hearty, channeling my dad's boundless enthusiasm. I remembered how eager Declan had been for driving practice. And like Wren, John was grieving. This was the least I could do. "How about we practice some parallel parking while we're out?"

"Sure thing." He returned upstairs with a small smile, leaving Denver and me to head for the kitchen.

"Nice goggles." Denver nodded at Wren. I hadn't been sure how he'd react to Wren's scientist outfit. Not everyone knew how to deal with neurospicy teens, but Denver did a perfect job of being accepting without seeming patronizing. "You wanna add bacon to the burgers since you're all prepared for grease?"

"Bacon." Wren made a happy noise before writing something in their notebook. "The answer is always yes."

The three of us made a happy cooking trio. Denver showed Wren how to use the griddle we usually used for pancakes for burger patties and let Wren do most of the work assembling the ingredients for the patty melts while I chopped potatoes for the home fries. Awkward uncertainty long gone, cooking with Denver simply felt right. Natural, like we'd been doing this for years.

"You're good at this," I said in a low voice when Wren went upstairs to fetch Rowan and John.

"Cooking?" Denver looked up from whisking the salad dressing. "I would hope so."

"No, teaching." I bumped his shoulder with my own. "For someone who gripes about not understanding kids, you're doing great."

My praise earned a rare flush from Denver. "Wren's a good kid."

"Yeah. They miss their late father a lot. We talked about

it earlier. First time I've gotten them to talk about it. I hope I said the right things." Admitting my doubts to Denver was another thing that felt natural.

"I'm sure you tried. That matters." After glancing up at the back stairs, he returned my shoulder bump, leaning in long enough to give me a most unexpected kiss on the temple. "Kids like Wren and the others here, they've been through a lot already. Foster kids often get so used to missing things that they get almost numb. It's a good sign they're opening up."

"Is that how it was for you? Numb?" I kept my voice casual but curious. Denver didn't often talk about his childhood, which was understandable, but I was hungry for any and all details about the man.

"Pretty much." He shrugged, setting aside the dressing to toss the salad ingredients with tongs. "A lot of moving from place to place. I was an angry kid, not exactly easy to place. Didn't care for rules and liked to push against them. I learned quickly not to get my hopes up with each new home, not to want too much. Easier to not care. If you don't care, it can't hurt."

There was a message in his tone, a warning of sorts. He wanted me to think he didn't care, couldn't care. But he did. I saw it in every interaction tonight, in each kiss and touch, in the way he listened and the questions he asked. The real warning was in how easy it would be to bruise the heart he kept so carefully hidden.

"I'm sorry." I touched his upper arm, where his sleeve met his meaty biceps. "You—and all kids in the system—deserve better. But caring doesn't always mean hurt and disappointment."

Denver's mouth pursed. "Like I said, some things become habits."

"Well, I'm here, and I care." My heart thumped against my ribs. Maybe if I said the words first, he could relax a little, but instead, his expression merely shifted from doubtful to sad.

"I know you do."

I glanced over at the stairs. The kids would be down any second. "On a happier note, the annual firefighter pancake breakfast is coming up. Think you could forgo a little Saturday sleep for a good cause?"

"Are you asking me out?" Denver's eyebrows knit together, dark eyes suspicious.

"Well, my dad put me in charge of bacon. I'm not sure that's wise. I could use an assistant."

"Ah. Not a date." Denver smiled, way more relieved than I liked. "You need a sous chef."

"It could be both a date and help." I didn't see what was so scary about dating, especially since tonight was going so well.

"With your dad there?"

Ah. Yeah. There was that. It was one thing for Wren and John to know and another entirely for my family and coworkers to meet Denver as my date. I inhaled sharply and let the breath out slowly. I could do this. "I'm going to come out. Eventually. Went okay with the kids tonight, right?"

Denver shook his head with something approaching pity in his eyes. "Sean—"

"Just say you'll come. Friends. Date. Whatever. I want you there."

Denver squished his eyes shut. Opened them. "I'll be there."

He sounded like he'd rather face a firing squad, but I'd take his agreement, especially since all three kids chose that moment to come clattering down the stairs. Denver had said yes. That was what mattered, not what label we gave the thing. And for all his warnings and worries over being unreliable, I knew I could count on him. I only wished Denver could trust himself the way I trusted him.

Chapter Eighteen

Denver

I was lost. Well, not literally. It was hard to get truly lost in Mount Hope. And while large, the downtown city park along the riverfront was hardly Central Park. I knew where I was headed: the annual firefighter pancake breakfast. Not only were the large white tents impossible to miss, but all the emergency vehicles lined up along the front of the parking lot were a clear giveaway that I was in the right place.

No, I was lost because I had no idea why I'd agreed to come. Friends. Sous chef. Random supportive citizen. None of those were accurate. Neither was date. Sean said he was going to come out, emphasis on going. Not out presently, and seeing as how his father was holding court at the front of the first tent, surrounded by his wife, the mayor, her wife, and other Mount Hope movers and shakers, I hardly expected Sean to grab my hand and make a round of introductions.

And I was also lost because I couldn't find Sean. The

advantage of being a professional nomad was that by belonging nowhere, I generally fit in everywhere, from concerts to dive bars, border towns to big cities. I wasn't used to feeling out of place anywhere, but here, among all these clean-cut first responders, I felt decidedly worn and grubby. And no way was I asking anyone for help locating Sean, but I finally found him over by a portable upright oven.

Ever the born leader, he directed a group of younger folks in blue *Pancake Breakfast* T-shirts on how to put bacon on baking trays. I liked watching Sean work, liked how effortlessly in charge he was, liked how good he looked in his own matching T-shirt. What I didn't like was how relieved I felt to have found him or how I instantly felt more comfortable in his presence.

Sean didn't deserve my grumpy mood, so I took a deep breath, located my seldom-used grin, and waited until he turned away from the group loading bacon trays. "Reporting for duty."

"Excellent." He beamed at me, a wide, genuine smile that made everything right in my world. Impossible to stay grumpy in the face of that smile.

"Hey, now, Murphy brought a ringer." One of the younger guys gave a good-natured finger wag in my direction. "I know you. You're the Honey's Hotcake Hut overnight cook."

"Murphy! You think we need pro help?" Suzy, the always sarcastic firefighter, was quick to join in the teasing.

Sean chuckled and held up his hands. "I think we need all the help we can get."

"He's not wrong." Of course Caleb was among Sean's bacon crew and, of course, he sprang to Sean's defense. "Last year, we had people lined up waiting. Lukewarm pancakes, burned sausage, not enough syrup. Yeah, this is a fundraiser, not a fancy Portland brunch, but people still deserve a quality breakfast."

"Thank you, Caleb." Sean nodded at him, and Caleb grinned like he'd won a race. I remained suspicious of him crushing on Sean, but I tried to keep my expression neutral. It wouldn't do to seem jealous.

"Besides, Tate brought Tennessee to help," Caleb added. "And Johnson and Luther brought their wives. Let Murphy bring his...friend."

The pause before friend was damning, as was Sean's too-enthusiastic nod, but luckily Suzy saved us by tossing me a T-shirt. "I guess he can stay. As long as he can take orders."

And with that, I found myself part of Sean's crew, which was both strange and cool. I was content to let him be in charge. Not only were these his people and his fundraiser, but I knew he'd freely give the control back to me later. The strange part was how much I liked the firefighter banter, the happy chaos of multiple voices and hands. After the initial round of teasing, they'd all easily accepted my presence. I felt included. Wasn't sure I liked that, but every time my back started to tense, Sean would catch my gaze and smile.

Lost. I was definitely lost. But at least the time passed pleasantly. The first responder crews produced mountains of pancakes, bacon, and sausage, and the crowds around the tents stayed thick.

"Denver!" I heard Wren call my name and turned to find Eric strolling in our direction with all three Wallace-Davis teens and the older kid, Maren, whom I'd only ever seen at the funeral. Sean had mentioned she was visiting for the weekend.

"Hey, Wren." I motioned them over. "Everyone."

"I'm not sure we've formally met." Stepping forward, Eric stretched out a hand. I returned the handshake while glancing around for Sean, who was occupied plating bacon for the line of customers. "I'm Eric. Super grateful for your cooking lessons for the kids recently."

"He ate all the leftover chili." Wren grinned.

Rowan rolled his eyes. He wore orange sunglasses, a lime-green hoodie, and teal shorts. "Probably because you actually defrosted the meat this time."

"Blow up one grill and hear about it forever." Wren made a put-out face before gesturing at the oven behind me. "Did Sean tell you I came up with a precise mathematical equation for determining the cooking time for each strip of bacon?"

"I generally go by instinct." I smiled at them, already anticipating the comeback.

"How unscientific."

"Wren." Eric rubbed his temples. "Wren is..."

"Pretty awesome." My chest was strangely warm. I'd been...*happy* to see the kids. Not as happy as I was with Sean, but a different sort of feeling, one I wasn't familiar with. "I've enjoyed spending time with your kids."

"Ah. Well, thank you." Eric jerked his head in Sean's direction. "And uh...take good care of Sean?"

"I'll try." My voice came out all gruff. Eric's request felt weighty. Me? Take care of someone? I didn't even travel with a cactus. Sean was a responsibility I hadn't wanted, but I also couldn't seem to quit.

After Eric and the kids departed, I put my promise into action, trying to make Sean's day easier by anticipating when the steamer trays needed refills. Producing mountains of bacon was hardly what Eric meant, but my shoulders still lifted when the crowd dwindled and Sean turned to me with a huge grin.

"We make a good team." He patted me on the arm. Friendly. Not date-like. I tensed anyway. "Couldn't have done it without you."

"Eh." As usual, I'd rather be the one handing out praise. "Looks like the event is a success, at least."

"Of course it is." Sean's father appeared in front of the folding table near us, seemingly by teleportation because he sure as heck hadn't been there ten seconds prior when Sean touched me. I hoped. "People look forward to this all year long."

"That they do." Sean's good mood didn't dip in the presence of his father, but he did subtly step away from me. "We did a similar event in Seattle, but Mount Hope sure does love its pancakes."

"And its first responders," I chimed in without thinking, and something in either my words or my voice must have given Sean's father pause because he frowned.

"I'm Joe Murphy. Fire chief. Sean's dad." He stuck out a hand. "You are?"

I shook his hand even though he knew full well who I was, having been in Honey's any number of times, and anyone with eyeballs could guess at his relation to Sean. Same shorter height, sturdy chest and arms, same piercing blue eyes. Joe's hair was more faded with a lot more white, but he was definitely a Murphy.

"Sorry, Dad." Sean sounded appropriately apologetic. "This is Denver..."

"Denver Rucker," I filled in for him. Despite our weeks of...whatever the heck we'd had going on, I'd never had reason to give him my last name. "Just helping out today."

"Thanks for your hard work." Expression distinctly uncomfortable, Joe sounded far too formal.

"Hey, we served everyone in record time." Sean clapped me on the shoulder, only to quickly drop his hand.

"Sean, your mother's been looking for you." Joe's tone was back to friendly, but his eyes remained guarded. "She has someone she wants you to meet."

"Dad," Sean groaned, drawing the word out to ten syllables like Wren or Rowan might.

"It's just a hello." Joe gestured vaguely as Sean shot me a helpless look.

"I'm..." He took a deep breath and squared his shoulders. My body went walk-in freezer cold, muscles stiff and icy, heart pounding sluggishly. I must have made some noise because Sean glanced at me again.

"I'll cover for you here," I said far too quickly. My words were warm, but the expression on Sean's face as he moved to follow his father was anything but. And I wasn't at all surprised when Sean sought me out a short time later.

"What was that all about?" he asked as he came over to the bench where I was sitting. Suzy had pushed a plate of food on me, so I'd taken the opportunity to escape the tent for a bit of quiet. The park still teemed with people, but none were paying attention to Sean and me.

"What?"

"Practically joining my father in matchmaking." Sean shook his head as he sat next to me. Not that I'd invited him, but I scooted over nonetheless.

"It wasn't the time or place for anything else." I kept my voice low but firm.

"Do you not want me to come out?" Typical Sean, going bluntly after the white elephant sitting between us. He'd been ready. I hadn't.

And I couldn't lie to him. "It's complicated."

"I see."

"I don't want to be responsible." I stared down at my empty plate, watching a puddle of syrup spread out. Eric's request from earlier echoed in my ears. I was failing already.

"You're not responsible." Sean's face was somewhere between furious and hurt, neither of which I wanted. "I am. And other people's reactions are on them, not either of us."

"Yeah." I wasn't sure I bought a word of that. If Sean's father reacted badly, that would certainly feel like my fault.

"Anyway, you probably need to get some shut-eye before your shift." He moved his hand dismissively, voice as disappointed as I'd heard it.

Disappointed in me. The easy thing would be to walk away now, let him have his hurt and anger, and be glad I didn't mess things up worse for him.

"Nope." My head shook, joining my voice in, not waiting for permission from my brain. "I traded days with one of the other cooks. It's my first Saturday off in forever. I was thinking we'd have some time after clean up."

"You asked for a day off? To spend more time with me?" Sean made the simple act of a shift change sound like a rare gift. He smiled slowly. "Bet I have some ideas for how to fill the time."

"I bet you do." Sex wasn't going to solve anything. It would probably make everything that much harder. Falling into bed rather than having the tough talk was a bad old habit of mine, but there was nowhere else I wanted to be with Sean. And maybe I couldn't take care of him out here in the real world, but I could damn sure take care of him in the sack, be what we both needed, if only for a moment.

Chapter Nineteen

Sean

"You made it." As soon as Denver opened the exterior door of the house, I hefted myself off the floor near the door to his studio, where I'd been lounging all of thirty seconds.

"The traffic coming back from the park was unreal." He tilted his head. "How'd you beat me?"

"Motivation." Putting extra swagger in my voice, I blew across my knuckles.

"That, and you have friends with sirens."

"I do." Actually, I'd caught a ride with Eric and the kids. Since he had the day off, they had plans to do a family hike followed by a big shopping trip. Them being busy was perfect for my own plans with Denver. But Denver thinking I had superpowers was fine by me.

"Well, get in here." Denver motioned me in ahead of him. As always, I went to slip off my shoes by the coat rack, but I barely had the second shoe off before Denver pressed me into the wall.

"What's this?" I grinned at him, totally happy to be caught.

"Making the most of my day off." He claimed my mouth in a kiss that was as possessive as it was sensual. We'd been at this for weeks, and the rush of energy I felt every time our bodies met only grew stronger. I'd assumed claw-your-clothes-off passion was a Hollywood myth, but Denver kept proving me wrong.

I simply couldn't get enough of the man or his kisses. I pulled his T-shirt loose from his jeans, shoving it up until he got the idea and sent it flying to the floor. My own shirt quickly followed. I'd had *goals* for this encounter, but the deep, drugging kisses were melting my brain.

"Shower?" I pulled back long enough to ask. I had a vague sense of being grubby from the breakfast work, not that Denver seemed to care. "We should shower."

I couldn't help myself and leaned back in for another kiss before he could reply.

"Keep kissing me like that and the floor will start looking plenty attractive." He tweaked one of my nipples before groping my ass. *Yeah. Want more of that.* For all our passion and urgency, Denver had been reluctant to fuck, and I was ready to end his mumblings about me not being ready and other distractions once and for all.

"We both smell like bacon grease." I shoved him toward the bathroom.

"Yummy." Denver laughed but let me grab his hand and tug him the rest of the way to the bathroom. I shed my jeans before reaching for his belt. "Okay, okay, you can wash my back again."

"Thank you." I gifted him with a sweet kiss before turning the shower on. I'd showered here enough times since that initial visit to know all the tricks of the old tub.

Denver pulled his ponytail loose and did a hasty wash with his shampoo before presenting me with his back.

And front.

I soaped him up in between more kisses. The scent of his soap held enough happy memories that it alone was enough to get me hard. I loved how his body felt under my palm. Warm. Solid. Alive and present. The contrasts between his fuzzy chest, soft belly, and hard biceps made my cock pulse. I couldn't get enough of touching him. He'd likely never been cleaner, but I kept soaping and touching, finding new spots to enjoy, like the planes of his upper back, the soft skin of his neck, and the ticklish spots along his ribs.

I was so entranced by washing him that I barely noticed when he started touching me as well, but when he reached for my cock, I batted his hand away.

"Wait. I don't want to come."

"Oh?" He raised an eyebrow, likely because I always wanted to come and had zero chill about that need.

"I mean, I do." Skin heating from more than the hot water, I chuckled self-consciously. "But I want to get fucked."

"We have plenty of time—" Denver offered me his most seductive smile, which had worked a dozen times to distract me. But today, I was determined.

"You always say that." I tried not to sigh too heavily. "And I was thinking on the way here..."

"Always a worry. You thinking." He smiled, but it didn't reach his eyes and lacked the warmth of his real grin.

"Why don't we fuck?" In our weeks of fooling around, I'd never asked him so directly. My pulse sped up. "Is that another responsibility you don't want?"

Harumph. Denver shut off the shower with a frustrated

noise. "What does it matter? If we both get off, does the how really matter?"

"Of course not. And if you're simply not into fucking, that would be fine. But you sure as hell talk about it enough." His dirty talk while playing with my ass never failed to get me off. "If it's something we both want, why not do it?"

Glowering, Denver threw a fluffy white towel at me. "Because then you might not have any use for me."

"Oh." Brain whirling, I barely caught the towel. I'd expected him to say he didn't want to be my first, but Denver—big, strong, capable Denver—being afraid was a shocker. Breathing heavily, I struggled to find a reply.

"Sounds stupid when I say it aloud." Denver made a pained face.

"Very stupid." I dried off with fast, jerky motions. "You think I'm only keeping you around for your dick and the prospect of getting fucked?"

Denver shrugged as he wrapped a towel around his waist.

My eyes were so wide they hurt, and I was torn between laughing, snorting, or sighing. In the end, I settled for grabbing his arm.

"We're going to fuck. Right the hell now." I steered him out of the bathroom. "And then I'm going to prove to you that I want you for so much more. I'm not sure what part of 'I want to date' you're not understanding."

"The part where it inevitably crumbles." Breaking away from me, Denver yanked lube and condoms from the drawer in his bedside table. My jaw tightened. He sounded so damn resigned that fucking no longer seemed like the right course of action.

"It doesn't have to fall apart." I touched his upper arm. "And we don't have to fuck right now."

"But you said—"

"I don't want to fuck as a result of you caving to some high-pressure ultimatum. I want you to want it too." He opened his mouth to reply, but I held up a hand. "And contrary to whatever you've been thinking, I don't want to get fucked simply to be able to say I tried it. I want it with *you*."

"Oh." Denver exhaled so hard his stomach muscles all drew in and his towel slipped. "That's a lot of—"

"Responsibility," I finished for him on a groan. "I know. Try not to break my heart."

"I can't promise that." He squished his eyes shut. I marveled at how he could doubt himself so much when I had a mountain of evidence along with my gut that said he was among the most trustworthy people I'd ever known. And the fact that he worried so much about hurting me was more evidence that he cared despite his best efforts not to.

"No one can." I opted for a pragmatic tone rather than continuing to argue. I stretched out on the far side of his bed, patting the mattress next to me. "How about you lie here and try not to think?"

"I thought we were fucking." His eyes narrowed like I was trying to sneak a cuddly nap past him. Which I totally was, so I simply smiled.

"Later." I smoothed the wrinkles from his gray sheet. "You worked last night and went straight to the pancake breakfast. You're exhausted, and this conversation isn't helping."

"But you want—"

"To lie here with you." It was my turn for a stern voice. "Obligatory fucking hardly sounds sexy. And we undoubtedly need more talking, but my brain hurts. You're tired. Let's take a breather."

"I suppose a little sleep won't hurt." He joined me on the bed, arranging both of us until he was curled around my back and my head rested on his lower arm as the upper one held me tightly against him. I wasn't planning on falling asleep with him, but I stayed quiet, listening to his breathing soften and deepen. My own breathing started to mimic his, an involuntary synchronization. I yawned.

No way was I tired enough to doze, except the next thing I knew, the afternoon sun was peeking through the blinds and Denver was dropping kisses all along my spine.

"How are you more awake than me?"

He chuckled and rubbed his erection meaningfully against my side. "I woke up hard with a warm you attached to me like a barnacle. Yeah, I'm awake."

He danced his fingers along the crease of my ass. I moaned and pushed more toward him even as I groaned.

"You can't fuck your way out of needing to talk."

"I can try." His laugh was so warm that I could practically see his grin without being able to glimpse his face. No way did I want to waste his good mood.

"I'm gonna let you, but I'm gonna keep you around after." I chuckled, but my threat was real. I wasn't letting Denver go.

He squeezed my ass cheek. "You don't have to prove a point."

"Neither do you." I rolled so I could stare him down.

"How about a ceasefire?" He dropped a kiss on the side of my neck as he gentled his groping of my ass, making me groan low. "I'd rather make you yell in a good way."

I dropped my head back to the pillow. "Consider me waving the white flag."

Yeah, we did need more talking, but his touch simply felt too good. Each kiss and caress had me caring less about conversation and more about coming. Later. Later, I would make him see that I wanted *everything*, but at the moment, I simply wanted him. His kisses turned more purposeful as he licked his way from the small of my back to my ass. I knew exactly where he was headed, and I was shamelessly moaning even before he reached my rim.

"Yes. That." My voice held an almost comical amount of relief. He licked and sucked, his attack made all the more devastating by how he'd learned exactly what worked to drive me wild. And how to make me beg. I loved his tongue, loved all his tricks with lips and teeth, but I adored his fingers even more. I rocked to meet his mouth, silently begging him to find the lube. And then not so silently. "Please."

"This?" He circled my rim with a slick finger before nipping my ass cheek.

"Yes. That. More." I didn't care how shameless I sounded. I only wanted more of him right that second, and when he finally reached for the lube and slicked his fingers, I moaned before he even pushed inside. And when he did, working me open with one then two fingers, my moans practically became a symphony. Every movement Denver made felt too good. I couldn't stop making sounds.

"That's right. Moan for me." Denver worked my prostate for maximum impact, making my head thrash against the pillow and my ass ride his fingers. My throat burned, but I still wanted.

"More." I shoved my ass upward. Denver worked his other hand underneath me, but I made a frustrated noise as he grazed my leaking cock. "No, don't touch my cock. Don't want to come."

"Oh, you're going to come." He chuckled darkly. "Gonna come all over my cock. God, I bet you could come untouched with a little practice."

"Let's see. Now." I rocked on his fingers. As good as this felt, I'd waited far too long to feel his cock. "Please."

Blessedly, Denver withdrew his fingers. He shifted, and the rustling sound of a condom opening was followed by the *snick* of more lube being squeezed out. My every sense was on red alert as Denver moved behind me.

"Up on your knees more." He arranged me with my ass up, head down, and the posture should have made me feel exposed. But the pride, adoration even, in Denver's voice made it so all I felt was sexy. "There you go. Show me that ass."

"Now." I was full-on begging, but Denver kept stroking my sides, groping my ass, and taking his own sweet time.

"You're so demanding." His voice was as affectionate as a hug. I loved how I didn't have to hold it together for him. He liked me needy and begging. He teased my rim with the head of his cock, and I gasped from the slick, warm, broad pressure. "Remember to breathe."

"Kinda...hard." I panted, more from anticipation than discomfort. My cock bobbed in the air, and I snorted at my unintended pun. "Ha." My laughter quickly turned to more moaning as Denver pushed in. His cock was bigger than his fingers, more solid, more *there*. "Oh. Oh."

The process of being filled by him, taking in his cock by degrees, was overwhelmingly good. My back and face went sweaty, my whole body heating. I had a flash of being younger, hanging out along the river in the Gorge, swinging out on a rope swing, and that first incredible hard-to-top jump. I'd probably jumped thirty times that first afternoon, addicted to the adrenaline rush and weightless feeling. I'd grown up, become responsible, forgotten how damn good leaping felt.

But now I remembered. A heady rush pumped through my veins. Each individual sensation was magnified. The stretch of my rim. The fullness of his cock. The pressure on my prostate. The weight of him against me with his thick thighs, fuzzy legs, and strong hands.

My head fell to the pillow in front of me as he started to thrust in earnest, a slow rhythm that had us both groaning.

"Goddamn, you feel amazing." His praise caused another rush of pleasure to surge through me. My cock pulsed, impossibly harder with every thrust from Denver. The cool room air was nowhere near enough friction, yet my body kept tensing like an invisible hand was stroking my cock.

"Fuck." I rotated my hips experimentally, testing how various movements felt. "What was that you said about coming untouched?"

"Overachiever. Don't you dare." Denver lightly tapped my side. "Not yet."

His grip tightened, and a hard shudder raced through me. Damn. Merely the way he held me like he meant it was enough to get me closer. "Trying."

I started to move with him, meeting each thrust, movements becoming more fluid. Denver groaned like he was the one on edge.

"That's it. Ride back on me. Move that ass."

"How does this feel so good?" I marveled, not expecting an answer and not caring how sex-drunk I sounded. "God. Denver. More."

"Demanding. Greedy." Denver chuckled, and I felt the laugh ripple through me as well. I'd never felt closer to another person, and the fondness in his tone made me feel special. Wanted. "Luckily, I like you."

"Denver." I made a low, distressed noise. "If one of us doesn't touch my cock soon..."

"Say please."

"Please." My reply was out almost before he finished the request. I trembled, thighs shaking, arms burning, fingers clawing at the sheets. "Oh God. I'm so close."

"I'm gonna go hard." If that was a warning, it was the best I'd ever heard.

"Please. That. Hard as you want." I arched my back farther, moaning as he pushed my shoulders down, exaggerating the angle. Now, every tiny movement enhanced the pressure on my prostate. "I can take it."

I hoped, at least. And if I couldn't, well, it had been a good life, and this was a hell of a way to go. But, of course, Denver didn't push too far. True to his word, he did go harder, thrusting faster, but he stayed in control, perfect grip on my hips, perfect slide of his thick cock, perfect stretch of my rim. I gave myself over to the fuck, the way I loved to do when I went down on him. Instead of hurtling closer to the edge, I rode a wave of pleasure. I was so deeply one with the fuck I almost missed the graze of Denver's hand against my aching cock.

"Now, baby." He stroked me with a firm, slippery grip. My body ricocheted back from make-this-last-forever to gotta-come-now. "Come. Come on."

I hardly needed the urging, orgasm rolling through me, shoulders and back undulating with the force of my climax. My ass spasmed with each spurt of my cock. It did that with fingering too, but having Denver's cock to clench against was another level of good. And he was still thrusting, drawing the pleasure out until my cock pulsed, valiantly trying to keep coming. Right as the sensations shifted from good intense to almost too much, his rhythm stuttered.

"Gonna..." And then I groaned with him because I could feel him come in the condom, the subtle increase in pressure. I also moaned because knowing he was coming was its own sort of pleasure. I'd pleased him that much. His orgasm was the most potent praise he offered, and my body gave one last shudder.

He was gentle as he pulled out, but I still winced as I rolled away from the wet spot. He grabbed one of our discarded towels and handed it to me. However, I was breathing way too hard to do much more than swipe at my stomach and the come on the bed.

"Sweet baby Jesus. I had no idea." My voice sounded fuzzy, throat suddenly parched. I stretched, intending to get up in search of water, but my body had other ideas. I yawned big as Denver settled behind me, holding me close. My limbs felt heavy, almost drugged. "Fuck. How am I so tired again?"

"You're cute when you babble." Denver kissed my sweaty neck.

"You fucked all the sense out of me."

"Good." He patted my torso. "Rest."

"We shouldn't sleep the day away." I yawned again, with absolutely zero intent of moving anytime soon.

"Sure we should." Denver wrapped me tightly in his arms like I was his personal body pillow. I was powerless to do anything other than doze until a meaty aroma crept into my dreams.

Chapter Twenty

Denver

I'd cooked in one-room cabins, ski lodges, diners, pizza places, hotel restaurants, and plenty of cheap rental kitchens, but I'd never cooked a romantic meal before. Hell, I'd never wanted romance, had run from any whiff of it, and I continued to think Sean's idea that we should date was laughably idealistic. And yet, here I was, wide awake while Sean snoozed on, making a post-sex meal for two, humming softly to myself while I worked.

I could have easily scrambled some eggs or offered some chips and hummus, but I wanted to impress Sean and do something nice for him. Romantic bribery? Oh, he said he wanted to keep me around and wanted more than sex, but trust remained in short supply.

"What's that amazing smell?" Sean sat up in the bed and stretched. He looked delightfully rumpled, skin flushed, hair messy, faint beard burns here and there, and kiss-swollen lips. The temptation to rejoin him on the bed was strong.

"A snack. Too early for dinner, too late for lunch."

"Tapas or happy hour?" Sean suggested in a goofy voice. "Happy for me, at least."

"You're cute, all sexed-out. Doesn't take much to make you happy."

"I'm a simple guy. Easy to please." Sean left the bed in favor of padding naked to the small dinette set where I'd set the food. Working with what I had in the fridge, I'd made some chicken skewers, small meatballs, spiced potato wedges, a couple of dipping sauces, and some cut-up vegetables. "Serve me meat, fuck me silly..." Sean took a seat, only to make another happy noise. "Oooh, is that peanut sauce?"

"Yeah." My skin heated. His obvious appreciation was both gratifying and unfamiliar. "Working at the diner, I don't get as much chance to experiment as I'd like."

"Outside of your favorite customer." Sean waggled his eyebrows at me as I handed him a plate.

"You always do present quite the challenge." I faked a stern tone. In reality, he was right that he was incredibly easy to please. He liked whatever food I put in front of him, liked whatever I dreamed up in bed, and liked spending time outside of it too. Could I be enough for him? The thought was as uncomfortable as his compliments, but if there was anyone on earth I could make happy, Sean might be it.

"And you like me." He served himself some of each of the dishes I'd presented.

I did like him, far too much. "Maybe."

"I see the sex didn't improve your mood much." Sean dropped his gaze to my black boxer briefs. I knew better than to cook totally naked, but Sean's obvious appreciation made me wish I'd skipped the underwear and T-shirt. "Perhaps we need to try it again?"

"You wish," I teased as I sat opposite him and helped myself to some food. "Later. Us old guys need recovery time. And fuel."

"Hey, you're younger than me!"

"My point stands." I gave him a firm look, but inside, I was smiling. I liked that Sean seldom acted his age around me. It was nice to be able to provide a break for someone who had taken on a ton of responsibility young. "Eat."

"Speaking of eating, what do you want to cook with the kids this week?" Sean asked between bites of the chicken satay. His tone was very offhand, like we had this routine now and merely had to sort out logistics. "I was thinking of teaching them some pasta basics like carbonara, but you've got me thinking stir fry now or something we could put more of this peanut sauce on."

"Everyone should know how to make rice." I stretched, unable to shake the tightness in my back. "And Wren will enjoy chopping practice, but..."

"But what?"

I sighed and set my potato wedge back down on my plate. "I don't want to give the kids the wrong idea."

"The idea that you're a nice guy who's a great cook and good teacher?" Sean gave me a pointed look. "Or the idea that you and I are dating?"

"Both. They've had a lot of loss. I don't want them thinking I'm sticking around."

"Admirable, but I think you're really talking to me. The kids understand dating, and besides, I'm only a family friend, honorary uncle type. You don't want *me* getting the notion that we might have a future."

Sean was right, and I hated that he was right. "It's not that I don't want to date you. It's that I don't want to hurt you. I've got terminally itchy feet."

"There might be a remedy for those." Sean grinned like my fears could be solved as simply as a pair of shoe inserts.

"I'm serious."

"So am I." Sean rolled his eyes, then squinted. His chair faced one of the front windows, and he stood, crossing the room to peer out the window. "Hey, what's that sign out front?"

I followed him to the window. All my appetite disappeared in a hurry. "Fuck me running. It's a for sale sign."

"Your landlord wants to sell?" Sean shrugged like this wasn't a sign from the Almighty that it was time for me to pack up. "I guess it's no surprise, given the history of this street and the value of land and property this close to downtown."

"Fuck land values." First, the ever-present threat of the diner selling, now my apartment.

"Take a breath. Everyone knows the real estate market around here is five-alarm fire hot, but even if your landlord sells, there's no guarantee you'll have to move. Tenants have rights."

"Uh-huh." I wanted to believe him, but my chest was cold and tight, that hollow feeling that had accompanied every move I hadn't asked for. Sure, I was an adult now, but my ears still rang with the voices of social workers telling me how this next placement would be so much better.

Damn it. This was why I tried so hard not to like any one place too much. Attachment fucking hurt. And I liked this little studio, liked its proximity to Sean, liked Mount Hope. But liking was seldom enough for guys like me.

As if to prove a point, Sean's phone vibrated along the floor where it had ended up. Somehow, I knew even before he picked it up that he'd be leaving. Likely with good cause, but my shoulders still drooped, hands and feet growing heavy and wooden.

Leaving the window and that fucking sign, I returned to the table and started packaging up the food while Sean talked into his phone.

"I'm sorry," he said after ending the call. He was already pulling his jeans on. "Eric got called into a shift. Maren, that's the oldest kid, asked if I'd come help her do dinner for the others. Wren's bugging her to be allowed to cook, and apparently, I need to play peacemaker."

"Go." I forced a small smile. "It's fine." Sean opened his mouth like he might be about to invite me along, so I quickly added, "I need more sleep anyway. We'll talk later. And here, take the leftovers. They can be appetizers for the kids."

"Are you sure? You didn't eat much."

"Eh. It was really for you." I handed him a neat stack of plastic containers.

"Well, I appreciate it." He set the stack back on the table to give me a quick kiss. "It was...special, having someone cook for me."

"I've cooked for you plenty."

"You know what I mean." He held my gaze, a palpable current of energy between us.

I nodded, not sure I trusted myself to speak. He was right in that this was so much more than sex, but right then, I hated that fact, wished like hell that this was only fucking.

"I'll text later." He leaned in for another kiss, this one soft and full of promises he had no business making.

"Thanks." I watched him leave, waiting until I heard the outer door close before I crawled back into a bed that still smelled like Sean. I breathed deeply, closing my eyes. It didn't take long before I fell asleep, chasing a state where I didn't have to think about anything. I had the talent or, perhaps more accurately, the experience of being able to sleep anywhere at any time. Now that I no longer partied, sleep was among my favorite escapes.

Too bad, then, that I was still alert enough to hear my phone vibrate with a message. Blinking the sleep from my eyes, I reluctantly felt around for it. Outside, dusk was falling. I hoped Sean's dinner with the kids had gone well. I hated that I missed him already and that he was the first thing on my mind. Sleep was supposed to ease the ache, not intensify it.

I unlocked my phone to find a message from Tammy at the top of my notifications.

> Gonna need you to work tonight. The replacement cook called in sick. Between that and a no-show meat delivery, the manager is fit to be tied. He called me because he couldn't find your number. Oh, and there's some sort of Honey family meeting brewing. Fill you in at work.

Already out of bed, I grabbed clean kitchen clothes. I was grateful for the distraction of work. If I couldn't sleep, at least I could cook, lose myself in the familiar rhythm of a Saturday-night shift. Maybe things were too familiar though. What with the pending sale of this place, more Honey family drama, and the risks of starting something with Sean, perhaps the universe was sending me a signal I couldn't afford to ignore.

Chapter Twenty-One

Sean

"Why is grilling season also idiot season?" Johnson asked as we surveyed a torched and still-smoking garage. We'd managed to save the majority of the house, but the garage, adjoining kitchen, mudroom, and deck were toast. Burned, soggy, smoldering toast that smelled like chicken.

"Be nice." I wasn't the captain on this call, but I could still remind Johnson that we were in earshot of the neighbors. It seemed like the entire cul-de-sac had turned out to watch this afternoon disaster unfold. "He's not the first homeowner to try to move a barbecue into the garage in the rain."

The homeowner had worked an early shift at the nearby shipping warehouse and returned home to place his carefully marinated-and-rubbed chicken on his fancy new grill. But it had been raining, hardly uncommon in May in Oregon, so he'd wheeled the grill from the deck to the garage. Big mistake.

"Nor will he be the last." Suzy shook her head, hair

hidden by her helmet. "He's damn lucky he didn't do more damage."

"He's lucky to be alive." Tate, our paramedic friend, loped over from where the ambulance crew had been working on the thirtysomething man.

"You taking him in?" I wasn't surprised to see the crew had loaded the homeowner into the ambulance. Smoke inhalation was nothing to take lightly, and his burns from trying to get the fire under control, even apparently minor ones, deserved another look. When we'd arrived, the man had been hopping mad at himself and the situation. It had taken Tate and Eric some serious cajoling to get the man to let them examine him.

"He'd rather not go, but yep. His wife arrived in time to make him." Tate laughed lightly. "Oh, and Eric said to tell you that Wren and Rowan made cupcakes, and hopefully, there will be some left for you in the morning."

"You and Eric got something going on?" Johnson frowned.

"They're roommates. Chill." Caleb, as always, was fast to spring to my defense.

"We about done here?" Our captain strolled over at the perfect moment to break up this gossip-and-complain session.

"Heading that direction." I gestured at the others. "Let's get a move on. Pack it up and be back at the station for dinner."

"As long as it's not chicken." Everyone laughed along with Suzy, and it wasn't long before we were back at the station. I was one of the last to shower and lingered near my locker, texting with Declan.

Up All Night

> Big race coming up in Washington, north of Vancouver. Think you can make it?

When he was younger, he'd asked me to come see him race all the time, but since turning pro, the invitations had been fewer. That he wanted me there was reason enough.

> I'll ask for the time off today. Everything good with you? Eating? Hydrating?

> Chill, Dad. I'm fine. Just thought it would be nice to see you. Feel free to bring someone. I'll get you two tickets.

Huh. Bring a friend. He was as bad as my parents at the none-too-subtle hints I should be dating. My finger hovered over my phone. I could bring Denver. He'd enjoy the raucous race atmosphere. Denver would be perfectly fine to go as a friend. I wanted more though. I was tired of keeping secrets. But I couldn't spring that on Declan between practice runs.

Yet another conversation I needed to have. And soon.

"Hey, sorry about Johnson giving you a hard time." Caleb emerged from the farthest shower, the one that always had the best hot water. He took his sweet time wrapping his towel around his waist, so I directed my reply to the wall of lockers.

"No problem. Thanks for sticking up for me."

"Anytime." Caleb plopped down on the bench near me. His locker was a few spots down. "So…you ever gonna let me take you to Pinball Pizza? Or are you kind of exclusive with the cook?"

I gulped hard. "I…um…"

Damn it, where had all the air gone? I'd wondered if Caleb suspected something at the pancake breakfast, but that had been a couple of weeks ago. Apparently, he'd been biding his time. Which I could sympathize with, seeing as I'd been doing much of the same with Denver. It was all too easy to stay caught up in the present moment, the great sex, the cooking lessons for Eric's kids, the string of easy texts back and forth, and avoid the conversations we really needed to have.

"It's not..." I tried again, but I hardly sounded convincing, even to my own ears.

"Oh." Caleb's mouth made a perfect circle before his expression went carefully neutral. Or as neutral as Caleb could muster. The others liked to tease him about how easy he was to read at cards, and right now, his attempts to hide his surprise were ruined by pink cheeks. Standing, he yanked open his locker, pulling out a fresh uniform. "Are you not out at all? I kind of assumed..."

"I'm..." I trailed off as excited voices from downstairs filtered up the stairs.

"Rodriguez must have arrived with the baby." Caleb smiled as he toweled off his short blond hair. I'd forgotten Rodriguez, the firefighter I was covering for, was scheduled to come by around supper time to show off the baby and see her work friends. Sort of a post-baby shower. I'd picked up a gift card earlier in the week and then promptly forgotten about the visit.

"Right. That's today." My voice sounded distant, almost floaty, as my brain whirred, finally piecing together that if Rodriguez's baby was a couple of months old now, she was likely coming back at some point soon. I needed to decide what I was doing with my future, stop coasting by, hoping that if I didn't raise the topic, Denver wouldn't be scared off. I had numerous reasons to stick around, but I wanted Denver to give me one more.

I breathed. In and out. The weight of the secret I'd been keeping pushed down on my shoulders, making me slump forward. Could I really make any decisions about the future if I kept holding back?

"You okay?" Dressed, Caleb sat back down, expression intent like he might check my vitals next.

"No, I'm gay." The words whooshed right out of my mouth, and all I felt was overwhelming relief, like a cool shower on a sweltering day. I smiled, small at first, then grinned, more than a little loopy. "Wow. I've never actually said that before."

"Congratulations, man." Caleb slapped me on the shoulder. "I'd say let me take you out and welcome you to the queer family, but I'm thinking you're taken."

"Yeah." My mouth twisted. "At least, I hope I am. It's complicated."

"Well, if it gets uncomplicated, let me know." Caleb gave me one of his patented flirty winks. "And I'm a decent listener. That offer is always open."

"Thanks."

More happy voices filtered up the stairs, summoning us to the party-like atmosphere below. Sylvia Rodriguez was a tall, stunning woman with big dark eyes that followed her baby as he was passed from hand to hand around our kitchen and break room. Our dining table was littered with cards and gifts, and I added my own to the pile before letting Caleb introduce me to Sylvia.

"Sean!" My dad summoned me before I had much time to make small talk with the new mother. Dad would usually be in his office at this time, finishing up his day before heading home to my mom. Instead, he sat in a wooden chair near the head of the table, bouncing the baby, totally content. "Look at this little boyo!" He held the baby up for me. He was a chubby, happy baby, full of gurgles and smiles, and I smiled back. "Your mom sent his wee little overalls."

"He's a cutie." I held out a finger for the baby to grab.

"I was just saying how we need more grandchildren."

I promptly pulled my finger back and blinked. "You have eight. My two, then Denise and Agnes each have three. I think you're good."

"Always room for one more. Or two." He winked at me like I might have a pair of twins in my back pocket.

"Dad, can we talk?" I jerked my head in the direction of his office. A calm resolve descended over me. Saying the words to Caleb had felt so *good*. I couldn't put up with my dad's teasing and matchmaking a second longer.

Dad passed the baby to Caleb, who started dancing with him, much to the delight of everyone in the room, giving Dad and me a decent escape route. I sent Caleb a grateful smile.

"What is it?" Dad asked as soon as we were in his office. "If you're worried about the job now that Rodriguez is coming back—"

"No, it's not that." I waited for him to take a seat at his desk. Already feeling far younger than forty-three, I opted to sit in one of the side chairs rather than continue to stand like I was making a request or had been summoned for a dressing down. "I mean, I like working here. Like being on the line again. Like working with you. But let me tell you what I have to say before you go figuring out if you want to keep me around the firehouse."

"Of course I want—"

"I'm gay." The words popped out, perhaps even more forcefully than with Caleb.

"What?" Dad frowned, thick whiteish-red hair falling

forward out of his usual neat slicked-back style. Apparently, his hair was as skeptical as the rest of him. "No, you're not. You were married to Maxine for what? Over twenty years?"

"Yeah, well, it was kind of a shocker to me too." I gave a rusty laugh, not expecting Dad to join me.

"So this is a recent...revelation?" He leaned forward, forearms on the desk. A spot of baby spit-up decorated one of his uniform lapels. "Maybe you're...confused? Grieving the divorce? Experimenting? I hear when some people get divorced, they dabble—"

I held up a hand before he could make this any more uncomfortable. "Dad, I'm gay, not trying party drugs."

"What about being bisexual?" Dad's voice was so earnest that an ill-timed laugh bubbled up in my throat. "Isn't that an option these days?"

"It doesn't work like that. I'm not attracted to women." Simply saying the words aloud was a relief I'd never realized I needed. Felt like removing two hundred and fifty pounds of gear after an hours-long fire call. I felt free. Buoyant. "I never once looked at another woman other than Maxine. Never tempted."

"You took your vows seriously."

"I did." I rolled my shoulders forward and back, flexing my newly freed muscles. "But I also lied to myself. For decades. And if I'm honest, I kind of did know. It shouldn't have been such a surprise. I simply never let myself consider the possibility."

"It's the cook, isn't it?" Dad's eyes narrowed, but I wasn't about to let him pin this on anyone else, look for blame rather than genetics.

"No, it's me. It's who I am, who I've always been." As Wren would say, science and facts mattered here, and I needed my father to accept the fact that being gay was simply a fact, like my blue eyes and Murphy spark-plug build.

"I meant—"

"I do want to date Denver. I want to bring him to dinner with Denise's and Agnes's crews. I want him and Mom to swap recipes. I want you both to be happy for me."

"I..." My dad's lower lip quivered. He sounded as close to tears as I was. Us Murphy men always did wear our hearts on our sleeve. He cared and cared deeply, but his voice remained hesitant. "This is a lot."

"I know. But this isn't a phase." I waited until he glanced up from studying the top of his desk to continue, willing him to understand. "The perfect woman isn't out there, no matter how hard you and Mom try to matchmake."

"We just want you to be happy."

"I am." My chest ached, so full it clogged my throat and made my voice husky. We might be an emotional family, but I still didn't want to cry in front of my dad. "Be happy for me?"

The phone on his desk buzzed, but he stayed rigid, in perfect posture, not reaching for it as it continued to ring, lights on the old-fashioned console flashing. A landline call was likely important.

I sighed and pushed to standing. This wasn't getting solved right now. "You should take that."

"Wait," he called after me as I crossed to the door. "We're Murphys. We don't leave angry."

It was a family rule borne of a lifetime of service, commitment, and risk-taking. We took our vows to the family seriously and knew full well how precious life was. Both he and my mother had never let us go to bed angry or upset, even in the trying teen years, and every phone call, every goodbye, was treated with respect.

"I'm not angry." I couldn't manage a smile, but I tried to soften my expression nonetheless. "I love you, Dad."

"I love you too, Sean. We'll talk soon."

What that meant, I wasn't precisely sure. I wanted to believe he simply needed a little time to digest this news. No guarantees though. But we had love on our side. I paused outside his office, not ready to rejoin the baby festivities. What I wanted was to talk to Denver, really talk, the way we'd been needing to for weeks now.

Chapter Twenty-Two

Denver

"Hello, Denver?" It wasn't the first time a ringing phone in the middle of the afternoon woke me, and it wouldn't be the last. This was, however, my first summons from a certain short, scientifically minded tween.

"Wren?" Rubbing the sleep from my eyes, I sat up in my bed. I didn't bother asking how Wren had gotten my number. I probably didn't want to know all of Wren's tricks. "Is everything okay?"

"No. I want to make a mousse." Wren delivered this news with the gravity of an oil spill closing a major highway. "Did you know there's a science to each precise element in a perfect chocolate mousse? It's more foam than solid but not liquid."

I stretched to make sure I was indeed awake. My arms hit the curved metal headboard where I'd had Sean... *Can't think about that right now*.

"Yes, I know. It's a challenging dessert, even for expert cooks."

"I like challenges."

"I know." I had a vision of the ways in which a mousse could end up exploding all over Eric's perfect kitchen. Leaving my cozy bed, I searched for a pair of jeans. Due to all the shift rearranging at Honey's, I wasn't on the schedule tonight. Might as well make myself useful.

"I need plain gelatin. John is at the gym with his football player friends. Rowan is at play practice. Sean will pick them up, and Jonas will be home soon from the hospital, but I want to surprise all of them. In a good way."

"I have some gelatin." Luckily for Wren, I had some left from my own experiments. And knowing how tricky it could be to work with, I was happy to show Wren what I'd learned. And strangely, I was happy for the summons and the excuse to leave my apartment and the endless cycle of thoughts that had plagued me for weeks. "I'm coming over."

"Excellent."

A short time later, Wren and I were in Eric's big kitchen, ingredients assembled, and working through the steps for mousse in a race against time to get it chilling before the others arrived home. Wren had had the day off from school for some sort of teacher workday and had also ambitiously attempted baked ziti. I'd arrived in time to help get the casserole in the oven, but I was impressed with how far Wren's cooking had come in a few short weeks.

"So, what made you think of mousse?" I asked Wren. They were doing most of the work, so I lounged against the island.

"Rowan went to prom. There was a fancy dinner. He said mousse was the perfect dessert." Wren did a decent imitation of Rowan's dreamy way of saying *perfect.* "I said nothing could ever beat ice cream, but Rowan said I've never had mousse. He's right."

Wren frowned like this was a grave shortcoming in their culinary education, and I suppressed a smile.

"Ah. I see. Definitely something to try. But I have to admit, good quality local ice cream wins for me. Especially strawberry."

Wren made a sour face as they expertly whipped heavy cream with a hand mixer. "Ice cream isn't fancy."

"True." I waited for Wren to tell me why fancy was important. I'd learned with Wren that if I stayed quiet but present, all facts eventually made sense.

"I wanted a fancy dinner tonight. I'm practicing."

"For?"

Wren took a deep breath, tongue coming out as they folded melted chocolate into the mixture. "Someday, my dad will probably date again. Maybe. And I'll make mousse."

Ah. Lord, help me. I glanced at the back door. No Sean or anyone else coming to rescue me.

"Sounds like a plan." I swallowed. What would Sean say in this situation? He was the A-plus dad and honorary uncle, not me. "But...it's okay if you have...feelings about your dad wanting to date."

"Oh, he says he's never dating again." Wren tossed a small hand dramatically. "Jonas went to this speed dating thing with some nurses. Dad said he'd rather have an unmedicated appendectomy. But Dr. Dad would have wanted him to have a person. Someday."

"Someday. When he's ready." I took a breath to try to ease my burning throat. Wren nodded stoically as I added, "When you're all ready."

"How did you know you were ready to date Sean?" Wren asked, conversational tone, completely unaware of the minefield they were wandering into.

Up All Night

"Um." I tried to think of an appropriate response. "He made it hard to say no."

"Ah." Wren crossed the kitchen to fetch their ever-present notebook. "Neurotypical allosexual dating habits are so weird."

"Uh. Pardon?" I took over dishing the mousse into serving dishes that would then go into the fridge.

"It's not an insult," Wren assured me as they scribbled away with a red pen. "I'm taking notes."

"Ah."

Blessedly, Sean and the two older kids chose that moment to come hustling in. Rowan was already on his phone and John was a sweaty mess, and both headed straight up the back stairs.

"Denver?" Sean glanced between me and Wren. "Wren? Why is Denver here, and why does he look so confused?"

"I called him a neurotypical allosexual. Which is accurate. You guys are dating. You kiss, and you likely have the sex—"

"Okay, that's enough of that." Sean turned fire-engine red as I made a strangled noise. "I like Denver able to breathe, thank you. Did you have a point, Wren?"

"I always have a point." Wren's tone was smug as they drew themselves up to their full, unsubstantial height. Taking the tray of small dishes from me, Wren crossed to the fridge. "And now, I have mousse."

"Help?" Sean looked to me for answers.

"Hey, don't ask me." I held up my hands. "I'm only here because Wren needed plain gelatin and a lesson on double boilers."

"Wren called you?" Sean smiled slowly.

"Yeah."

"And you came?" His smile widened like I'd given him some treat.

"Yeah."

"Thank you." While Wren's back was to us, he gave me a fast, soft kiss.

"Oh, hello!" Naturally, as soon as we kissed, the back door opened again. A tall, broad bear of a late-thirty-something dude in nursing scrubs strode in to hold out a hand. "Denver? We finally meet. I'm Jonas."

"Hey." My grip felt clammy. My hands, along with the rest of me, were totally uncertain as to what was happening here.

"Wren, what smells so good?" Jonas asked as Wren returned from placing the dishes in the fridge.

"Baked ziti. And there's chocolate mousse for dessert."

"I should leave you all to it." I scurried toward the backdoor, but Wren gave me a stare worthy of a dictator giving orders.

"You're staying."

"I am?"

"Of course." Wren nodded sharply. Jonas was already fetching plates, and I felt like I was on one of those moving sidewalks, powerless to get off. "How else am I supposed to know if this is an appropriate date meal?"

"Uh. Sean and Jonas could give their opinions—"

"They're not chefs. Get the silverware."

"Yes, general." I laughed because that seemed my only alternative.

"Eureka!" Wren grinned wide, their wild hair askew and snaggle tooth smile giving them even more mad scientist vibes than usual. "That's the nonbinary term for leader that I've been searching for. None of this sir or ma'am nonsense."

Up All Night

"General or maybe mastermind would suit too." Sean teased as the three adults made quick work of setting the dining room table. I supposed I was having a family meal whether I wanted it or not.

And in the end, it was a surprisingly fun, loud, chaotic meal. Sean didn't speak much, but all three teens more than made up for his uncharacteristic lack of chattiness. As always, Wren scattered in plenty of scientific facts. Rowan did impressions of all the other leads in the play while John reported on upcoming football fundraisers, including a car wash. Apparently, the local team was notoriously bad, but John had high hopes for the fall season. I liked the way Sean and the rest of the kids encouraged him to think positively.

The baked ziti and mousse were both huge hits, and after dinner, Jonas shooed the teens upstairs for homework and waved Sean and me to the back deck so he could take charge of kitchen cleanup.

"Are you sure we shouldn't be helping?" I asked as Sean took over one of the large Adirondack chairs on the deck.

"I offered. Jonas has a very particular method for loading the dishwasher. That and he probably wanted to offer us some alone time." Sean shrugged and gestured to the chair next to his.

"Ah." I lowered myself to sit, not particularly comfortable. "I suppose we could get some work in on the carriage house tonight since we're both off."

"We could." Sean didn't sound in a hurry to tackle one of the many in-progress projects at the carriage house. Instead, he stretched, taking in the cool late-spring evening. Flowers were in bloom all around the yard, and June strawberries were just around the corner.

"Weather's nice, at least." I couldn't believe I was making small talk about the weather, but Sean had had a weird vibe ever since arriving home with John and Rowan. I didn't know how to ask about his mood, though, so the weather it was. "Maybe I should go, let you—"

"I came out to my dad yesterday." Sean's voice was remarkably matter-of-fact, to the point of being unreadable.

"Oh." Well, that explained the weird vibe. I glanced over at him, but his expression was as emotionless as his tone. And he stayed quiet, not providing any additional information. "I'm...I'm not sure what the right thing to say is."

"Congrats?" Sean leaned back in his chair. "Or say how you really feel? I know you didn't want me to do it."

"I didn't want to be the reason." My voice came out far too defensive, and Sean sat forward, his body tense. "Wait. I don't want to argue."

"Then don't." Sean sounded not unlike one of the teens, but I supposed I deserved it. I gazed over at him, really looking. His eyes were weary, and the lines around his mouth were more pronounced. I'd never been where he was, never had to come out to someone I cared that much about because there hadn't been anyone.

"I'm proud of you," I said softly, hoping it wasn't more of the wrong thing to say. "I know it wasn't easy."

"What?" Sean's tone was more curious than combative.

"I'm proud of you," I repeated, only to have Sean launch himself at me for a hug. My chair creaked under our combined weight as he straddled me.

His expression shifted from tense and tired to grateful. "Denver—"

"Hey, don't get all sappy at me." I held him as tight as I dared, to protect him if the chair collapsed under us but also because I needed the grounding.

"And saying the words wasn't the hard part. Waiting for his reaction..." Sean quirked his mouth.

"How bad was it?" I kept my tone cautious.

"Not horrible. Not great. We're talking more...sometime." Sean shifted against me. "I have a feeling he thinks it's a phase. But I have hopes that once he sees us together, once it just becomes a normal thing that's not going anywhere, everyone will understand, and—"

"Sean." My voice croaked. His reliance on a permanence I couldn't provide was exactly what I'd wanted to avoid.

"What?" His eyes were big and soft. "Things won't be awkward forever, right?"

My heart cantered along like a Clydesdale trying to make up time. I had to tell him and tell him now. "The Honey family wants to sell. Land values, just like my rental. Guess nothing good lasts forever, huh?"

Chapter Twenty-Three

Sean

"So?" I gave Denver the harshest stare I could muster. I knew where he was going with this piece of news and already hated it.

"What do you mean, so?" Denver returned my stare with a firm look of his own. "The family is meeting at long last to discuss sale options. And the land and location are worth far more than a struggling twenty-four-hour diner. I'll be out of a job soon enough. And if the apartment house sells..."

"So what? Let them sell. Let your landlord do what they're going to do as well. You're a great cook with other skills as well." Warming to my pep talk, I added more enthusiasm to my voice. "There's more than one job in Mount Hope, more than one apartment. If you need a loan—"

"I won't take your money." Denver's tone was bitingly dismissive, and I made an involuntary noise. I'd thought we were at the point where we could help each other. Like couples did. I started to move off his lap, but Denver tugged me back. "It's not about money. Ever since I stopped partying, I don't spend nearly as much as I make. I've got savings."

"Then you'll find something, land on your feet." I struggled to keep my upbeat attitude in the face of his dour resignation.

"That's not how it works for me."

"Because you don't stay and fight." I was done tap dancing around the real issue. Not bad luck, rising land values, or even nomadic natures. I didn't buy Denver's theory that he simply wasn't capable of roots.

"Why?" Denver shrugged, body rolling under mine. "Why fight to be someplace that doesn't want me? All the signs point to it being time to move on."

"Maybe you're looking at the wrong signs." I shifted against him, ass grinding as I gave him another pointed look.

"Good sex isn't a sign."

"This is more than good sex, and you know it." I hopped off his lap, and this time, not at all surprisingly, he let me.

"I warned you I wasn't sticking around."

"Is this how it always goes for you?" I wanted to be sympathetic, but I was having a hard time reconciling his choices. "You find a place, start to feel comfortable, make some connections, and then...what? Cold feet?"

"More likes signs. Something pushing me on my way." His tone was pragmatic and distant like it was all the universe's doing and out of his control. "There's always a sign that it's time to move on. And when I've ignored those signs, I've regretted it."

I made a frustrated noise. I was mad at the foster system that had failed him as a kid and also furious at the people who had hurt him as an adult. However, I was desperate for him to see that I was different. "I'm not your closeted musician guy."

"I'm well aware of that." His voice echoed my frustration.

"I'm not going to leave you hanging for years. I came out—"

"I told you not to do it for me."

"I did it for me." I wasn't sure how many times I'd have to remind him he wasn't responsible for me and my choices. Further, his stated desire to move on and not get attached was at odds with how responsible he acted. He cared, and his inability to see that rankled. "It doesn't matter if you move on. I'm still gay. I still want to live my truth. No more hiding, including from myself."

"See? You said it there. It doesn't matter if I move on."

"You're being dense on purpose." I'd paced away from his chair, but now I returned to glare down at him. "Of course it matters. I want you here."

"You could come." Denver's whisper was so low I had to strain to hear it.

"What?" I dropped to a crouch, both to hear better and to stop looming over him.

"You could come." He said the words slowly, like he was still mulling each one over. "Your dad didn't react like you'd hoped. That firefighter is coming back from maternity leave soon, right? Maybe you'd be up for an adventure?"

He sounded so uncertain that I had no clue what he'd do if I actually said yes. But if I'd learned anything over the past few months, it was where my place was.

"All the adventure I need is right here. I'm not going to run away. My dad still has a few months before retirement. Worst comes to worst, I'll work in a nearby town. Eric and the kids need me."

"I ne—" Right as I was sure Denver was about to say that he needed me too, he shook his head and scowled. "Never mind. Doesn't matter."

"Of course it matters." I reached up to cup his face, fingers trailing along his fuzzy jaw. "You matter. *This* matters."

He remained statue-still even as I pressed a soft kiss to his mouth.

"What are you doing?" he whispered.

"Showing you what matters."

Chapter Twenty-Four

Denver

"Come with me?" Sean held out a hand as he stood.

"Where?" I asked like it mattered. When he kissed me like that, soft and slow and dreamy, I'd go anywhere with him, from a supply closet to the Arctic.

"Carriage house." He pointed, already tugging me out of the chair. "It's closest."

He waited until I was standing to kiss me again, this time more aggressively. And damn, I liked it, liked it when he showed me everything he wanted. He nipped and sucked at my lips and tongue, sending blood rushing straight to my cock. He made everything seem so simple.

I knew better.

"Sean." I pulled away slightly but kept my hand linked with his. Weak. I was so weak that even my voice was less than convincing. "Sex isn't going to solve everything."

"Can't hurt." Sean was wrong, of course. It could hurt plenty. Every kiss. Every meal. Every moment was a few feet closer to heartbreak. Yet, I let him lead me down the steps of the deck because disaster might be worth it for another few of those kisses. "And maybe it'll show I'm worth sticking around for."

"Of course you're worth it." I stopped short, directly in front of the carriage house, which was looking far cheerier these days with clean windows and new exterior lights. "That was never in question."

"Then what's the problem?" Sean grinned, but I forced myself not to smile back.

"Other than the fact that you're worth a heck of a lot more than someone like me?" I held up a hand as he opened his mouth, undoubtedly ready to sing my praises. "And you haven't exactly looked around. You've been out all of three minutes. I'm your first...male partner."

"You could say boyfriend." He continued the light tone and cheeky smile before sighing. He opened the carriage house door, ushering me in. "And none of that matters. You seriously think I'd cheat on you? Or get bored and move on?"

"You're not the cheating type." I had to admit that. Loyalty was one of Sean's best qualities. His loyalty made me that much more protective of him. I wanted to make sure he didn't give it to the wrong cause. Or the wrong person. "But you might get resentful. You deserve to experiment, to get out there and see what options you have, meet different people."

"Harrumph." Sean made a rude noise before shoving me in the direction of our favorite chair. The rest of the interior of the carriage house was much improved. A thorough cleaning had gone a long way, as had some fresh paint on the walls and updated cabinetry. The biggest project had been updating the bathroom with all new fixtures, including a new one-piece shower with a modern glass door.

But through all the sprucing up, we'd kept that giant old chair exactly where it was. "And I keep telling you I have no desire to sow oats just so you can be more comfortable being my only field."

"That's a terrible metaphor." I groaned, unable to keep from laughing, which was exactly what Sean wanted. He chortled along with me before dropping to his knees.

"It's the truth. You're the one I want."

"For now." My retort sounded a lot more like a plea as he unzipped my jeans and slipped my cock out. He palmed it slowly, holding my gaze before licking a wide stripe up the shaft.

"Okay, that's no fair." I moaned, but I sure as hell didn't look away.

"Who said I fight fair?" He did a swirly thing with his tongue that had me panting.

"We're not fighting."

"We're disagreeing over whether your recent streak of bad news is some sort of sign." Sean made a clucking noise like one of us preferred pie and the other cake. Then he gave my cock a series of diabolical little nibbles. "But I'd rather give you a different sign than keep arguing."

"The sign that you're among the best oral I've ever had?" I let my head fall back against the chair. He'd won. He was always going to win. And damn if I could argue with that outcome.

"High praise." Sean released my cock long enough for a smug smile. "Not stopping till I'm number one."

He went deep, sucking hard on each upstroke, extra friction around the head, tongue action on the underside, each piece of the choreography exactly calculated to bring me to the edge.

"Keep doing that, and you just might be."

Up All Night

Sean slowly built up speed until my hips were rocking to meet his mouth and I reached for his head. But right as I was about to pass the point of no return, he pulled back, releasing my cock with a wet, slurping sound.

"Wait. Don't want you to come this way." He dug around in the pocket on the side of the chair, coming up with a small bottle of lube and a condom. "Want to fuck."

"Since when do we have lube and condoms stashed out here?" I might be dazed and sex-drunk, but I'd remember if we'd fucked in the carriage house before.

"Since now." Sean peeled off his clothes. "This may be my favorite chair in the world. The star of many of my recent fantasies." Naked, he gestured at me to remove my clothes, which were already tangled around me, shirt up, pants down. "You also star in all my fantasies. I don't need anything else. Just this."

He waited for me to finish undressing and sit back down in the chair before deftly straddling me. I held out a hand for the lube, intending to play with him a bit for prep, but Sean was already rolling the condom on my cock and generously slicking it with lube.

"Hey, you can slow down." I grit my teeth as he positioned himself over my cock, teasing himself with my cockhead against his rim. Sexiest fucking thing ever, and I was reduced to repeating multiplication tables in my head to not come before penetration. Sexy as it was, though, I wasn't so sure about prep-less fucking. "Don't hurt yourself."

"I'm not." Sean continued his tease, small movements, lowering by degrees before retreating, only to repeat the torturous pleasure all over again. "Feels amazing. Love this, using your cock to stretch me out."

"Yeah, use me." I groaned as my cockhead finally sank fully into his tight, welcoming heat. Sliding more freely now, he braced his hands on the back of the chair above my shoulders, rocking with a fluid motion. Watching him move was hypnotic, all his muscles and strength from his firefighting job on display, coupled with a surprising grace. His cock bobbed in front of him, bouncing with each movement, and a flush spread up his neck from his chest, highlighting his sparse reddish chest hair.

"Need this." He moaned as I moved my hands to hips, not guiding but rather hanging on for dear life. Usually, he was the one with the fast trigger, and I could easily wait him out, but the edge kept rushing closer as he rode me harder and harder.

"Take it. Whatever you need." I reached for his cock, intending to help him along, but Sean batted my hand away.

"Don't distract me." He gave me a sexy glower as he ground against me, milking my cock with his ass muscles. "Want to focus on this."

"It's pretty fucking amazing." Reclining more in the chair, I reveled in the sensations of him on top of me, the faint sheen of sweat on both our bodies, the scent of sex hanging in the air, our moans mingling, every perfect detail.

"Like always." Sean offered me a look so tender my heart gave a weird twinge.

"Sean..."

"Come on. This has to be top ten for you? Top five all-time?" Sean's eyes twinkled.

"Stop fishing." I yanked his head down for a kiss, which was a mistake because it took the smoldering pleasure between us and turned it into a full-blown inferno in three seconds. A deep, pleased rumble escaped my chest. "God, yes."

"Please. Keep kissing me," Sean begged like I could do

anything else. Add in his please, and I could easily kiss him for the next decade or three. However, soon enough, he started to shudder, body bucking, cock dragging against my stomach. Tense lines appeared around his eyes and mouth. "Damn it, I wanted this to last."

Me too. On so many levels. But I didn't, couldn't, say that. Instead, I encouraged his motions, hands returning to his ass.

"Just go, baby. Ride me. Get us both there."

"Denver. Denver," he chanted my name, voice wobbling as his body shook. I'd had a feeling for some time that he could come from fucking without a hand on his dick, but actually witnessing it was the hottest thing ever. His cock pulsed harder, head brushing the trail of hair on my stomach, the barest of contact, yet it left a shiny, wet trail of precome. "Close. So close."

"It's okay. I've got you." And in that moment, I did have him, had him in my arms and head and heart all at once. I held him tightly as he came, come dripping onto my stomach.

"Yes. Yes." The sexiness of his orgasm pushed me closer, but it was his obvious joy at climaxing that did it for me, the way he said, "Yes," like it was an affirmation of being alive. Even as his cock spurted and his body trembled, he grinned widely.

So happy. And for an instant, I was the reason. I couldn't help smiling back as I thrust upward in quick, short bursts until I came with a shout.

"Sean."

"You said my name." He preened. "That's a first."

"So is you coming damn near untouched." I chuckled, a near-giddy afterglow replacing the intense rush of the climax. Sean untangled our bodies and handled the condom, locating a towel before he snuggled back into my lap.

"Funny how much I love this position now." His voice was sleepy, almost enough to lull me into a nap along with him.

Me too, I wanted to say, wanted to ask him to stay like this forever, but nothing this good, this special, ever lasted. I held him tightly anyway, like that could stem the inevitable parting. He rested his face against mine, both of us breathing deeply for long, glorious moments.

"I can't stay." I finally managed to get the words out.

"I know." Sean yawned. "We can't sleep here, much as I might like to."

"I meant—"

He cut me off by dropping a delicate kiss on my lips. "We're not fighting, remember?"

I groaned. "What am I going to do with you?"

"Something good, I hope."

I wish. I wanted to give him only good things, only good memories, only good feelings, yet I'd never doubted my abilities less.

Chapter Twenty-Five

Sean

I wasn't at all surprised to find Eric awake at not even five a.m., nursing a cup of what smelled like mint tea at the kitchen island.

"You up late too?" he asked with a salute of his mug. "Or is it up early?"

"Early." I suppressed a groaning yawn. Eric looked like he'd had even less sleep than me. In the couple of days since my carriage house sex with Denver, the quality of my sleep had been directly proportional to the number of messages from Denver. Which was to say, sleep was spotty and not nearly enough. "Gotta be on duty soon enough."

"Yep." Eric took a long sip of his tea, wincing like it was too hot and swallowing anyway.

"You okay? Rough night?"

"They're all rough lately." Eric dragged a hand through his short hair. "Sorry. That sounded depressing, even for me. Rowan called me Eeyore the other day. He's probably not wrong."

"You're allowed to have hard nights." I took the stool next to him. We'd been friends for over two decades, and there were still times I felt I didn't know Eric well enough. I lacked my mother's ability to always know the right thing to say to comfort someone, and for all that I knew the right actions on the job, I felt adrift in knowing what to do for Eric. "I just wish I could help."

"You do help by being here. The time with the kids and the cooking lessons with your guy—"

My turn to wince. "Not sure he's my guy."

"Ah. The cause of your sleeplessness?" Eric managed half a smile.

"Yeah, but we were talking about you." The last thing I wanted to do was unload on Eric about my love life.

"I'm boring." He shrugged, the motion revealing slim shoulder blades. He'd lost too much weight. "Same old grief. I keep expecting it to get better, but it doesn't. Maybe it won't."

"It will." I clapped him carefully on the back.

"You don't know that." His tone was more matter-of-fact than argumentative, but the rebuttal still stung.

"I have faith." I tried for a brightness I wasn't feeling.

"Sean, buddy. Of course you have faith." Eric clearly wasn't buying my assurances either. "You haven't had your faith tested. You've led a fairly charmed life. Which is awesome and good for you, but not everything is fixable with a pep talk and one of your mom's casseroles."

"Oh." I took a long breath, let his words sink in. I had led a pretty blessed life. Both my sisters were still living, my parents had been married for forty-five years, and while middle class, we'd always had a certain stability I often took for granted. I'd lost a few good coworkers over the years, and those tragedies left a mark, but I couldn't say as I carried many scars other than my failed marriage. *Oh,* indeed. I was scared of failing with Denver. I kept arguing with him about dating, but was I holding on so tightly because I didn't want to fail again?

I didn't know.

And more importantly, I kept acting like Denver's past and Eric's grief were minor inconveniences. Fixable, like Eric said. Maybe some wounds went too deep for a little Murphy optimism and a quick repair job.

"That's fair. I'm lucky." I measured my words, careful to not sound defensive. He was right. "And I guess I want that same luck for others. I want to fix things even when I don't know how."

"I know you want to help. It's one of your best qualities, and I'm sorry if I sounded snappy." Eric swirled the tea in his mug. "But one of the lessons I've had to learn as a parent is that sometimes we can't make it better."

"I get that. Not being able to keep Declan safe keeps me awake plenty of nights. Bridget too. I hate knowing there's little I can do to protect them from pain." I stared down at my hands. Strong hands. Capable. The same hands my dad and grandpa before him had, but they weren't magic. I couldn't protect Denver from his past any more than I could will Declan safely over the finish line.

"Exactly. As a prime example, Wren had another nightmare tonight. They've had them for years."

"That sucks." My mouth twisted and double layers of helplessness made my shoulders and neck knot up. I couldn't save Wren from a nightmare and couldn't save Eric from the parental stress of dealing with it.

"It does. And I can't take away the past, the nightmare, or the fear that caused it. All I can do is meet them where they are, hold space in the present. So when I say you help by being here, I'm not being trite. You do help."

"I get what you're saying. I'm only human," I said slowly, flexing my hands. Human. Not magic. "Damn it, I knew I forgot to pack my superhero cape."

"Ha." Eric smiled. Holding space. That was what he was doing for me here too, giving me space to come to my own conclusions rather than lecturing me about my rose-colored outlook on life. I wasn't exactly sure how to apply these new insights to my present standstill with Denver, but I felt better having talked with Eric.

On my way into the station for the six a.m. start of my shift, I passed by the diner. I slowed, knowing full well I didn't have time to stop and wouldn't know what to say even if I did have time to catch Denver at the end of his night shift. I wished I knew how to make things right, not simply between us, but also for Denver, how to make him feel safe and secure and *want* the same things I did, like a future.

But maybe he didn't. Couldn't.

I didn't care for that line of thinking, so I drove on and pushed my personal problems aside for the shift change meeting. The prior shift reported having a slow day and night, but we had barely settled into our morning routine when a call arrived about a cloud of smoke coming from a dispensary on the edge of downtown.

"A pot shop is lit?" Johnson was quick with the jokes, as always.

Not to be outdone, Caleb whistled the refrain from a seventies song about getting high as we all loaded up.

"Let's roll."

By the time we arrived on the scene, the shop owners had been located—an older hippie-type man with a long gray ponytail and tie-dye pajamas and his more business-minded daughter, who'd arrived fresh from yoga class. Both were understandably distraught, and several other onlookers from nearby businesses and apartments had joined them on the sidewalk in front of the dispensary.

It was a low dark-green building with small windows that had been an aquarium shop and costume store in prior lives. Smoke billowed out the back windows into the alley.

"Anyone inside the premises?" The captain approached the owners. Our shift captain today was a tall, string bean of a man around my age and balding but not very talkative. I didn't know him well because he usually worked a different shift, but he was covering for our regular captain.

"Just Jimmy," the male owner wailed. "Please let me go get him."

"On it." Caleb headed closer to the building, shouting for Jimmy.

"We'll get Jimmy out," the captain promised, motioning me over. "How old is Jimmy? Description?"

"He's seven—"

"Dad." The daughter swiped at her eyes, but she had a far calmer demeanor. "It's a cat. Jimmy Buffet. Large gray-and-brown cat. Let's not risk anyone's life."

"We'll do our best to find him and get him out," I said quickly to head off a father-daughter argument.

"My beloved good luck charm. Store mascot." The father wrung his hands and shuffled his feet as the thick, pungent scent of burning weed filled the air.

"Jesus. All the spectators are gonna get contact highs." Johnson shook his head. "Everyone try not to inhale."

"Funny."

"Murphy, make sure everyone knows it's a cat we're on the hunt for," the captain ordered. I took off at a run, trying to find Caleb, who wasn't responding on the comm lines. He'd already entered the smoke-filled building.

"Caleb! It's a cat we're looking for!" I called out.

"In the front." Caleb's voice finally crackled over the comm set.

I made my way through the rapidly thickening smoke to one of the front rooms of the store, where Caleb stood in front of a tall display case.

"Think I found him." He pointed at the top of the case, where a large cat was lolling around on his back. "And I think he's high as a kite. Apparently, they also sell several varieties of custom catnip blends in addition to organic cannabis strains."

"Of course they do." Because of the dense smoke and increasing heat, we needed to get us and Jimmy Buffet out of there in a hurry. "Here, kitty kitty."

The cat, naturally, made no move to leave his perch.

"I'm going up after him." Caleb gave a decisive nod. "I'm lighter than you."

"Gee, thanks." I hated that he wasn't wrong. He was taller but way more dedicated to the weight room and cardio. However, Caleb was also both younger and not exactly known for coordination. I tried for a diplomatic tone. "I don't think those shelves will hold either of us."

"Gotta try." What I could see of Caleb's expression under his gear was determined. Time was of the essence, and the space around the display was cramped. Getting a ladder in would be tricky, but I didn't like watching Caleb climb one bit.

Helpless. That was the feeling. No way the shelves would hold us both, so all I could do was watch and wait. I sucked at waiting. Also, I had to trust Caleb, trust his skills, his reflexes, and, most of all, his judgment. *Huh.* Had I been trusting Denver enough, or had I been reacting from a place of fear? Trying to cling to control when a better option might be to wait and—

"Whoa, he's on the move!" Caleb shouted as the cat sprang from the display case to a lower shelf.

Pay attention, Murphy. I gave myself a mental shake.

"Hey, kitty kitty." I pitched my voice as coaxing as possible.

"Murphy, need you and Caleb out of there." The captain's voice sounded on my radio.

"Almost got Jimmy Buffet."

"Now, Murphy." The unmistakable urgency in the captain's voice sharpened my senses, but I wasn't going anywhere without that cat.

"Almost." I reached toward the lower shelf as several things happened all at once. Caleb descended the display case, which wobbled precariously. I moved to steady it right as the cat leaped from the other shelf and the ceiling in the back hallway behind us collapsed.

"Guess we're not going out that way," Caleb yelled as he swung down from the display case. Hardly elegant, but at least he was in one piece, which was more than I could say for the building around us.

"Where'd the cat go?" I looked around.

"Clear out," the captain ordered again.

"There." Caleb pointed behind me at another case. I reached for the cat, but he leaped back toward Caleb. Nimble, high as balls on catnip, and scared. A wonderful combination, but I wasn't leaving him behind.

Not leaving. Not letting go. A deeper realization teased the edges of my consciousness, but I had to focus on getting Caleb, Jimmy Buffet, and myself out in one piece.

Hold space. Eric's voice rang in my ears as I crouched

low under the shelf where the cat was. Rather than lunging for him, I held my arms open and pitched my voice calm and soothing.

"Come on, Jimmy. Who's a pretty kitty?"

"Are you seriously trying to reason with a cat?" Caleb asked, eyes going wide as Jimmy took a delicate flying leap directly into my outstretched arms.

"Got you." I tucked him against my heavy jacket, claws and all, as Caleb and I battled our way out the front. The front door was blocked by more falling debris, but a side window beckoned. I boosted Caleb up and through before the cat and I made our escape, pulled through by several crew members.

"My baby!" The older owner guy was only too happy to take Jimmy Buffet from me as soon as we were clear of the building. Mere seconds later, while the owner continued to cuddle and check the cat over, the remainder of the building collapsed, settling into a smoldering, pot-scented heap.

"Well, that was close. Glad we made it out." Caleb grinned. The captain didn't, and I spent the remainder of the fire waiting for a lecture on not following orders fast enough. We finally made it back to the station some hours later, the blaze thoroughly extinguished, fire investigators and insurance people on site, and I wasn't surprised when the captain headed my way in the break room.

"I'm sorry—" I started, but the captain waved my apology away.

"Not now, Murphy. Your father wants to see you." He motioned toward the chief's office. My dad usually kept his fire business and personal lives separate, but I wasn't terribly surprised by this summons. Ever since I'd come out a few days earlier, our greetings had been strained, and we hadn't had any real conversations.

"You requested to see me?" I asked after knocking on his office door. I shut it behind me before heading toward the same side chair I'd sat in the other evening. *Huh*. I chose the other one to sprawl in instead, trying for a relaxed body language even as my brain churned and my heart thumped.

"I hear you had quite the morning," my dad said, infuriatingly conversational, expression placid. "High times?"

"Ha. All worked out in the end, Chief. No injuries. The building had insurance. I'm sure the captain can give you a full report."

"The captain isn't my son, who, if rumors are correct, barely escaped." Dad narrowed his gaze.

"I'm fine."

"You sure?" Dad's tone was sharp, and his breath came in frustrated huffs. "Damn it, Sean. I don't know how to make things right between us. But I want to try."

Opening a folder on his desk, he handed me a thick stack of papers.

"What's this?" The top page looked like a copy of the job announcement for the new chief. "I told you I don't want to apply for chief."

"That's only one option." Dad motioned at the stack of papers. "City council finally voted to fund another firefighter position for us. And Henderson, your usual captain, just accepted a job in Portland. Bigger station. So we'll have a captain opening too. Chief, captain, firefighter. Take your pick. I support you, whatever you choose. We're honored to have you serve with us, and I'm proud of you, no matter what."

Oh. This was some sort of noble gesture, but instead of relief, my insides twisted. He was undoubtedly trying, but was my value linked to the job? I didn't know the answer, and a bitter taste gathered in my mouth.

"And if I don't fill one out?"

"Then I'm still proud of you." His expression wavered slightly, emotions I couldn't label flashing in his eyes. "I love you. Unconditionally. Firefighting is in our blood, but you're my blood, no matter what."

"Good." I squished my eyes shut, trying to stem the flood of gratitude.

"And I saw the duty roster. You're off on Sunday. Your mom's expecting you and your fr—boyfriend for lunch after church. Better warn your cook that your sisters will be there too."

"I...uh..." I wanted to accept in the worst way, but I had no idea where things stood with Denver. We needed to talk. Again. "Thank you. Things are...a bit...complicated with Denver right now, but I'll let Mom know."

"Well, uncomplicate them. You're a Murphy. You don't back down from a challenge."

"I'm a Murphy." My voice came out thick and croaky. "And I'll be there."

I hoped I wasn't lying. I needed to take the jumble of thoughts in my head and figure out how to give Denver what he needed. Because what I needed was him in my life. My dad was right that I'd never backed down from a challenge, but winning Denver might be the fight of my life.

Chapter Twenty-Six

Denver

It was another slow night shift at the diner in a week of too-slow shifts. Business was down, which sucked for the upcoming meeting on the fate of Honey's, but it also left me with far too much time for thinking. Tonight, though, I had a minor distraction in the form of Tammy, who'd brought a slim laptop to the diner, one of those cheap, smaller-style ones good for surfing but not much else.

Despite the diner having Wi-Fi, I'd never known Tammy to play around on her phone, let alone a computer, but during a lull with no customers, she sat at the far edge of the counter and typed away.

"What are you working on?" My curiosity and the need for a distraction got the better of me. "Applications in case the family votes to sell?"

"If I was smart, I would be." She gave me her version of a stern look, which was not unlike a bossy kid. Tammy might be older, but her youthful demeanor often made me forget her true age. "You too, hot stuff. Gotta stay ahead of bad news."

"Trying. Can't wait for shit to hit the fan." As I said the words, I wondered if perhaps I tried too hard to outrun messy endings. How many times had I left before a job was truly over? Ended a fling before it had run its course? Skedaddled out of a city I liked? And usually, I'd be on the road by now, but here I was, still at the diner, still in town, still responding to Sean's short texts, unsure what to do with any of it. "Gotta figure out my next plan, same as you."

Tammy snorted. "Ha. You're not a planner type, and we both know it."

"I could be." I knew I wasn't. I wasn't like Sean with his calendar, Tammy with her stack of private dreams, or Wren with their future in science all planned out. My only real plan ever was to avoid disaster, minimize hurt feelings, and not get attached.

"Oh? What's your big plan for if—when—the Honey family votes to sell?"

"Not sure," I mumbled. I didn't have a pep talk in me right then about how the family might not sell. They would. That was simply how things went. "Hey, I thought we were talking about you suddenly taking up typing practice."

Tammy pursed her lips like she was about to tell me off, then sighed and looked at the computer. "It's an email to my daughter," she said softly.

"I'm sorry. I shouldn't have said anything. I didn't know you had kids." This was why I sucked at small talk. Given how long we'd worked together, I should've known more about Tammy. I knew she was sober and had heard about a comical string of exes, but never any mention of kids.

"I don't talk about it much. I've never met her." Tammy studied her bracelets, her typical stack of gaudy costume jewelry at odds with her somber tone. "I was seventeen and scared, and back then, adoption felt like the most loving thing I could do. Tried not to think about it after that. Outrun it, outdrink it."

"I get that." God knew I had my share of stuff I'd tried to outrun and out-party.

"But you can't outrun hurt. It comes out eventually." Tammy's voice strengthened, adopting a sager tone. "Learned that in my meetings. So I sat with my hurt for a good while. Wrote a letter to the adoption agency, but it folded years ago. Then I saw a commercial for one of those DNA tests."

"You took it?" Wow. I couldn't help my wide eyes. I was stunned by her courage. I'd seen the same ads and had flipped the channel every damn time. There was plenty I didn't want to know.

Raising her gaze, Tammy nodded. "Biggest leap of faith I ever did take. But she was out there. Waiting. Sent me a message as soon as my sample processed. She's a bit older than you. Married with teenagers. Three of them."

"Are you going to see them?"

"Dunno." Tammy exhaled hard. "Gotta write back first."

"Oh." This was that new, and I'd wandered right into the thick of her dilemma. I was laughably ill-equipped to offer advice.

"Maybe I shouldn't. Shouldn't open the past back up."

Hell. I personally would rather eat gravel than dig through the sandbox of my past hurts and regrets. But I tried to think what Sean, my always-optimistic, always-encouraging, smiling guy, would say.

"She reached out. She wrote to you. That's a sign." I swallowed hard. *Signs.* Sean thought maybe I was looking at the wrong ones, and for the first time, I considered what I might be missing.

"You and your signs." Tammy scoffed. Huh. I guess I did talk a bit much about signs, usually negative ones.

"Well, I think this is a good one," I said stubbornly. Stubborn. I had a flash of my conversation with Wren about Eric dating and big feels. "It's okay to feel...whatever you're feeling. Scared?"

"Well, hell yeah, I'm scared. Scared spitless." Tammy made a frustrated noise for good measure. "She's a nurse practitioner. Practically a doctor. I'm just a waitress. About to be an unemployed waitress."

"Hey, now." I hated seeing her this down, hated how much the sale of Honey's was weighing on her, and now this big decision that made my own worries seem rather trivial.

"Just stating the truth." She shrugged, ample chest moving under her apron. "I'll land on my feet. Somewhere. The other day, I counted my pennies, thought about whether my little savings account could maybe make a go of a diner of my own..." Her mouth twisted into a wistful smile that made my chest clench. "But no. What would I know about running a place?"

"More than any manager we've had here," I said firmly. And damn it, Tammy *deserved* a business of her own. She was a good-hearted woman, the best server I'd ever worked with, and a better friend than I likely deserved.

"You're sweet." She reached across to pat my jaw.

"And you're a damn fine person. Your daughter would be lucky to know you." I didn't know a lot about my own origins, didn't much *want* to know, but I'd bet Tammy was better than whatever gene pool I'd sprung from.

"Oh." Tammy made a soft noise, eyes going glassy and

mouth drooping. "Thank you, but I don't know the first thing about mothering."

"You mother every customer who comes in." I met her gaze because it was true. She bravely wore her heart on her sleeve. Just like Sean. Who was also brave, and not only on the job. He was brave enough to go for what he wanted, to ask me to date, to want me to stay. I was the coward who still didn't know what to say to him, but I did know what to tell Tammy. "Write the email."

Biting her lower lip, she nodded and got busy typing.

A short while later, we finally got a trio of customers, a group of EMTs mid-shift. They parked their rig out front and ambled in. I craned my neck to see whether any fire department vehicles were joining them. Nope.

I headed to the grill, but not before Tammy whistled low. "Someone's pissy it's not the firefighters."

"Stop." I gave her my best glower, but she merely laughed.

"If you can give advice, so can I." She flipped her shoulders like a teen. "Call him."

It wasn't that easy. And it wasn't that we weren't talking. We texted. Okay, we texted some. I hadn't seen Sean in days, and whether a call or an in-person conversation, I had no clue what to say. My talk with Tammy had only confused me more.

"Hey, Tammy, did you hear about the dispensary that caught on fire this morning?" Tate, the EMT who was also friendly with Sean and Caleb, called out as the three EMTs took seats at the counter.

"Is it the punchline of a joke?" Tammy narrowed her eyes. I shared her confusion because Tate was always joking and in a good mood. "Or was it an actual callout?"

"Both." One of the other EMTs, a woman in her forties,

shook her head, burgundy curly hair dancing. "And geez Louise, what a blaze. Sean Murphy and Caleb Endicott barely made it out, thanks to a cat."

Murphy. My breath stuttered, an audible catch, and Tammy glanced at me.

"A cat, you say?" Tammy asked, louder than normal, undoubtedly for my benefit.

"Yep. More complicated than some human rescues." The curly-haired EMT laughed, as did the other two EMTs. "Cat was high on catnip. And more than a few onlookers got baked on pot fumes. It was a mess."

"I bet." Tammy made a sympathetic clucking noise. "Any injuries?"

She glanced my way, more sympathy in her eyes. I'd already figured Sean was fine, given the high spirits of the EMTs, but I appreciated her asking.

"Just some treat-and-release bystanders for smoke inhalation and a few scrapes." Tate set aside his menu to gesture. "Murphy is lucky he was in full turnout gear because otherwise, that darn cat would have flayed him. Menace of a cat."

"Says the guy who adores his boyfriend's cat." The third EMT, a younger man, gave Tate a pointed look.

"Guilty." Tate shrugged. "But I'm a dog person."

"Your dog thinks it's a cat," the curly-haired EMT teased before I returned my attention to the grill. Well, most of my attention went to prepping their orders. But a good chunk of my brainpower was worrying about Sean. Did he have something to put on those scrapes? And more importantly, how close of a call was the cat rescue?

I'd known from the start that Sean was a firefighter. Like all first responders, he faced certain risks, but I hadn't dwelled on those dangers. But for the first time, it hit me:

Sean could leave *me*. I was so concerned with when to leave him, how not to hurt him, and why we couldn't get attached that I'd forgotten.

Sean could have died.

And yeah, he hadn't, and apparently, he and the cat were both safe, but he could have. And then what? I'd be back where I'd started. Alone. But changed because, damn it, I *was* attached, despite my best efforts. Losing Sean would gut me. Losing Sean and him never knowing...

Well, I simply couldn't finish that thought. I made myself focus on the familiar pace of filling orders until our shift was nearly over, and Tammy and I were faced with an empty diner as we waited for Amos and the rest of the day crew.

"You send your email?" I asked as I plated some eggs and toast for her with a side of marionberry jam.

"I did. Thank you, sweetie." She smiled up at me as she sat at the end of the counter again. "I'll miss you."

"Where are you going?"

"Me?" Her eyes went wide, eyebrows rising to her dyed-red hairline. "You're the one who always talks about moving on. I figure after the Honey family meeting tomorrow, you'll be hitting the road. Especially since you don't want to take my advice to call you know who."

"Oh." A stone sack smacked into my gut, stole all my wind. I leaned against the counter, hands digging into the counter. *I don't want to go.* A voice from my past, the younger self I tried so hard to block, rang louder than a siren in my ears. Huh. Maybe all this time, I'd been outrunning myself.

"Figure I'll get on with one of the chain places." Tammy was still talking, oblivious to the seismic shift in my brain. "

I'll keep myself busy, don't you worry. Keep adding to the rainy day someday fund."

I had one of those, a seldom-touched bank account. Funny how fast it grew without drinking and partying to drain it and with working long hours with few expenses. I took a breath, head tilting as I studied Tammy. And thought. And thought some more.

"About that someday fund."

Chapter Twenty-Seven

Denver

"Is that a suit?" Tammy eyed me critically as I stepped out of my truck at the downtown hotel where the Honey family was scheduled to meet in one of the event spaces, having outgrown gathering at one of their houses, what with all the kids, grandkids, and a few scattered great grandkids.

"It would appear so." I bent to inspect myself in the side-view mirror. I'd slicked my curly hair back the best I could, trimmed the facial fuzz, and even put on a splash of seldom-used cologne from some long-ago impulse purchase. "According to the checkout clerk at the thrift store, it's a designer brand."

It had also been the only suit at the used clothing store that fit my wide shoulders and long legs, but hey, I looked decent in the gray three-piece number. The clerk had helped me find a white dress shirt, and I'd opted to skip the tie. My throat was tight enough on its own.

"Well, you look good." Tammy pronounced this with the sort of firmness Wren used for sharing scientific facts.

"You too." I gestured at her black dress. A bit dated in style, she nonetheless managed a regal air with her hair piled even higher than usual and red lipstick. "Are we ready to do this?"

"Nope." She cackled, grinning widely. "But we're gonna. Hey, what's that?"

Tammy pointed across the parking lot where a large contingent of folks had gathered near the entrance to the hotel conference center. A big percentage of the people appeared to be first responders—EMTs, firefighters, nurses, and police officers in uniforms. I recognized many of them from late-night meals at Honey's. There were also a number of suits—management types. Near the front of the group, I spotted Sean's father, along with the police chief and the mayor, who was accompanied by her library-director wife.

"Is that the mayor?" Tammy marveled as she grabbed my elbow and hauled me closer to the group.

"It appears so." I continued scanning the crowd as we approached, knowing exactly who was behind this. And yup, there was Sean, stepping out from behind his father.

"What are you doing, Murphy?" I said as Tammy led me right to him.

"I could ask you the same thing." He grinned, gaze doing an appreciative once-over of my suit. "I'm here with a group of concerned town leaders and citizens to ask the Honey family to reconsider selling to developers for the land value. There aren't nearly enough twenty-four-hour eating options for shift workers in this town."

"Exactly." Tammy nodded. "Honey's is too important to lose."

"You also came to ask them not to sell?" Sean asked.

"Nah." Tammy gave a wide, secretive smile. "We're here to offer to buy the place."

Up All Night

Sean's shocked look was worth all the sleep I'd sacrificed to work on this plan with Tammy.

"You—*both* of you—want to buy Honey's?" Sean's eyes were wide and confused. Good. We could be confused together.

"Well, lease. We probably don't have enough for an outright purchase. But we're hoping they might consider a mortgage or a lease." I did a pretty good job of sounding all professional. I hoped I could keep it up when it counted, not give in to the inner voices that kept mocking my efforts. Who did I think I was?

However, in front of me, the crowd was nodding, including the mayor.

"That's an excellent idea." The mayor beamed, gesturing widely with perfectly manicured hands. "I think that's one plan we could all get behind."

Plan. Ha. For the first time ever, I did have one, and it felt itchy and a little tight, not unlike my suit and new shoes. And now I had to worry about letting down more folks than just Tammy. I hadn't expected support, and all those smiling and nodding faces added pressure to my shoulders and chest, a heavy, unsettled feeling.

An unfamiliar dark-haired woman came to the double glass doors of the conference center. "They're about to start."

She led us to a medium-sized meeting room, and between the Honey family members and the town contingent, every seat was quickly filled. Tammy and I found seats off to the side but near enough to the front. Not surprisingly, Sean stuck close beside me and ended up sitting next to me.

At the front of the room, the oldest members of the Honey family sat at a table. An older woman with hair the color of peaches was first to speak, surveying the crowd. "Well, this is...unexpected."

"We should have reserved a bigger room," the man beside her added in a perplexed tone. He had a Hawaiian print tie that contrasted with his crisp dress shirt and balding head.

"There are a lot of people in Mount Hope who care about Honey's future." The mayor had sat right down in front, opposite the table.

Next to me, Sean added in a low whisper, "And a lot of people who care about yours, Denver."

"Is that why you came?" I whispered back. "To convince me to stay?"

"Not exactly." Sean's tone was cagey. "I wanted you to have the option, but I mainly wanted you to see how many people care, and not only about the diner."

"I see." Around us, introductions were being made, but my attention was far more on Sean than the proceedings.

"Like I said, I want you to have the option of staying. A choice. Not staying for me, but a reason to stay for *you*."

"Oh." I swallowed hard, unsure whether to be irritated with him for undervaluing himself or touched that he understood a little of where I was coming from. "Thank you."

We were both quiet as the meeting got underway. The family lawyer addressed the terms of the original owners' wills and the legalities around selling. Then, a Realtor, who was clearly friends with the peach-haired woman, judging by her chummy demeanor, spoke about buyer interest in the land and its value to developers. A low hiss swept through the room as she finished. Various Honey relatives laid out their opinions until finally, one of the younger relatives, a stout thirtysomething man who'd been one of the rotating crew of managers, suggested hearing from the representatives for the town as well as the concerned employees.

Show time. Concerned employees. That would be Tammy and me. I drew myself up straighter as the mayor launched into a lengthy monologue on the value of Honey's Hotcake Hut to the community.

"If this goes south, I'll go with you," Sean whispered.

"You'll what?" I turned to give him a sharp eye.

"I'll go where you go. I'm not giving up on you. If you need to move on, I'm moving on with you."

"Your job? Your family? Eric and his kids?" I shook my head. It was a nice and not entirely unexpected offer, and although I'd been the one to propose it the other night, I was also well aware of how unrealistic it would be for Sean to go anywhere other than Mount Hope.

Up front, the mayor droned on, followed by an executive from the hospital, speaking on behalf of the nurses and other shift workers. Next to me, Sean leaned closer.

"I'm not going to say it would be easy. But I'd work it out because it would be worth it to be with you, to try to find a compromise. I don't have all the answers, but I know I want to be together."

I inhaled sharply, my brain sizzling like an egg on the griddle.

"Mr. Rucker? I understand you wanted to speak?" the peach-haired woman called out before I could reply to Sean.

"Go." He pushed my shoulder. "I've got your back."

Someone had my back. That was a first. Like Sean, I didn't have all the answers, but the warmth of someone caring enough to want to compromise filled my chest, giving me hope and courage. I could do this.

Chapter Twenty-Eight

Sean

As Denver stood to speak, my own knees trembled and my belly wobbled. I'd had bystander nerves before at Declan's races or Bridget's school events, but this was different in that my future—*our* future—seemed to hang in the balance, and all I could do was watch.

"I don't belong here," Denver mumbled, then cleared his throat. "Let me try again. I don't belong in Mount Hope. I'm not a lifer like many of you. But I've worked in a lot of places over the years. Honey's is special."

All around the room, people nodded. And I agreed, but I also thought Denver was the special one. After all, he was why I'd kept coming back.

"I see it every shift. And it's not only that the diner is open late. It's where folks come after a rough night or a good one. We're there for our regulars, and they're here for us." He gestured around the room, a ruddy cast coming over his skin. He was embarrassed by the support, undoubtedly thought it was all my doing, but the truth was it was *him*.

Sure, people liked their hotcakes and omelets late at night, but they also liked the good people working at Honey's, like Tammy and Denver.

"I know our offer isn't what you could get from selling the land. But this place means something to a lot of folks. Me too." His voice dipped, a subtle waver most would miss, but I knew Denver, knew what it cost him to admit to an attachment to anything. And if Honey's meant something to him, perhaps there was hope for us as a couple. Maybe I could mean something too. My stomach twisted, nerves and want and need all mixed up. Denver looked so good in his suit and tamed hair. He glanced down at me like he was looking for something. I nodded at him as he continued, trying to send reassurance. I wished I could promise him it would all work out, that his efforts would pay off. But the faces of the Honey family at the front of the room were hard to read, even in light of Denver's heartfelt speech that had much of the room murmuring in agreement as he laid out more of his and Tammy's plans and the specifics of their offer.

"It would be an honor to carry the Honey's tradition forward, to keep giving people a place to belong. Thank you." As he finished, Denver nodded at each of the Honey heirs, then sat back down.

"Wow." I clapped him on the shoulder, not caring where we were or who could see. "That was amazing."

"Thanks." Denver shifted in his chair, lips pale, skin chalky. I didn't need my training to know he was having a post-stress reaction, not unlike after a race or accident.

While Tammy said her piece next, I quickly fetched Denver some water from the pitcher at the back of the room and pressed a cup into his hand.

"Thanks," he said as Tammy finished. The audience

applauded, and several people swiped at their eyes. She and Denver had made a great case for keeping the business going.

"Now we're going to vote." The older woman who'd done much of the talking for the family shooed everyone else from the room so the Honey family could deliberate in private. Denver, Tammy, and I made our way into the hallway with the rest of the crowd.

Tammy excused herself to the restroom while several of the town leaders, such as the mayor and my dad, took the opportunity to head back to work. My dad saluted me from across the crowded space, mouthing, "See you Sunday."

Oh yeah. *Sunday.* I still had to ask Denver about dinner with my folks. Just the little matter of convincing him we had a future first. That he was here and fighting for Honey's was a good start, but I wanted him to fight for *us* as well.

Too much adrenaline zoomed through my veins to even think about sitting.

"You want coffee? A cookie?" I motioned at the table that had been hastily set up in the hallway with some store-bought cookies and a coffee station. "I'm gonna get you a cookie."

"Think you're more nervous than me." Denver managed a tight smile as I brought back a chocolate chip cookie for him.

"Obviously." I tried for a joke, but my voice came out too strained.

"Hey." Denver grabbed my upper arm, steering me into a doorway that afforded us a small amount of privacy. "Look at me." He moved his hand from my bicep to thread his fingers with mine. "No matter what the vote is, I've decided. I'm staying."

"You are?" My relief was so profound that I had to press my back against the nearby door.

"I found a place to belong, and it's not only at Honey's. It's with you." His voice was soft, more uncertain than I'd heard it, almost as if he expected me to disagree.

"You do belong with me." I squeezed his hand. "I belong with you too. I know you think I've always had a place—my family, the firehouse, my friends. And it's true, I've been blessed. But I never truly belonged until you. With you, I can be myself."

"Yourself is pretty awesome." Denver shook his head as he gazed back down the hall at the various townsfolk waiting to go back in. "Can't believe you got all these people to show up."

"They wanted to." I licked my lower lip. "And...my dad helped. He knows everyone."

"Oh." Denver's eyebrows drew close together as he narrowed his eyes. "He's...okay? With everything?"

"We're talking more. I'm lucky."

"No, he is," Denver corrected, his sudden loyalty making me grin.

"In fact—" I opened my mouth to tell Denver about the Sunday dinner invitation, only to be interrupted by one of the younger Honey kids sticking her purple-streaked head out of the meeting room.

"You can all come back in."

"I feel like there should be a drumroll," I joked to Denver as we found seats again. He'd said he was staying no matter what, but I wasn't sure I believed him. The town would survive if the Honey family voted to sell the land, and Denver and I might as well, but I'd rather not test that theory.

He'd shown so much courage, standing in front of the

group, showing us all a part of his huge well-hidden heart. He deserved to have that bravery rewarded. I stared down the Honey family at the front of the room, willing them to see that Denver and Tammy deserved this chance.

"Well, we had quite a...spirited discussion." The older woman glanced down the row at the other family members. "But after much deliberation, we kept coming back to what Lionel and Loretta would have wanted."

"Oh, thank God." I kept my voice low, but I turned my gaze skyward.

"Lionel and Loretta cared about family first, but they also cared deeply about Mount Hope. And the answer was clear: they'd want Honey's to continue while also preserving the future value of the land for the family. And thus, we've decided to lease the property to Mr. Rucker and Ms. Deevers as part of their business plan."

"Reluctantly." The man in the Hawaiian print tie frowned as the assembled crowd cheered the news.

I turned toward Denver with a big, dopey grin, not even trying to hide my relief. "I guess you're a business owner now."

"I guess so." Denver sounded dazed, eyes staying glassy even as the Honey family leader announced the business sale details would be worked out by the lawyers at a future date. The room started to empty, and Denver and Tammy accepted congratulations from various folks, but Denver was the far more stunned of the two.

"Yippee." Tammy did a little dance toward the door. "Now I have to skedaddle. I'm expecting a phone call from my daughter."

Denver's face went uncharacteristically soft. "Go. I'm so happy for you."

"And I'm happy for all of us." Tammy wagged a finger in my direction. "Don't let this one get away."

"Hey, I'm trying my best." I wasn't sure whether she'd meant me or Denver, but I was grateful for the order either way. "And thank you for convincing him to offer for the place."

"Oh, he convinced me." Tammy cackled as she exited, leaving Denver and me to head toward the parking lot.

"Need a ride?" Denver gave me a knowing smile.

"Always." I followed him to his truck, but Tammy's words continued to echo in my ears. "Offering to buy the place was your idea?"

"It was." Denver put the truck in Drive before continuing, voice emotional, "For the first time, I didn't want to run away. I realized I didn't want to leave, and as Tammy would say, I sat with that feeling a while."

I swallowed hard. "I hate that I can't take the pain of the past away for you."

"But you make it easier to bear." Denver turned toward Prospect Place.

"I guess that's my goal—not fixing the past or your hurts, but being there to sit with you."

"That's a good goal." He nodded solemnly as he parked near his place, which still had the blasted for sale sign out front. "Did you mean it about coming with me if I did leave?"

"I did." I put a hand on his shoulder before he could exit the truck, making him turn to meet my gaze. "I want to show you that I'm here, and I'm not going anywhere, and I want to give you the time and space to trust me. Trust us. And trust that even if you need to go—for a week, a month, longer—you'll always have a place to come back to."

"Yeah." He exhaled hard, and I couldn't tell whether he

was actually agreeing or simply overwhelmed. My pulse sped up, that urge to fix a hard habit to quit. Denver wasn't the only one working on trust.

"Can I show you something?" I asked, my voice as shaky as my hand.

Chapter Twenty-Nine

Denver

Sean led me across the street to the carriage house. The main house was quiet, sitting majestically in the early summer sun. The kids were still in school for another week or two, and Eric and Jonas were both at work. Meaning, there was valuable daylight Sean and I were wasting. I had gallons of adrenaline surging through me like three quad-shot coffees and a powerful need to fuck Sean through the nearest mattress. But Sean wanted to show me something, so I supposed sex could wait.

Or I could drag him onto our chair again...

My brain started to spin up a fantasy as Sean unlocked the carriage house, and I followed him in, not really paying attention until Sean cleared his throat. "Well?"

"Oh." I looked around. A few days prior, when we'd had sex in our chair, the place had already looked much improved but remained very much a work in progress. Now, Sean had cleaned up the various construction and cleaning supplies. The counters and sink gleamed and a new apartment-sized fridge and stove had joined the kitchenette. Someone had fixed and polished the little dinette set we'd found while working on the space. "You finished everything?"

"Hardly. There's plenty to do." Sean gave an uncertain laugh as I continued to look around. A braided rug sat in front of the wood stove, and while our chair remained near the stairs to the loft, a few other pieces of furniture had been added, including a plant stand near the front window with pots of herbs. "The herbs are for you," he said like he hadn't done this whole darn thing for me.

My tongue felt thick and unwieldy as I struggled for words. "Oh?"

"I fetched a few furniture items from my storage unit, but a couple of things are new, like the plants. And the bed." He pointed at the loft area. "And I wanted to show you this."

He dug a piece of paper out of his pocket and handed the handwritten receipt to me.

"You paid Eric for a year?" My mouth twisted as my head spun. "I thought you said you'd come with me if I decided to leave."

"And I would." Sean patted my upper arm like I'd been replaced by a nervous poodle. And perhaps I had. After today, nothing could shock me anymore. "I paid Eric rent, so we'd have a place to come back to, no matter what. A home base, so to speak. Like I said, I'll go where you go, but I also want to give you a place to come home to."

A home. The one thing I'd never had, and had stopped letting myself wish for decades prior, and here Sean was, just handing one to me.

"I'm..." I was no closer to being able to speak. "I'm not sure what to say."

"You don't have to say anything." Sean stretched to give me a soft kiss on the mouth. "And you can wait until your landlord sells before deciding whether you want to stay here with me. Like getting the people to speak at the meeting, I'm not trying to force your hand. I only want to give you options."

"This is a pretty good option." I looked around the space again. *A home.* Not a pre-furnished apartment or room to rent. He'd made me a home. I kicked off my dress loafers and placed my suit jacket on one of the dining chairs. "I think I'll take you up on it, but I better inspect that bed to be sure."

"You should." Sean enthusiastically tugged me toward the narrow stairs. I was a big dude, but luckily, the stairs were solid and didn't creak. I did, however, have to bend to stand in the loft, but the bed beckoned invitingly. It was a huge king-size mattress on a low platform, piled high with puffy comforters more suitable for winter nights. *Home.*

I stretched out to save my back and because I no longer trusted my knees to hold me.

"Well?" Sean asked, hovering near the bed.

"Nice firm mattress. No idea how you managed to get it up those stairs, but this is quality."

"Rowan and Jonas probably won't speak to me for a week." Sean grinned as I pulled him down to the mattress. "And I owe John a lot of hours of driving lessons, but we managed. Barely."

"I approve. It's cozy." I snuggled against Sean, breathing deeply. He smelled like minty shampoo and bracing shaving cream and Sean himself, and I couldn't get enough of his unique scent and warm body.

Sean stretched against me, ass rubbing against my groin, leg hooking me even closer. He exhaled along with me, almost like he was ready for a nap, but the way he was wiggling said otherwise.

"What would you like?" I asked indulgently.

"Make love to me?" Smiling, Sean rolled so we were face to face.

"Huh." I made a surprised noise. "You haven't called it that before."

"Yeah, but we've done it." Sean held my gaze, memories of the past few weeks in his eyes.

"I suppose we have." I nodded slowly. "And now that we have a giant-ass bed in here, we should break it in."

"We should." He grinned at me. "But you're always asking what I want, making sure my bucket list is met. What's on your list?"

"Well, you are the newbie. And I'm still not convinced you wouldn't be better off experimenting—"

Sean cut me off with a deft move to flip me to my back. "I don't need to experiment to know you're it for me. It's like having amazing prime rib. I don't need to rack up a stack of restaurant tabs simply to know a good thing when I find it. And this is a good thing."

"It is." I had to agree.

"So, I'll ask again." He pinned my arms loosely above my head and smirked down at me. "What would you like?"

I groaned. "What am I going to do with you?"

"Hopefully, it involves your—"

I stretched to silence him with a kiss, letting go when he started to laugh.

"Heart. I was gonna say heart."

"Uh-huh." I kissed him until he loosened his hold on my arms and started moving more purposefully against me. "And I'm not sure I have a list. Or a favorite thing. Each time with you is better than the last. Love your mouth. Love grinding like this. Love all of it."

Love you. I didn't say it, of course, but I let myself think it for the first time. Merely letting the words trot through my head made my pulse speed up and my palms sweat. But someday. Someday, I might say them aloud.

Sean continued to gaze expectantly down at me, apparently not letting me off the hook.

"You coming pretty much untouched the other night? That was damn hot. Tell me you stashed some lube and condoms up here?"

"You know it." He pulled a laughably large bottle of lube out from behind a stack of books and a lamp. "And do we really need condoms?"

I worried the inside of my cheek with my tongue. "I've never skipped the rubber. Even when high or drunk. Always played it safe and got tested on the regular too."

"Okay." Sean shrugged and reached toward his hiding spot again, but I stopped him.

"I trust you," I said simply. Trust. It was such a fragile, delicate thing. And not something I had a lot of experience with. But he was offering me his trust. Also, for the first time ever, I was staying. Denver Rucker was putting down roots. Business owner. Seemed like the right day for another first. "And there you go, that's my wishlist item."

"Yes." Sean's eyes flared wide and hot. He rolled off me long enough to remove his clothes with admirable speed. I managed to pull my suit pants and dress shirt off, only bumping my head on the low ceiling twice.

We collapsed back on the bed in a heap of laughter and naked body parts.

"Hopefully, we get used to that ceiling before anyone gets a head injury," Sean joked before sobering a little. "But, seriously, even without the exposed beams knocking me over, I'm falling for you."

"Guess I'm gonna have to catch you." I gathered him close for a long kiss, trying to let him know that I meant it. I'd catch him, give him a soft landing place. He was always so brave, heart right there for the taking. He had mine, had for far longer than I wanted to admit. And maybe I couldn't give him much, but I could whisper, "And I'm falling too."

"Good." Sean tipped his head back, inviting more kisses, which I happily provided. In each kiss, each touch, each moment, I found more peace than I'd ever known. *Home.* It wasn't this town or this carriage house or even Sean's gesture. It was Sean himself, this feeling we created together.

Make love to me, he'd asked, and that's exactly what we were doing. Making something extraordinary out of two rather ordinary humans. I'd had more than my fair share of bodily experiences—crowd surfed, snowboarded, hiked, and fucked—but what happened with Sean was so much more than skin and neurons.

I gazed down at Sean, in awe that we were here. We traded kisses as I swept my hands all over Sean's torso. He was so damn responsive, with the slightest touch making him shudder or gasp. And he delightfully liked it all, soft caresses on his sides, tweaks of his nipples, strokes across his chest and belly.

"Now." Of course Captain Impatient eventually had enough of waiting, arching toward me and using his legs to yank me closer. "Now."

He handed me the lube like there was any doubt as to what he wanted.

"We're getting there," I scolded, even as I slicked my fingers.

"Not fast enough." Spreading his legs up and back, he wriggled his ass. "And feel free to skip the prep. Don't wanna come too soon."

"That's always a risk with you." I chuckled. "And I happen to like the prep. Love making you go crazy on my fingers, love making you beg for it."

"Well, okay then." He tilted his hips as I started to tease his rim, clearly on a mission to make this fast. But I was having none of that, teasing with slow, deliberate circles before working him open.

My personal favorite thing was the way Sean was so damn greedy for my fingers. I didn't have small hands, and watching him take one, then two, and then work for that third never failed to make my cock throb and my pulse pound. Sean might be the one who could come fast, but he was so hot taking my fingers that I could almost get there simply from watching.

Almost.

"Want you in me," Sean moaned while riding my fingers. "Please. Wanna come on your cock."

"When you put it that way..." I withdrew my fingers to slick my hard and waiting dick. Sean's cock bobbed invitingly above his abs, a drop of clear fluid on the tip, and I bent to give it a quick lick.

Sean made a low, needy noise. "Thinking about doing it bare, you coming inside me... God, I'm so turned on."

"I like that thought too." And how. All my blood seemed to have been redirected to my cock, which pulsed harder every time Sean spoke. I arranged him on his side so I could spoon him from behind, the way we often slept. Seemed cozier, like this bed.

"This is different." He smiled over his shoulder at me,

already getting the idea by hooking his top leg over mine, giving me easier access.

"Yeah. Seems like a day for different. Firsts."

"I like that." He tilted his head back for the softest of kisses. "And I like this." He shuddered as I pressed in. Took a little bit of adjusting to get my angle right, but once I slipped in, Sean groaned, a satisfied noise I felt in my cock. "Oh God, I really like it."

"Yeah, this is perfect." The lack of a condom had me making a similar noise. His ass was warm and tight, but the unexpectedly wonderful part was how I could feel his pulse, feel even subtle reactions. After the initial penetration, I could hold him close, kiss his face and forehead, and watch as he reacted to each thrust. He never held anything back, joy and awe crossing his expression before his eyes drifted shut and quiet moans escaped his lips.

"Feels amazing." Sean started moving in rhythm with me. My thighs and stomach tensed, my body hurtling far closer to climax than I wanted, yet Sean was right. It simply felt that amazing. I reached for his cock, loving the noise he made. Part relief. Part desire. All need. "Tell me you're close because I so am."

"Wait for it, speedy." I managed a strained chuckle, slowing my thrusts and my strokes of his cock. "Let's make this last."

"Can't." He bumped his ass back against my groin, encouraging me to go faster, an invitation my body was all too eager to accept. But my brain wanted more, another few moments of anticipation.

"You can." Even as I said the words, my thrusts sped up, the weight of his cock in my hand, the sounds he was making, and the squeeze of his ass combining to push me closer and closer. "Because I'm going to come in you, going to come inside you, fill you up…"

"Not helping." Sean released a shuddery laugh. His cock pulsed harder in my grip, more precome gathering at the tip. "God, I'm gonna—"

"Me too." I finally gave in to the inevitable, thrusting hard and fast as Sean matched my every movement. Perfect rhythm. Perfect person. Perfect moment. "Now."

The rising wave of orgasm stole my breath and made my hips stutter as I came deep inside him. The first spurt made everything hotter, slicker, more intense, and I thrust hard, riding out my orgasm.

"Oh my God. I feel it. I feel you." Sean's amazed voice pushed me that much higher. I came and came as his ass milked me as he too came. "Denver."

We both shuddered and shook, and I reveled in the pleasure of holding him like this as we both climaxed and drifted back to earth. Not having to worry about the condom, being able to stay inside him, was also an unexpected bonus.

"Have I told you I love how you say my name?" I mumbled sleepily against his neck as I readjusted our positions.

"No. But I like your name."

I shook my head, nuzzling his hair. "My whole life, I kind of hated my name. There's undoubtedly a story behind the name my dad picked, but I never knew more than that he picked it and my mom hated it. Denver felt like something I was saddled with. But you make it feel…special."

"Good. I'm glad." Sean shifted so he could press a kiss to my mouth. "And you are special.

"Thanks." I released another big yawn. "Think I'm gonna sleep all afternoon after that."

"Good." He settled down against my shoulder before popping his head up again. "We have till dinner time. I might have volunteered us to help."

I gave a good-natured huff. "Well, as it happens, I have the night off."

"Hey, as part-owner, you'll be able to set your own schedule."

"I will." I grinned at him, weeks and months stretching ahead of us when I might be able to coordinate our days off. For the first time, the thought of a future with him wasn't terrifying. It was reassuring, the idea that we'd have time to figure things out.

"Think you could get this Sunday off? Or at least be awake around lunchtime?"

I raised my own head to give him a stern look. "What else did you volunteer me for, Murphy?"

"Nothing big." His sheepish smile said otherwise. "Just family dinner with my folks."

"No big deal." I gathered him close again, but it was a big deal. A very big deal. Suddenly, the reassuring thought of a future transformed into a tight pressure across my chest. What if I screwed this up before we even got started?

Chapter Thirty

Sean

"Nervous?" Denver asked as I parked on my parents' street under a tree a couple of houses down from the one where I'd grown up. We'd driven together since parking could be tight in this subdivision, especially when multiple Murphy family members were visiting. As was the case with most Sunday afternoons, my parents' end of the cul-de-sac and driveway looked like a used car lot.

"Nervous? Me?" My voice sounded high and tight, and my pulse had been revving since I'd woken from a morning nap. I'd been on duty until six, then home, that lovely new word, to the carriage house with Denver, and gotten a good five-hour snooze before it was time to get ready for the gathering at my parents. "I'm not nervous. Why? Are you nervous?"

"Sean. Take a breath." Denver set a hand on my thigh. His tone was soothing, but his mouth and eyes were tense. He'd also changed shirts twice, finally settling on a short-sleeved blue one with buttons with a vaguely tropical vibe that worked with his pulled-back hair and trimmed beard. "It's okay if you're a little...on edge. I get it. I'm afraid I'll fuck things up as well."

"Oh." I swiveled to meet his gaze. Because Denver carried himself so confidently, it was easy to forget he struggled with self-worth. And those issues hadn't magically gone away when he'd decided to stay in town. He had the ridiculous notion that I could do better. My neck tightened. I was the one who was at risk of not being a good boyfriend, not him. "I'm not afraid about anything you'll do. I'm worried the Murphy clan is about to run you off. We can be a bit...much."

The volume level alone of most family meals had me concerned that someone like Denver, who'd ridden solo for so long, would head for the hills. "I've told you about my mom's Disney obsession, right? And each of my sisters' various kids play different sports. Keeping track can be hard and—"

"I'm not going to hate your family, okay?" Denver squeezed my leg again. "And if they're rude about us being together, I'll simply quietly seethe until we can be alone later."

"So far, everyone seems cool. Which is cool, right?" Hell. I was rambling again. And yeah, I was nervous, had been nervous ever since Denver had accepted my invitation. And this whole coming-out thing was weird. After I'd talked to my father, I'd talked to my mom, who'd talked to my sisters, who'd likely talked to the whole darn town. But all that talking meant a lot of texts and calls. Even when things went well, the number of awkward conversations took a toll. "Sorry. I just don't want to mess this up. Or make you regret deciding to stay."

There it was. My real fear. Denver struggled to believe

Up All Night

he was good enough for me, while I struggled to believe I could be reason enough for him to stay. My worry wasn't simply about Denver's nomadic ways but rather my own self-worth battles. For so long, I'd tried to be who others expected of me, so I was getting used to being with someone I could be myself with without an invisible measuring stick.

"Hey." Denver looked deep into my eyes, a level of compassion there that worked to instantly settle my nerves. Moving his hand from my leg, he laced our fingers together, resting our joined hands on the truck's middle console. "I'm staying for me. Because I want to save Honey's. Because I want to see who I might be if I stay somewhere for a change. Who I can be with you. One family dinner isn't going to make me flee."

"Good." I closed my eyes, taking a deep, grateful inhale. When I opened my eyes, Denver was still smiling. I leaned in for a kiss, making it fast because two different sets of neighbors were out doing yard work. Time to go in. "The faster we make it through lunch, the faster we can get back to the carriage house and get naked."

"Sounds like a plan." Denver chuckled as we exited the truck and made our way to my parent's front stoop. As usual, my mom had said I didn't need to bring anything, but I'd spotted a fun flavor of local soda at the store. I had that, plus some cookies for what was sure to be a loaded dessert table.

"Sean!" My mother opened the door with her usual flourish, immediately seizing the bag with the food. "And this must be Denver!" Bag dangling from one arm, she swept him into a hug. Like my sisters, she was a natural hugger, so I wasn't surprised by her greeting. Denver, however, made a startled noise before she released him. Turning back to me, my mom flashed a gleaming grin that matched the cartoon characters smiling across the front of her T-shirt. "And we have a surprise for you!"

Oh, please no. I'd been pleasantly surprised so far by the reactions to my coming out. If this were an intervention or, worse, more matchmaking, I was going to lose the calm I was so known for.

Mom ushered us into the sunken living room of the split-level house. Three generations of Murphy family photos lined the mantel and the walls. Happy chaos reigned throughout the older home, with the sound of the kids filtering back from the kitchen and yard. My sisters and their husbands were in the living room, but my gaze went right to the couch centered by the front window.

"Declan." My heart lifted as my son stood and crossed the room toward me. His auburn hair was shaggier and more styled than our last visit, and he looked to have lost a little weight. Probably training too hard. He gave me a fast hug and a back slap. He was taller than me—had been for years now—but I still wasn't used to having to look up. "What are you doing here?"

His presence was indeed a surprise, and as happy as I was to see him, my head spun with a fresh new set of worries.

"I came in early for the race next week in Washington. Told Grandma not to tell. I figured I'd get a little extra practice at the track and cruise down here to see the fam. Introduce y'all to Stacey." He returned to the couch and a model-perfect young woman in a tight black V-necked tee advertising an energy drink. The red can on her shirt matched her lips and manicured nails, while her blonde hair was almost longer than her tiny denim shorts. Declan threw an easy arm around her shoulders. "Stacey runs promo for one of our sponsors. And she's why we've been playing text and phone tag lately."

Declan had a smug smile, but my stomach clenched.

"Ah. That's...awesome." I nodded at both of them. Declan had a revolving door of girlfriends, going back to his middle school years, and had always been one to have a lot of female friends and dates. "Nice to meet you, Stacey."

"Of course." She gave a pageant-worthy smile as Declan looked expectantly at Denver, who was still by my side. Undoubtedly, awaiting introductions, which would have been far easier had Declan picked up the phone any of the dozen-plus times I'd tried to reach him over the last week.

"And uh...this is Denver. My...um..."

"Fr—" Denver's mouth opened at the same time that three of my tween-aged nieces came running through the room.

"Uncle Sean's boyfriend is here," the oldest shrieked, red curly hair spilling down her back as the other two giggled. My sisters tried to quiet the trio, but I was actually a little relieved. Grateful even.

Denver had been ready with the save because I'd had an attack of nerves. But now the news was out, and I was strangely calm amid all the laughing and carrying on.

"That's right. This is my boyfriend." I grabbed Denver's hand and held on tightly.

"Wow." Declan went pale, classic Murphy freckles standing out in stark relief. He tilted his head, then shook it like he was testing reality.

"I wanted to tell you first." Despite the crowded room, I directed my attention to Declan. "That's why all the phone messages. Didn't want to leave this news in a text or as a surprise."

"Oh, I'm surprised." His tone was flat, as hard to read as his expression.

"I'll just go check on lunch." My mother bustled off, my sisters fast on her heels, all of them likely in a hurry to give Declan and me privacy. We were Murphys. We didn't yell or make scenes, but this was unchartered territory for all of us.

"I'm sorry you had to find out this way," I said to Declan. Denver kept ahold of my hand, but his posture was rigid.

"Does Bridget know?" Declan asked, raking his hair, ruining its careful style.

"We talked on the phone last night. She said she was happy if I was happy. And I am." I glanced at Denver, who was eyeing the door. "We both are."

"Yep." Returning his attention to the living room, Denver gave a sharp nod.

"Happy is good." Stacey nodded enthusiastically. "Love is love."

Declan shot her a look I couldn't decipher before frowning at me. "Guess we know why Mom left for the Antarctic."

"Declan." I recovered my ability to use a stern parental tone. "My sexuality isn't why your mother and I divorced."

"I know." He scrubbed at his smooth jaw. "Sorry. Bad joke. This is…gonna take some time. You and a dude. Wow. Never saw this coming."

"Can't say as I did either." I offered what I hoped was an encouraging smile. "But what I told Bridget is right. I'm happy. Really happy."

"And we're Murphys." My dad chose that moment to stride into the living room in a fire department polo shirt. "We stick together."

"You're okay with this, Grandpa?" Declan eyed my father closely. And I did too, especially when he took a moment to respond. He'd been warmer since our second talk at the station, but I wasn't sure *okay* would have been my word of choice.

But then my dad clapped both Denver and me on the shoulders. "I love your dad a lot, Declan. And I don't know how many more years I have left to tell him that. None of us do. Like your sister said, if our Sean is happy, I'm happy."

"Thanks, Dad." Blinking hard to not tear up, I gave him a grateful smile. Next to me, Denver finally exhaled, grip losing tension and posture relaxing.

"Exactly. Our Sean is happy." My mom came back into the room wearing giant Disney oven mitts. "And there's mac-n-cheese for an army of Murphys."

Declan crossed the room toward the dining area and kitchen, dragging Stacey with him.

"Love you all, but I need a drink." Almost out of the room, he turned back toward me. "You need one, Dad?"

"I'm good." I glanced over at Denver. "Well, I suppose that could have gone worse."

"Give him time." My dad used the same sage tone he used for all parental advice. "And speaking of time, have you filled out any job applications yet?"

"Job applications?" Denver's expression went from stoic to confused.

"The firefighter I've been covering for is coming back from maternity leave. I can apply to stay though. And Dad wants me to apply for the chief position."

"Help me convince him." Dad gave Denver a conspiratorial grin. "The wife and I are going to be snowbirds. Winter in California, summer here. Ideal retirement. Just need my ideal replacement."

"Like you said earlier, Sean needs to be happy." Gaze going tender, Denver squeezed my hand. "And he's a damn good firefighter."

"He is," my dad agreed.

"I'm honestly happiest on the line with the crew right now." Voice not wavering, I met my dad's gaze. "And right now, I want to do the things that make me the happiest, so I put in for the firefighter opening. And told Suzy to apply for both captain and chief. You want someone who's excited to lead."

"I can respect that decision." Dad didn't sound particularly joyous, but at least he wasn't fighting me on the job issue. "Now, let's eat."

He headed toward the dining room, leaving Denver and me more or less alone. Well, as alone as one could be in a house full of Murphys.

"Doing okay?" I asked.

"I was about to ask you that." He chuckled and tugged me a few steps closer. "You've got a good family, Sean."

"I do."

"They love you, and they want you to be happy. Like me."

"Like you." I was dying to ask whether he meant to imply he loved me, but my earlier nerves over being enough for him kept me from asking. "You do make me happy."

"Good." He smiled, glancing down at my mouth. We didn't kiss, but the promise was there for later.

Later. Time was a beautiful thing. Like my dad said, none of us knew how much time we'd get, but I knew I wanted to spend mine with Denver, wanted to take time to get this right, make it last.

Chapter Thirty-One

Denver

Sean's text came right as I was finishing cleaning my station and turning things over to the day crew.

> Meet you at home.

I still wasn't used to that word and what it did to my insides. Busy few weeks, what with moving into the carriage house and taking over the diner, but Sean was at the center of it all. And that word. *Home.* Each day, I grew a little more secure in what we had going.

"Have a good one, boss," Tammy called from the breakroom door. The transition of ownership wasn't quite complete, but Tammy took great delight in calling me boss and letting me handle any chore she wasn't in the mood for. As we went through the process of taking over the daily running of the diner, we worked out a pretty good division of labor. She sweet-talked all our suppliers while I handled unruly employees. Honey's was running smoother than ever, and Tammy's wide smile said it all.

"See you later, Tammy." I waved her on. "Enjoy your night off."

"I will." She was taking an overnight trip to Portland, meeting her daughter in-person for the first time after several long phone calls. "More jumpy than a pot of frogs, but I'm excited."

"I'm happy for you," I said, and I meant it. I may never be ready to do my own DNA looking, but her experience gave me hope that healing was possible.

"Thank you, sweetie." She waved back. "Now you get on home to your man."

"That's the plan."

"Bye, boss!" Great, now Amos and the day crew were doing it too. But rather than be irritated, I smiled. Maybe I could get used to this. I made it to my truck in record time. The sun was up, and June was in full swing with longer days and shorter nights and the sort of weather that made me glad to be staying in Mount Hope.

Home. I parked on the street because Eric's wide driveway could only hold so many cars, and the kids would be leaving for school soon. In fact, as I made my way around the house, I discovered the three of them on the back deck with a colorful tablecloth on the picnic table with a homemade sign that said *Congrats*.

"It's the last day of school!" Rowan called out. He wore a silver mesh top more suited for a club than high school.

"Last day of school." Wren was far grumpier as they tugged at their T-shirt featuring some sort of periodic table joke. "But Dad made bacon. Want some?"

Wren gestured at the table as John brought out a platter heaped with pancakes.

"Thanks, but I think I had enough bacon at work." I grinned, though, grateful at how easily this household had accepted me. Sean and I cooked with the kids most nights when he wasn't on duty, and I'd come to really look forward to the rowdy family meals. "Besides, Sean is waiting on me."

"Go on." Eric smiled back as he waved me on with a spatula. Good to see him smile, something he was doing a little more often these days.

"Come over after school," John called before I could walk on. "We're having the last day of school ice cream cake. It's a tradition."

Huh. Traditions. I didn't have many of those. Sean and the Murphy clan had a whole stack of them, though, from Sunday dinner to birthdays to holidays. Eric and the kids also had their traditions, and it was both weird and wonderful to be included. The idea that I might—*would*—be around next year at this time made me need a deep breath, but I didn't tense in the way I would have a few months ago.

"Will do. I'll bring Sean," I promised. "How's driving practice going?"

"I'm driving to school." John smirked.

"With me. Slowly," Eric added as he served up pancakes to the kids. "Oh, and, Denver, tell Sean I heard from Tony. He'll be here in time for—"

"Dad's birthday barbecue!" Wren crowed.

"Which is so not a big deal." Eric gestured with the spatula.

"Denver already said he'd help with the chicken." Wren was not to be deterred in their enthusiasm for Eric's upcoming birthday.

"Thanks." Eric nodded at me before turning back to Wren. "No explosions, please."

"We'll try." Wren grinned as the rest of them groaned.

"Get some sleep," Eric ordered as Jonas came striding up the walkway in scrubs, yawning wide as the dog came to greet him.

I exchanged a quick hello before heading on to the carriage house.

I opened the door and didn't immediately spot Sean, so I called out, "Hey, I'm home."

I paused, heart thumping. I sounded like something out of a sitcom, a life that wasn't mine. And then Sean emerged from the bathroom in only a towel, and all was right in my world. This was my real life, and this was home.

"You are." Sean crossed the room to give me a kiss that had me very grateful for the thick blinds we'd installed.

"And you're already showered." I ran a finger along the edge of his towel, dipping lower over his hipbones.

"I am." Sean steered me toward the small bathroom, which, while updated, was still smaller than many closets. Multitasking, Sean kept tugging at my clothes as we went. "Your turn."

"Our next house is going to have a shower for two. Walk-in, tile, dual showerheads," I mused as I finished stripping, only to turn when Sean gasped. "What?"

"You said next house." Leaning against the corner sink, Sean's eyes were wide and surprisingly emotional.

"Well, yeah, down the road a piece, when Eric and his kids need us less..." I trailed off because Sean's smile became as wide as his eyes.

"I love you." Tone offhand, he beamed at me. He was so easy with his feelings that I wasn't sure whether he meant the words casually or as a more serious declaration.

Ever cautious, I went for joking. "Because I'm dreaming of a bigger shower?"

"Because you're you." Sean pushed away from the sink to come cup my face. Serious. He was definitely serious. My pulse sped up. "And you're dreaming of a future together."

"You make the future less scary." I sucked my lips inward, swallowing hard. I knew the expected reply, but the words were stuck behind a boulder in my chest. "Thank you. And I..."

"It's okay. You don't have to say it back." Sean pressed a sweet kiss to my lips.

"I don't think I've ever said it. Like ever." I tiptoed through my memories, but no, nothing I could recall. I clenched and unclenched my hands, moving them to Sean's sides, pulling him closer.

"I get it." He stroked a hand down my bare shoulder.

"But I'm pretty sure I feel it," I whispered. It was easier to talk into Sean's hair, not have to see his face, but having him near enough to give me strength. "That's what this is, this feeling of being home even when I'm not actually here."

"Yeah." His voice was muffled against my collarbone. "It is. Now to the shower—"

"I love you." The words came out in a dazed rush, but I got them out.

"Oh wow." Sean embraced me tighter, face damp against my neck. "Thank you."

"Don't you dare cry." I faked a stern tone to cover my own lack of composure.

"I'm a Murphy. We get emotional." Sean raised his head to give me the softest look I'd ever seen. If love had a look, that was it. "Someday...never mind."

"Someday what?" My heart hammered, but I wanted to know.

"It's too soon. Way down the road, like the next house

and all that, but in the future..." He inhaled sharply, then whispered, "Maybe someday, you'll be a Murphy too."

"Yeah." I kissed him because there was nothing else left to do. Kiss him, love him, and try like hell to trust in that future we both wanted.

Epilogue

Caleb

This doesn't have to be awkward. As I exited my truck at the park, I tried to remember why I'd agreed to attend the birthday celebration for Eric Davis, one of our lead paramedics. Most of our crew was attending, and my absence might have been noted, but as I surveyed the city park, I was tempted to get right back in my truck.

"I shouldn't have come," I muttered. And, of course, my friend, Tate, chose that moment to stride up next to me.

"Why?" Tate asked. Like me, he wore a white T-shirt and jeans. Unlike me, however, he had an adoring lawyer boyfriend holding his hand and hanging on his every word.

"Did you forget a gift?" Tennessee asked, holding up a small bag. "I can put your name on ours—"

"I have a gift." I held up the card I'd picked up on the way to the town park. I had no idea what the appropriate gift was for a recent widower, but a funny card and a gift certificate for pizza would have to do.

"And no offense, guys, but too many happy couples and families." I gestured at the park. Seemed like not only the whole fire and rescue community but also the whole darn town of Mount Hope had turned out. Teens swarmed across the green space, younger kids packed the playground, and multiple grills were already smoking. No matter which direction I looked, I encountered more couples toting picnic baskets and holding hands like Tennessee and Tate. "I get why they had to move the barbecue to the park instead of the house."

"Too crowded for you? Our resident party animal?" Tate made a show of inspecting me like I might be ill. "Are you still salty that Murphy got away?"

"No, I'm happy for him," I lied. I'd spotted Sean right away, over near a big grill on wheels, his boyfriend beside him. Tate was one of the few who knew about my prior and all-finished crush. "Let it drop, okay?"

"Uh-huh." Tate didn't sound convinced as the three of us walked toward the barbecue. I guessed I was doing this thing.

"Like you said, I'm a party animal." I forced a wide grin. I hadn't truly partied in years, but my rep had stuck and could be helpful in moments like these. "I'm not really interested in a relationship anyway."

"Tate, Tennessee, and Caleb." Eric greeted us, his smile as strained as mine felt. He accepted my card and Tennessee and Tate's gift before gesturing toward the folding tables full of chips, burgers, hotdogs, and more. "You made it. Help yourselves to some food." A group of teens came zooming by, narrowly avoiding knocking us over. Eric chuckled fondly, though, pointing at the pack of kids. "Oh, and John's organizing a game of flag football. Rowan's setting up the volleyball net, so pick your poison."

"I'm not really that athletic..." I tried to find a spot for my gaze that wasn't directly at Sean and Denver over by the nearby grill. Too damn close for my comfort.

"You? You're ripped." Tennessee sounded as shocked as most people when I confessed to my lack of athletic talent. "You spend more time in the gym than Tate."

He patted Tate's generous bicep. Tate was shorter than Tennessee, but like me, he spent plenty of hours in the weight room. Tate's and Tennessee's adoring gazes at each other made my stomach clench.

"Gym time doesn't mean much," I mumbled as I headed toward the food. Anyone could log hours on the elliptical or weight bench, but team sports required coordination I didn't have. One of my instructors at the fire academy had speculated that since my reflexes were fine on the job, perhaps I had some sort of phobia around sports. He wasn't that far off the mark, not that I'd ever admit it. "Think I'll start with some food."

I assembled my plate, already calculating how quickly I could make my escape.

"Ketchup?" Wren, Eric's youngest teen, stood behind the condiment table, ketchup bottle at the ready.

"Sure." Easier to agree, but as I held out my plate, the bottle gave an ominous slurping noise. No ketchup came out. "That's okay—"

Wren gave the bottle a mighty shake, sending a large dollop of ketchup flying into the center of my shirt.

"Oh no!" Wren looked close to tears. "Sorry!"

"It's fine," I lied. I was getting far too good at that, which was for the best because Sean came rushing over with a stack of napkins.

"Hey, sorry about that." He dabbed at my shirt, then abruptly dropped his hand. Yep. Awkward. "You need a place to sit? You're welcome to join Denver and me."

Fuck me, no. I pasted my fake smile back on as one of the teens came by with flags for football.

"Wanna play?"

"I—" I glanced over at Sean, who was waving at Denver. He'd moved from the grill to a nearby small table. Oh, hell no was I joining the happy couple. Instead, I held out my hand for a flag. "Sure. Why not?"

"Great." The stocky teen handed me a flag. If nothing else, I needed to start learning the names of area teens for when my brother returned from camp. Scotty already complained that I sounded like a boomer. Maybe meeting potential friends for him would help Scotty love it here more. Or so I told myself as I followed the kids to the part of the green space usually used for soccer games. But after an unusually rainy June, the field was practically a swamp.

"Isn't it a little muddy?" I asked no one in particular.

"Aren't you a firefighter?" Johnson, a fellow firefighter and the frequent bane of my existence, shot back. Naturally, our crew's resident dude-bro was first to line up for football with the kids. "Scared of getting dirty?"

"Of course not," I snapped, the sound of every school bully I'd encountered ringing in my ears. Gym class had been the absolute worst, with dudes like Johnson lurking in every game of dodgeball.

Just a game. I was an adult, a trained first responder, and a valued member of my crew. Johnson was annoying, but I could suffer a few minutes of flag football, especially if it meant making some contacts for Scotty. Unlike me, he'd fit right in with all these jocks.

Of course, through the universe's crappy sense of humor, I ended up on Johnson's team, along with Tate. Predictably, Johnson appointed himself captain and took everything far too seriously.

"Geez, drop the ball again, and I'm asking to switch teams," he yelled at one of the older teens.

"Calm down, Johnson." I took a cue from Sean, who could go from calm to commanding in a single syllable. "It's just a game."

"That we want to win."

"And we will." Tate attempted to make peace. "Throw it to Caleb instead next play."

"Oh, uh—" I didn't have time to protest before we were lining up again. I followed Tate's instructions on where to run as Johnson lobbed the ball in my direction. It was an ideal pass, headed right for my chest, an easy catch.

Well, an easy catch for anyone other than me.

I ran backward, arms outstretched. Was I still in bounds? I wasn't sure, but I kept going, sliding in the mud, crashing into something large and solid behind me.

"Watch where you're going, kid," a voice sounded behind me. Fuck. I hadn't been a kid in years, but before I could argue, I slipped farther, taking down the man I'd run into.

"Crap." We both went spiraling to the dirt, no ball, no touchdown. And there I was, lying in a mud puddle, ketchup stain on my white T-shirt, dirt everywhere else, as I gazed up into the most gorgeous set of eyes I'd ever seen. The dark-haired dude was older than me, probably close to forty. I cared less about our age difference and more about fixing my absolutely horrendous first impression. "Oh my God, I'm so sorry."

"Tony!" Sean and Eric both came running over to haul the guy off me. And, of freaking course, this was *Tony*. Their much-talked-about special forces friend. My soon-to-be coworker if the rumor mill was right. Apparently, Eric and Sean had helped him get a maintenance position at the fire station while he completed the last of his fire certification requirements. Army Ranger to rookie firefighter was a heck of a leap, but this guy looked more than capable of leaping into anything he chose.

"Are you okay?" Sean asked.

"I'm fine." Tony had a deep, melodic laugh, which I would have enjoyed far more if it hadn't been directed at me. "Did I squash you, kid?"

I wish. "I'm fine." Another white lie in an afternoon filled with them. I wasn't fine. My pride stung worse than the muddy scrapes along my arms. I wasn't a kid. And no way was I going to allow myself another hopeless crush on a coworker.

* * *

Dear readers,
If UP ALL NIGHT left you hungry for more Mount Hope stories, never fear! OFF THE CLOCK is coming soon. Caleb and Tony's coworkers-to-lovers tale is going to be epic, and I can't wait to share it with you all. Preorders are so very much appreciated!

Want more UP ALL NIGHT with Sean and Denver? I've got a sexy bonus chapter for you on Ream, free to follow and read!

Love,
Annabeth

Acknowledgments

UP ALL NIGHT starts a new series for me, which is always such a leap of faith, trusting that readers will make the leap with me into this new universe. I'm so grateful for my readers. Never doubt that your purchases, borrows, and support make a huge difference in authors' lives, now more than ever. I appreciate each and every one of you. If you loved this book and are excited for the rest of the series, please tell a friend!

This series also marks a new venture for me into the world of reader subscriptions. I'm so grateful for my Ream followers and supporters at all levels. Because of you, audio for this series and other extras will be possible. If you're not yet following me on reamstories.com/annabethalbert, it's free to follow!

Sean and Denver are both starting over in midlife. I dedicated this book to fresh starts after forty because I know firsthand how scary and exciting and paradigm-altering such changes can be. In my personal life, I'm so grateful to my own friend group for helping me navigate my fresh start after forty. To anyone contemplating a big leap, build your support system and lean on them for a softer landing, but don't let your fears stop you from leaping. Also, your continued readership makes such changes immeasurably easier, and I don't take your support for granted either!

A huge thank you as well to Lori at Jan's Paperbacks. She makes providing signed copies to my readers so painless, and she's an amazing beacon in the romance community to boot! Her tireless advocacy for romance, queer fiction, and small businesses inspires me.

Reese Dante made my cover dreams come true. Furious Fotog provided the perfect picture of model Caylan Hughes, but Reese truly worked cover magic to create the ideal look for this whole series. I can't wait to share the rest of this friend group with all of you!

Finally, a big thank you to Abbie Nicole, my PA, friend, and fabulous editor. My work is easier, better, and more fun because of you. Rae Marks provided early feedback on the opening that helped bring Sean's character alive. Katie B held my hand during a critical time in revisions.

It really does take a village to bring you the stories of my heart, and I'm so fortunate to be able to do so.

Also By Annabeth Albert

Amazon Author Page
Many titles also in audio and available from other retailers!

Mount Hope Series

- Up All Night
- Off the Clock

Safe Harbor Series

- Bring Me Home
- Make Me Stay
- Find Me Worthy

A-List Security Series

- Tough Luck
- Hard Job
- Bad Deal

Also By Annabeth Albert

- Hard Job

Rainbow Cove Series

- Trust with a Chaser
- Tender with a Twist
- Lumber Jacked
- Hope on the Rocks

#Gaymers Series

- Status Update
- Beta Test
- Connection Error

Out of Uniform Series

- Off Base
- At Attention
- On Point
- Wheels Up
- Squared Away
- Tight Quarters
- Rough Terrain

Frozen Hearts Series

- Arctic Sun
- Arctic Wild
- Arctic Heat

Hotshots Series

Also By Annabeth Albert

- Burn Zone
- High Heat
- Feel the Fire
- Up in Smoke

Shore Leave Series

- Sailor Proof
- Sink or Swim

Perfect Harmony Series

- Treble Maker
- Love Me Tenor
- All Note Long

Portland Heat Series

- Served Hot
- Baked Fresh
- Delivered Fast
- Knit Tight
- Wrapped Together
- Danced Close

True Colors Series

- Conventionally Yours
- Out of Character

Other Stand-Alone Titles

Also By Annabeth Albert

- Resilient Heart
- Winning Bracket
- Save the Date
- Level Up
- Sergeant Delicious
- Cup of Joe
- Featherbed

Stand-Alone Holiday Titles :

- Better Not Pout
- Mr. Right Now
- The Geek Who Saved Christmas
- Catered All the Way

About Annabeth Albert

Annabeth Albert grew up sneaking romance novels under the bed covers. Now, she devours all subgenres of romance out in the open—no flashlights required! When she's not adding to her keeper shelf, she's a multi-published Pacific Northwest romance writer.

Emotionally complex, sexy, and funny stories are her favorites both to read and to write. Fans of quirky, Oregon-set books as well as those who enjoy heroes in uniform will want to check out her many fan-favorite and critically acclaimed series. Many titles are also in audio! Her fan group Annabeth's Angels on Facebook is the best place for bonus content and more! Website: www.annabethalbert.com

Contact & Media Info:

- facebook.com/annabethalbert
- x.com/AnnabethAlbert
- instagram.com/annabeth_albert
- amazon.com/Annabeth/e/B00LYFFAZK
- bookbub.com/authors/annabeth-albert

Made in the USA
Columbia, SC
19 April 2024